THROW IN THE TROWEL

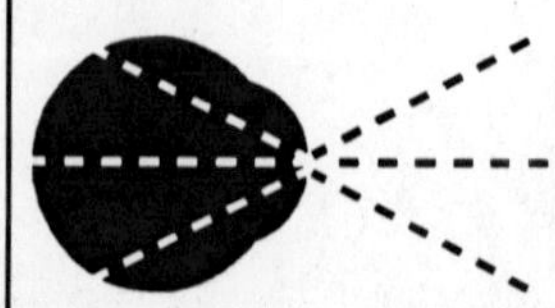

This Large Print Book carries the Seal of Approval of N.A.V.H.

A FLOWER SHOP MYSTERY

Throw in the Trowel

Kate Collins

KENNEBEC LARGE PRINT
A part of Gale, Cengage Learning

Farmington Hills, Mich • San Francisco • New York • Waterville, Maine
Meriden, Conn • Mason, Ohio • Chicago

GALE
CENGAGE Learning

Kennebec Large Print, a part of Gale, Cengage Learning.

Kennebec Large Print® Superior Collection.
The text of this Large Print edition is unabridged.
Other aspects of the book may vary from the original edition.
Set in 16 pt. Plantin.

LIBRARY OF CONGRESS CATALOGING-IN-PUBLICATION DATA

Collins, Kate, 1951–
Throw in the trowel : a flower shop mystery / by Kate Collins. — Large print edition.
pages ; cm. — (Kennebec Large Print superior collection)
ISBN 978-1-4104-7083-6 (softcover) — ISBN 1-4104-7083-0 (softcover)
1. Knight, Abby (Fictitious character)—Fiction. 2. Florists—Fiction. 3. Newlyweds—Fiction. 4. Missing persons—Fiction. 5. Murder—Investigation—Fiction. 6. Women detectives—Fiction. 7. Large type books. I. Title.
PS3603.O4543T48 2014
813'.6—dc23 2014013845

Published in 2014 by arrangement with NAL Signet, a member of Penguin Group (USA) LLC, a Penguin Random House Company.

Printed in the United States of America
2 3 4 5 6 18 17 16 15 14

To my son, Jason, who knows my characters' voices as well as I do and has a knack for finding the humor in a scene.

To my daughter, Julie, who embodies the energy and enthusiasm for life that my main character, Abby Knight, has and, like Abby, can't resist a challenge.

To my gifted editor, Ellen Edwards, who has an unerring sense of what makes my stories sparkle.

To my fellow Cozy Chicks, Ellery Adams, Deb Baker, Lorraine Bartlett, Julie Hyzy, Maggie Sefton, Leann Sweeney, and Heather Webber, for their constant support and encouragement.

As always, to my beloved husband and soul mate, Jim. Even though you're not physically with me anymore, I feel your spiritual love and support and hear your marvelous voice through Marco.

And to the many fans of the Flower Shop Mystery series, I leave you with this quote and hope you find its essence in this book. Maybe not so much the wrinkles.

"With mirth and laughter
let old wrinkles come."

— William Shakespeare

Prologue

Marco

Sun is shining. Day is young. Time to get up and make the coffee, soldier.

Problem was, I couldn't stop gazing at my lovely wife. She was lying against my side in the middle of our bed, red hair fanned out around her face . . . My *wife.* I was still having a hard time absorbing that. Abby Knight — make that Abby Knight *Salvare* — was *my* wife, which made me ping-pong between being unbelievably happy and utterly overwhelmed by my new responsibility.

As a private investigator and former Army Ranger, I was used to the inherent risks and hazards of those occupations. But now, with Abby insisting on being my partner in the PI business, the risks loomed large and sinister. I couldn't even begin to think what I would do if something bad happened to her. I'd sooner lose my life.

I had to blame Abby for that. Before I met

her I was fiercely independent. A loner who liked it that way. Sure, I dated, or at least made the effort, but the women I met bored me. They were flirty and giggly, snapping photos and texting their friends about me, attracted by my looks, *supremely* fascinated about my life as a private eye — until they weren't. *You follow people? How dull is that?*

And then a small ball of fire opened a flower shop two doors down from the bar I'd just bought, and my world changed overnight. I knew Abby *liked* my looks — not meaning to brag, but that was what first attracted women to me. Not for Abby, though. My investigative work intrigued her, drew her like a moth to the flame, as her assistant Grace Bingham would say. My buddy Reilly called Abby a trouble magnet. I called her Sunshine, because she was all that and more to me.

So my new policy was hands off any investigation that even hinted of danger. I didn't care if a hole opened up in the earth and threatened to swallow the town, nothing was going to darken my Sunshine.

I eased off the bed and crept out of the room, our little mutt, Seedy, at my heels. Once I had Seedy fed, I ground the coffee beans so Abby would have a fresh brew. I wanted my apartment to feel like home to her.

Don't forget, Abby's a breakfast person.

Oh, right. There had to be oatmeal in the kitchen somewhere.

Chapter One

Tuesday

Hey! You there. Abby Christine Knight! Snap to it, girl. You've got to get to work. The honeymoon is over.

Correction. Let's make that Abby Christine Knight Salvare.

Pep talk over, I yawned, scratched my head, and squinted at my reflection in the bathroom mirror. A short, sleepy, freckle-faced redhead squinted back, a bit bleary-eyed but generally happy. No, make that extremely happy, because I was a married woman now. Me. *A married woman.* Hitched to my dream guy in a fantastic wedding ceremony followed by an incredible honeymoon in Key West, Florida. Wow.

I sighed wistfully at the thought of those stunning sunsets over the Gulf of Mexico, primrose pink, goldenrod yellow, pansy purple — a florist's dream — as I'd stood arm in arm with my new husband watching the sun melt into the ocean. I remembered holding Marco's hand as we parasailed high over the island and neighboring Sunset Key, pointing out the places we knew. I sighed again, recalling how we'd biked along the Atlantic side of the island as pelicans dove for fish, and strolled along Duval Street licking chocolate gelato cones, and toured the coral reef in a glass-bottom boat, and Jet Skied across turquoise wat—

I leaned closer to the mirror. Could those be bags under my eyes? Did people get bags at the age of twenty-seven?

Confession time. I was extremely happy and also extremely tired and, if truth be told, just a little bit — minuscule even, hardly worth mentioning but, yes, I'd have to say it — annoyed. Marco had rolled to the middle of the bed during the night, taking up more than half of the mattress, forcing me to squeeze onto one edge and sleep fitfully. Plus his bedroom had too much morning light coming in behind the old window shades, waking me at the crack of dawn. And forget about prying my clothes from his small bedroom closet, where I hardly had room for two shirts and a pair of jeans.

I splashed my face with cool water, hoping that would rev me up.

Okay, then maybe coffee would do the trick. Marco would probably have a pot already brewed and a cup waiting for me on the kitchen counter. I just needed to look presentable for my gorgeous groom. Unlike him, I didn't roll out of bed looking camera ready. I didn't even roll out of bed. It was more like a tumble.

I balanced my hairbrush on the edge of the sink, shoved the hand-soap dispenser as far back into the corner of the narrow countertop as possible, zipped open my flower-print makeup kit, and laid out my blush, eye shadow, mascara, and lip gloss. They barely fit in the small space.

"Good morning, Sunshine," Marco said, standing in the doorway, looking indecently hot in his pajama bottoms. "Coffee's made. Want to join me for a bowl of oatmeal?"

"Lottie makes breakfast at the shop on Mondays, remember?" I always looked forward to her delicious scrambled eggs with thick slices of toasted homemade bread. My stomach growled just thinking about the feast that awaited.

"Today's Tuesday."

The stomach growls turned angry. "Oh, right. Do you have toast?"

He shook his head. "Oatmeal is it. You like oatmeal, don't you?"

Had he ever seen me eat oatmeal? At my apartment I had kept a box of oatmeal for *him.* Why didn't he have toast for me? But, hey, this was Day One of our brand-spanking-new life together (honeymoons didn't count), so I forgave him and gazed at him with tired but adoring eyes. "I'd love to join you. And maybe we can shop for groceries after Bloomers closes today."

Marco stepped in behind me for what I thought was going to be a hug. Instead, he opened the medicine cabinet in front of me with one hand and began to rummage through it with the other.

"Let me get out of your way," I said, trying to duck under his arm.

"No, you're fine. I'm making room for your things."

How considerate was that? "Thank you, Marco."

He removed a box of bandages and a bottle of ibuprofen. "There you go."

If he thought that would do it, my helpful hubby had a whole lot to learn.

My hairbrush slid into the sink. I grabbed for it and knocked over the tube of lip gloss, sending it plummeting to the floor. "You know what we need in here?" I pointed to empty wall space above the toilet tank. "A cabinet."

"We need a house, Abby. A cabinet isn't going to give us the kind of space we want."

"In the short run it will. We're not going to find a house overnight."

A wet tongue licked my ankle. I glanced down and saw Seedy gazing up at me as if to say, "Hey, don't leave me out!"

And doggy makes three.

Marco had adopted Seedy the day before we got married as a surprise wedding gift. She was the homeliest dog I'd ever seen, with brown, black, and tan patchy fur, large, pointed ears with tufts of hair that fanned out at the top, a small pointed muzzle, protruding lower teeth, and the kicker — pardon the pun — only three legs. I'd first seen the dog while investigating a murder at the animal shelter. My niece, Tara, had wanted to adopt both Seedy and her adorable pup Seedling to keep them from being separated, but her parents had said an emphatic no. They'd let her have the puppy but not his mom.

Abused, malnourished, timid around most people, and scared to death of men — Marco being a recent exception — Seedy had instantly bonded with me, even though I'm more of a cat person. From that moment on, I wasn't able to get the little pooch out of my mind, especially after I'd learned that she was in danger of being put down due to her unadoptable status. Because I hadn't thought Marco would want to start off our new life with a dog, and because I'd known that his landlady wouldn't accept pets, I'd tried my best to find her a home. But eventually I'd run out of options. That was when my hero had come to Seedy's rescue.

Fortunately, Marco's landlady was allowing the dog to stay with the understanding that we would find a new dwelling as soon as possible. And now that we were back from our honeymoon, the house hunt would begin.

While I was spooning oatmeal into a bowl from the pot on the stove, Marco's cell phone rang. He took the call in the living room, where I could hear the floorboards creak as he paced. His apartment occupied the second floor of an old two-story house, and while it had high ceilings, decent-sized rooms, and sturdy plaster walls, it also had noisy floors, drafty windows, and scant counter space in both the kitchen and bathroom.

I heard Marco grumbling to the person on the other end. Whatever the call was about, it couldn't be good.

"That was Rafe," he told me a few minutes

later, pouring himself a cup of coffee.

Two things instantly jumped to my mind. First, Rafe, Marco's younger brother, called only when something at Marco's bar, Down the Hatch Bar and Grill, had gone wrong. Second, Rafe was not the most reliable person you'd ever want to meet. Which was why Marco's next statement was alarming.

"He said there's a plumbing problem in the basement, but he's been handling it."

"So the problem is ongoing?"

"Apparently it's in the process of being repaired. Rafe wanted to prepare me because the old cement floor had to be torn up to locate the problem. I'm heading down to the bar now to see what they found."

A hard shudder ran through my body. That happened when I was cold or when my sixth sense vibrated a warning. Since I wasn't cold, I said, "Marco, be careful."

"Abby, it's an old basement. No boogeymen down there, I promise."

"I've just got a bad feeling about it."

He gave me a kiss and hugged me close. "You worry too much."

Seedy let out a little yip and leaned against my legs. As Marco headed for the door, I scooped her up, felt her trembling, and wondered if she had picked up a bad vibe, too.

Chapter Two

With Seedy in my arms, I stood on the sidewalk outside of Bloomers and gazed up at the sign over the yellow framed door.

Bloomers Flower Shop

Abby Knight, Proprietor

"See that?" I directed the dog's gaze upward. "That means this little shop belongs to me." She licked my chin. Okay, so she couldn't appreciate what those words signified. To me, though, they were proof that I'd overcome great adversity in my life — getting booted out of law school, effectively ruining my career plans, and subsequently being dumped by my then-fiancé, Pryce Osborne II, two months before our wedding. His family, scions of our cozy college town of New Chapel, Indiana, hadn't been able to bear the social stigma of my failure.

Humiliated, discouraged, but not defeated, I'd returned to the little shop where I'd spent summers happily delivering flowers and doing odd jobs for the owner, Lottie Dombowski. I'd asked to be taken on as her assistant only to learn that Lottie, a forty-five-year-old mother of quadruplet teenage boys, was looking for a buyer. Her husband had had major heart surgery that had overtaxed her medical insurance policy and was about to plunge them into bankruptcy. So I'd used the last bit of college money my grandfather had left me, bought up the mortgage, and now Lottie worked for me as mentor and assistant. She was still paying off those medical bills.

"From now on," I told Seedy, "you're going to be Bloomers's mascot. Are you ready to see your daytime quarters?"

Before I could get the door open, it was flung wide and two women rushed forward to embrace me. One was Lottie, of course. The other was Grace Bingham, my sixty-something assistant, who ran the coffee-and-tea parlor.

"How lovely that you're back," Grace exclaimed in her charming British accent, ushering me inside. "We've missed you, dear. And welcome to you, Mistress Seedy.

We have toys and even a treat for you. Homemade doggy biscuits. And come see the comfy bed we've tucked under the worktable."

She took the dog from my arms and carried her off toward the parlor, while Lottie spun me around and enfolded me in a bear hug. Being a woman of substance, she gave a substantial hug.

"How're ya doing, sweetie?" She held me at arm's length and smiled. "Honeymoons sure must agree with you because you look" — she paused as she searched my face, her enthusiasm waning — "well, like you have a glow — or something."

"Bags under my eyes," I said.

Her cheeks turning pink, she said, "I didn't want to say anything. You *have* been on your honeymoon after all."

"And the honeymoon was wonderful, Lottie. Honestly, it was a dream come true. I'll tell you and Grace all about it later — I have a ton of photos on my phone — but these under-eye bags are from a bed problem that Marco and I —"

"TMI!" Lottie cried and stuck her fingers in her ears.

I tugged at her elbow. "You didn't let me finish. The problem is with Marco's old mattress. It dips in the middle, so he rolls into it, and I end up hanging on to the side."

She fanned her face, a broad, friendly visage framed by short, brassy curls. "Whew. You had me going there for a second. Well, then, that's easy to solve. Buy a new mattress. You don't want to start off your marriage being mad at your new husband."

"Angry at Marco already?" Grace asked, gliding through the purple curtain that separated the shop from the workroom with Seedy in her arms. Grace had short silver-white hair and a trim body, which she kept in impeccable shape. She was my role model for what an older woman should look like.

"Mattress problems," Lottie said.

Grace handed the dog to Lottie, then took hold of the edges of her pale green wool jacket and cleared her throat. It was her classic lecture pose. " 'O bed! O bed! Delicious bed! That heaven upon earth to the weary head.' "

I wasn't sure what point she was making but I clapped anyway. Lottie put Seedy on the floor to join me in the applause, and Seedy immediately began to check out her surroundings.

"That was Thomas Hood, in case you're curious," Grace said.

I wasn't, but she'd never know by my expression.

"What it means, love," Grace said, "is that you can't afford a cheap mattress. There's nothing healthier for a relationship, as well as for a body, than a good night's sleep."

"Then I definitely need to discuss a new mattress with Marco," I said.

"Talking about beds," Lottie said, "come back to the workroom and see what we fixed up for Seedy."

"Come, Seedy," I called, following the women through the shop. The little dog looked up, saw me on the move, and began to trail after us. "So you're both okay with Seedy being here during the day?"

"You bet," Lottie said. "A mascot is a great idea. Customers like well-behaved pets, and she seems very well-behaved."

"She's a love," Grace said. "It's amazing how she gets along on three legs."

Hearing a crash, I spun around to see a tall ceramic floor vase filled with silk roses lying on its side. The obvious culprit backed under a wicker settee, her little body trembling as she gazed up at me with guilty eyes.

So much for well-behaved. "I guess she has to get used to the place," I said, and crouched in front of the settee to coax her out.

I spent the hour before we opened working with Seedy. I thought she might sit in the big bay window with the floral arrangements so she could watch people passing by on the sidewalk outside. Since we were directly across from the courthouse on the square, the window offered the perfect vantage point. But when the first customer entered and set off the bell over the door, Seedy leaped from the window and ran with her awkward gait as fast as she could across the tile floor to the purple curtain. In the workroom, I found her cowering beneath my desk.

I calmed her down until the next person entered the shop and then had to start all over. As more and more customers came in, Seedy grew increasingly distraught. I ended up counting how many times the bell rang, and pretty soon my nerves were jingling, too.

"Seedy needs a nice walk in the park," Grace said. "She's had enough for one morning."

"What about all the orders waiting?" I asked.

"I've got it covered," Lottie said. "Now scoot!"

Since I'd heard nothing from Marco about the plumbing crisis, after a long walk, Seedy and I headed up the street to Down the

Hatch Bar and Grill, one of the most popular watering holes on the town square. The bar had the advantage of being across the street from the courthouse and within walking distance of New Chapel University, drawing in a diverse clientele of attorneys, judges, secretaries, clerks, business people, and college students.

Marco had purchased the bar nearly two years ago but hadn't touched the decor at all. Last outfitted sometime in the sixties, Down the Hatch had a big, polished wood, L-shaped bar that ran down the left side of the building and a row of booths with orange vinyl cushions opposite. A large fisherman's net hung suspended from the ceiling in one corner, and a big blue plastic carp occupied a space of prominence above the bar, along with old photographs that ranged from the 1940s to the present. I thought the place needed a makeover, but customers seemed to like the ambience, so Marco was reluctant to change a thing.

As soon as Seedy and I walked inside, the bartenders and waitstaff came over to congratulate me. They looked at Seedy askance at first, but after they learned of her history and saw how sweet-natured she was, Seedy won them over, even if she did hide behind me. People made her nervous.

Men absolutely terrified her.

"Where's Marco?" I asked Gert, the waitress who'd worked at the bar for over thirty years.

"In the basement with the plumber," she said in her gravelly voice. "Too bad he had to come back to such a mess. I told Rafe to go ahead and have it fixed, but he refused to make any decisions without his brother's okay." She rolled her eyes. "It's a leak, I told him. But he wouldn't budge. It's like he has no confidence."

"Is Rafe downstairs, too?" I asked.

"He's in the office doing some tasks Marco gave him." In a low voice Gert added, "I think he's keeping a low profile, if you know what I mean."

Obviously Marco wasn't pleased with the way that Rafe had handled things in his absence. But what else was new?

I picked up Seedy, followed the hallway to the back of the building, and descended the old wooden steps. Basements in buildings that had been constructed in the early nineteen hundreds were not pleasant places to be. As mine was at Bloomers, so was Marco's — dank, chilly, dimly lit from the poor electrical wiring, and, in this case, smelling of musty earth. By the time we reached the bottom, Seedy and I were both shivering.

We entered a large room filled with deep, sturdy wall shelves that the previous owner had installed for storage. Marco kept that room neat and clean, but through the doorway beyond, the basement was a horror. The windowless cellar had a stockpile of broken barstools, pieces of slatted benches, stacks of ancient wooden crates, and rusty tools, including some old wooden-handled garden tools. I doubted if anyone had cleaned it in a century.

Marco was standing at the far end with Stan, a plumber from Greer Plumbing, whom I had used on many occasions. Both men were gazing up at the ceiling while Stan gestured. I was about to start toward them when Marco called, "Abby, watch out!"

I froze. Then in the dim light from an overhead bulb, I saw that the center of the old concrete floor had been excavated, exposing a mixture of damp sand, stone, and dirt. I circumvented the exposed area by stepping carefully along one side and joined Marco on the far end. Seedy was wiggling in my arms, so I set her down, unsnapped the strap from her collar, and let her explore. She hobbled into the storage room, then peered fearfully around the corner at Stan.

"What's the problem?" I asked.

"Old pipes," Stan said, hitching up his brown work pants. "When ya got old pipes, ya got old problems."

"He's going to have to replace this whole section of plumbing," Marco said, pointing upward.

"Might have to follow the pipe up to the next floor," Stan said, "but I won't know that until I get started."

"Why is the floor torn up?" I asked, looking back at the mess. Seedy ventured out of the storage room, her nose pointing toward the corner beyond Marco.

"Drain pipe's clogged," Stan said. "We're gonna have to clean it out."

"Will your insurance cover the cost?" I asked Marco.

"Yeah, good luck with that," Stan said. "Insurance companies hate these old buildings."

"It doesn't look promising," Marco said. "I'll probably end up eating a lot of the cost."

Didn't look promising for a new mattress, either.

"Your dog likes it down here," Stan said with a chuckle.

I glanced around for Seedy and saw her digging in the dirt. "Seedy, no!" I cried. But she was having such a good time, she ignored me. It was too late anyway. I'd just have to wash her paws before I took her back to Bloomers.

"So what's the game plan?" I asked.

"I think we've got enough of the cement up to get to the old drainpipes," Stan said. "If I have your okay, Marco, I'll get my guys down here this afternoon to start digging."

Seedy gave a little yip to get my attention. When I glanced down at her, she dropped a dirty, old-fashioned wooden-handled garden trowel at my feet, then wagged her bushy tail, looking exceptionally pleased with herself. So pleased, in fact, that she forgot to be terrified of Stan.

"Did you find a treasure?" I asked her.

She gave another yip and hobbled back to her dig site, while I dropped the trowel alongside the other garden tools amid the junk farther back in the room.

"How long do you think the job will take?" Marco asked.

"That depends on what I find up there." Stan pointed toward the ceiling.

Seedy returned to drop a twig at my feet. "Good girl," I said, giving her head a pat. She waited, tail wagging as though she wanted something else from me.

"I think she wants you to throw it," Marco said.

I picked up the twig and tossed it onto a part of the floor that wasn't torn up. Seedy watched it go, then looked back at me expectantly.

"Maybe she doesn't know how to play," Stan suggested.

I pointed to where it lay. "Go get it!"

Seedy watched it for a moment, then looked up at me and tilted her head, as though puzzled.

Now all three of us were in on it. While Stan crouched down to give Seedy a lesson, gesturing to show her how to run after the twig, causing her to back away in fear, Marco retrieved the twig and knelt in front of her, holding it out for her to sniff.

"Ready to go for it?" he asked her.

I grabbed his shoulder. "Marco."

"I think she understands this time," he said.

"Marco, that's not a twig."

Both men leaned close to look at the object in his palm. I stood up and brushed my hands on my pants, feeling as though I'd touched something disgusting. "That's a finger bone."

Chapter Three

"It came from over there." I pointed to a small pile of dirt in the middle of the floor as both men got to their feet. Marco walked across the excavated area and crouched down a good twelve inches from Seedy's hole. He brushed away more soil and plucked something out of the dirt.

"Another finger bone," he said, holding it up. "Abby, hand me that broom behind you."

I glanced around and saw an old straw broom propped in one corner. I handed it to him from the sideline, and both Stan and I watched as Marco swept away a thick layer of dirt, uncovering a skeletal hand and then an arm bone. After watching him follow the bone up to the shoulder, I said, "We'd better call the police."

"I don't believe it," Marco muttered. "A hole in the earth." He pulled out his cell phone and tried to hand it to me. "Phone

Reilly and let him know we found human remains."

"Right, and give him more reason to call me a trouble magnet? You'd better do it."

Sergeant Sean Reilly was Marco's buddy from the one year he'd spent on the New Chapel police force. After graduating from college and serving with the Army Rangers for two years, Marco had joined the force and trained under Reilly, who, as a rookie, had trained under my dad. But a bad sergeant and too many rules had soured Marco's taste for police work, so he quit, bought Down the Hatch, got his private investigator's license, and, in a stroke of pure serendipity, met the short, feisty, but ultimately irresistible redhead who'd just gone into hock to buy Bloomers.

While Marco talked to Reilly, I picked up Seedy and carried her upstairs to wash her paws. I didn't want to take the dog into the kitchen, so Gert brought me a handful of damp paper towels. I ducked into Marco's office to clean Seedy up and met Rafe coming out.

"Hey, hot stuff," he said with a big smile. "Looking good! Married life agrees with you."

"Save it, Rafe. I know I look tired."

"I didn't want to say anything. Hey,

puppy!"

Seedy buried her head under my arm. Clearly, Marco's charm hadn't rubbed off on Rafe.

Raphael (Rafe) Salvare was ten years younger than Marco and looked like Marco must have looked at twenty-two. He was broad shouldered and lean hipped, with dark, wavy hair, dark eyes, olive skin, and a faint shadow of a beard that women found sexy. After dropping out of college one semester short of graduating, Rafe had moved back to New Chapel on orders of his mother, who sent him to Marco to be straightened out. But Rafe had decided to settle permanently in his former hometown, so Mama Francesca put her Ohio home up for sale and followed. She was still in the process of selling her house, but now resided with Marco's youngest sister, Gina, so she could be close to her two grandchildren.

"How did Seedy get dirty?" Rafe asked, as I finished wiping her paws.

"You know that big hole in the basement? Seedy started digging in it and uncovered what looks like a human finger bone."

"No kidding?" He seemed delighted.

"No kidding. There may be a whole skeleton buried under the floor. Marco's on the phone with Reilly right now."

"So it's a good thing I didn't have it fixed," he said, nodding as though he was quite pleased with himself.

"Stick with that story, Rafe," I said, giving his arm a pat.

Marco came upstairs with Stan to wait for the police, but Seedy was getting antsy, so I got a sandwich to go and took her back to Bloomers. Motioning for my assistants to gather close so the customers in the shop wouldn't overhear, we huddled behind the cash counter where I shared the startling discovery.

"Was there any identification with the remains?" Grace asked quietly.

"Not that I saw," I said in a whisper, "but we stopped looking after we realized what we'd found. Maybe the police will uncover something."

"Could you tell how long the body's been there?" Lottie asked.

"Long enough to decompose," I said. "Only the bones are left, and they looked pretty old."

"Any clothing?" Grace asked.

"None that I saw," I said, "but we uncovered only one arm."

"I'll bet someone was murdered down there," Lottie said. "No one's going to bury a loved one in a murky old bar basement."

"Exactly what I was thinking," I said.

"In which case I doubt there'd be any identification or clothing to be found," Grace said, "which leaves a mystery to be solved."

Also what I was thinking.

"If that turns out to be true," Grace said, "I suppose you and Marco would want to investigate."

"You'd think so," I said, "but Marco wants us to take a break from private investigations."

"Considering that you're both new to marriage, that's wise of him," Grace said.

Not what I was thinking at all.

Lottie gave me a discreet wink. She knew that a mysterious skeleton would be an irresistible draw for me, a puzzle that needed to be solved, justice that had to be served. Plus, I enjoyed investigating closely with Marco, watching his savvy mind at work. He'd taught me a lot about being a private eye, but I was still green, still learning. If the police weren't able to ID the body, a cold case like this might be just the practice I needed.

In the meantime, I had orders to fill, flowers to arrange, customers to make happy. Seeing all the gorgeous tropical flowers in Key West had made me eager to try new designs. I hadn't had time to fill my creative well that morning, so I could hardly wait to get back to my slice of paradise and dig in.

"Francesca will be in tomorrow," Lottie reminded me, as I headed to the workroom with Seedy in the crook of my arm.

"Do we still need her?" I asked in surprise. Okay, dismay.

Marco's mom, Francesca Salvare, was a beautiful Italian woman who ate, drank, and lived with gusto. She loved her children passionately and had graciously accepted me as one of them. With that said, Francesca could also be overbearing. She was used to running things, so I'd had to struggle to keep hold of the reins of my wedding plans. Her insistence on being in control was one reason I'd balked at having her work at Bloomers. But our business had picked up to such an extent that my assistants had needed the extra help while I was away.

"If we stay as busy as we were last week, yes," Lottie said. "And by the looks of the orders that came in yesterday, definitely yes."

"I have to admit that Francesca's been an asset," Grace added. "Quite efficient at organizing, too."

"She's not bringing in food anymore?" I asked.

"You were clear on that subject," Grace said.

That was a relief. When we'd first asked Francesca to help, she'd decided to ramp up our business by bringing in platters of homemade Italian food for the customers. As soon as the news got around the square, she'd drawn in people by the busload, but mostly those who came solely to eat, not to buy. The shop got so ridiculously crowded that I finally had to lay down the law and ban her food, but I had feared a revolt in my absence.

"If you want Francesca here," I told my assistants, "I trust your judgment." I'd just have to make sure she stayed up front. Some places were sacred, and my workroom was one of them.

"I wasn't sure how much you wanted to be at the shop during your first few weeks back," Lottie said, "so I scheduled her for Monday, Wednesday, and Friday mornings this week."

"Whatever you think will help," I said. "Seedy, it's time to get down to business. You're going to have to be a good girl this afternoon, okay?"

She licked my chin. Either that meant yes, or she liked the taste of my moisturizer.

"You might notice that a few things are

different back here," Lottie said, following me through the curtain. "Just keep in mind that what's done can be undone."

That sounded foreboding.

I set Seedy down then scanned the room to see what had changed. *Hmm.* Not the position of the two big walk-in coolers on the right side of the room or the slate-covered worktable in the middle. Not the computer on my desk or the silk flowers that stood in tall containers next to the coolers. Nothing seemed out of place on the countertop that ran the length of the left wall either.

Then I glanced up at the shelves on the end wall and saw that my large stock of vases had been arranged by material rather than by shape and color, which went totally opposite of the system Lottie had taught me. "Why did you change them?"

"I didn't," Lottie said sheepishly. "Francesca came in on Saturday morning to help Grace and decided to organize things. I didn't find out until yesterday morning when she showed me what she'd done. And what could I say? She thought she was being useful."

It was the platters of Italian food all over again. Irritated, I said, "She should have asked first. It'll be a pain to change everything back."

"I completely agree with you," Lottie said. Then her face scrunched into a you're-not-going-to-like-this expression. "She organized the drawers, too." Lottie pointed to the row of tool drawers along the underside of the big table.

I opened the drawer near the spot where I always stood to create, where I kept my florist knife, stem stripper, crimper, snippers, scissors, and pruners. Instead of tools, however, I found packages of deco mesh, deco stems, enclosure cards, and envelopes.

"Why did Francesca do this?" I asked in exasperation, yanking open the next drawer. In it I found my florist's knife, along with glitter, glues, moss, mascot trinkets, and packets of preservatives. "How am I supposed to find my tools when they're mixed in with the floral supplies?"

"Francesca thought it would be easier if everything was arranged alphabetically," Lottie said.

"She *alphabetized* my stuff?" I stalked to the far end of the table and opened the first drawer. Sure enough, there were packages of adhesive lettering, balloons, butterfly picks, clay, and my crimper. My Garden of Eden had been invaded.

I shut the drawer with a bang. How did

Francesca think I could work with my tools scattered all over?

"I'm sorry, sweetie," Lottie said. "I knew you wouldn't like it, but I didn't want to hurt Francesca's feelings by putting everything back before you saw it."

Had Francesca thought about *my* feelings before she'd delved into my drawers?

"I'll have to put it all back before I do anything else," I grumped. "I can't work with everything" — I gestured widely — "all over the place."

"What's all over the place?" Marco asked, stepping into the workroom.

In as calm a voice as possible, which might have come out through gritted teeth, I said, "Your mother decided to *organize* my tools and supplies. I don't know where anything is now."

"I'll find them for you," Lottie said, clearly chagrined. "I know where everything goes."

I felt bad for making Lottie feel bad, so I said, "It's not your fault. I'll take care of it, Lottie. You're needed in the shop."

"Are you sure?" Lottie asked.

As if on cue, the bell over the door jingled. "Go," I said lightly, motioning for her to leave. "I can handle this."

As soon as Lottie was gone, Marco pulled me into his arms. "I'm sorry, Sunshine. I was afraid something like this would happen."

"Your mom didn't even ask, Marco. She just did."

"You know you're going to have to fire her."

"How can I fire her? She's your *mother.* And Lottie and Grace think she's an asset."

"She's not an asset when she causes extra work for you. Time to let her go, babe."

"She'll be crushed. She'll hate me."

"Tell her you don't have enough business."

"That's the problem. She knows we do."

"Then tell her to stay out of the workroom."

Ah, if only it were that easy. Marco simply didn't understand how fragile a brand-new mother-in-law/daughter-in-law relationship was.

"I'll help you put everything back," he said, rubbing my neck.

"Thanks." I laid my head against his chest and slipped my arms around his sturdy rib cage. How good it felt to know I had someone who would always be in my corner. I closed my eyes and sighed, feeling suddenly drained. I wished I could curl up somewhere for a nap.

Before I fell asleep on my feet, I said,

"Okay, time to get down to business. How about if I go through all the drawers to locate my tools and you empty out this drawer right here?"

"Whatever you need, Abby."

As we worked, I asked, "What happened with the police?"

"They taped off the excavated area, so all work on the plumbing beneath the floor had to be halted."

"That's a bummer. Did they dig up any more of the body?"

"They're still taking photos and soil samples, laying out a grid. When I left, they were waiting for the coroner to arrive."

"Have they mentioned murder?"

"They're just calling it a crime scene, but what else can it be besides murder? An old graveyard? I don't think so. Okay, this drawer is empty."

I handed him the tools I'd located. "Are you curious about who's buried there?"

"No."

"Seriously?" I knocked the third drawer closed with my hip. "I am."

"Big surprise there."

I sorted through the drawer he'd just filled and sighed in relief. It was now stocked with my important tools. My world made sense again. "*Now* I can work."

"I'm going to head back to the bar, then. I just stopped by to update you."

"Marco," I asked, before he could slip through the curtain, "aren't you even just a *little* curious about the bones? It's *your* bar they're in after all."

"Abby."

"What?"

Marco picked up my hand and kissed the center of my palm, then nibbled his way along my wrist and up the inner side of my arm, which always gave him unfair advantage. "We've got better ways to occupy our time now."

Better than investigating a murder? Well, at the moment, yes. But I'd have to ponder that question more seriously when he wasn't kissing one of my erogenous zones.

Seedy gave a little yip. She was sitting in between us, gazing up expectantly.

"I wasn't talking to you," Marco said, crouching down to scratch her behind the ears.

The bell over the door jingled and Seedy scooted back under the table. "Does she do that every time?" Marco asked, rising to his feet.

"Every. Time. I have to find a way to get her accustomed to the sound."

"Do you want to have dinner at the bar or

take something home to eat?"

How odd to think of Marco's apartment as my home. Seedy wasn't the only one who had to get accustomed to new situations. "Let's eat at the bar. Then we can shop for groceries afterward."

"Sounds like a plan."

Seedy did better in the afternoon, reacting with not quite as much trepidation when the bell jingled. She finally grew brave enough to venture out from beneath the table to explore the workroom and small kitchen in the rear of the building. Later, while I worked on orders, she curled up in the pink-and-green-plaid doggy bed Lottie and Grace had bought and took a nap.

At five minutes till five, I came out of the workroom to close up shop and heard Grace and Lottie chatting in the coffee-and-tea parlor while they prepared the machines for the next morning.

"I've been thinking about the body in the basement," Grace was saying. "There's a story way back in a cubbyhole in my mind of someone who went missing years ago, but I haven't been able to retrieve it."

My ears perked up. I paused just outside the doorway to listen.

"Same here," Lottie said. "Danged if I can

call it up, though."

"A search of the newspaper's archives might bring up a name," Grace said, "if I could remember how long ago it was. Bother! I hate when that happens. I may just have to ring up my friend Caroline. Old girl has a memory like an elephant."

"You're not going to suggest to Abby that she and Marco investigate, are you?" Lottie said.

"Oh, heavens no," Grace said. "I would never suggest that." There was a pause, and then she said, "On the other hand, we know our Abby, don't we? She won't rest until she has answers, and the detectives will be in no great rush to work on it, not with this current rash of bank robberies to investigate. Not that I blame them. They have their priorities, and this is a cold case after all."

I hadn't even considered that. According to the latest news, the entire police force was working around the clock to find the pair of armed robbers that had hit three banks around the county in the past four weeks. The detectives certainly wouldn't drop everything to investigate a bundle of old bones.

"How long do you think it'll be before Abby is champing at the bit?" Grace asked.

How about I was already there?

"You know Marco won't be for it," Lottie said. "Abby's already told us that."

Grace sighed. "Sad, isn't it, knowing how our Abby enjoys a challenge?"

"On the other hand," Lottie said, "she could investigate on her own time. Wait. Never mind. Forget I said that. We don't want her to go against Marco's wishes."

"Well, he's not the king, is he?" Grace asked with a sniff. "Shouldn't Abby have an equal say in the matter?"

Yes, Abby should. Make that would.

The women had stopped chatting, apparently having finished their chores, so I knew they would be appearing momentarily. I cleared my throat as I walked to the door to turn the sign to CLOSED.

"All set?" I asked when they came through the doorway.

"You bet," Lottie said.

"Big plans for this evening, love?" Grace asked.

"*Big* plans," I said. "Eat dinner and buy groceries."

Lottie and Grace glanced at each other with looks that said, *She'll be champing at the bit in no time flat.*

When Seedy and I got to the bar, Marco was working in his office, so I peered around his door to let him know we were there.

"Did the police finish downstairs?"

"They're done photographing and taking samples, but the coroner wasn't able to get here today because of a fatal accident on the toll road involving multiple cars. He's coming tomorrow, but no one could give me a time frame for when the detectives would be out to sift through the dirt. They're focused on the robbery investigation."

Grace had certainly called it.

"They did assure me that the bones will be removed tomorrow," Marco said. "I want them out of here as soon as possible."

Tomorrow? Yikes. If I were going to snoop around — I mean investigate — I'd have to do it soon. "What about your drain problem?"

"There's nothing I can do about that until the detectives finish." Marco shrugged. "It is what it is, I guess."

But it wasn't what it could be.

And who knows how long it will take detectives to make those bones a priority? I wanted to ask him. But all I said was, "That's annoying," because I knew the smartest thing to do would be to let Marco draw the conclusion I had already reached.

"I'm just finishing up here," he said. "Give me about fifteen more minutes."

"No problem," I said, checking the time on my watch.

I shut his door and headed straight for the basement.

Chapter Four

I put Seedy down in the storage room and tucked the end of her leash under a box of paper towels on a low shelf. "I'll be right through that doorway," I told her, pointing. Seedy sat on her haunches and gave me a perplexed tilt of her head as I took a penlight from my purse.

In the next room, yellow crime scene tape circled the excavated area starting about three feet from the doorway. To avoid it, I'd have to edge along the wall for about twenty feet before I reached solid concrete on the far end. Fortunately, I had no such plans.

Shining the beam on the ground in front of me, I ducked under the tape and picked my way through gravel and dirt until I was close enough to see the skeleton without disturbing anything. Marco had warned me often enough not to tamper with evidence.

Detectives had pushed the soil that had covered the bones off to one side, so I crouched on the opposite side near the head and aimed the light at the skull. It took only a moment to spot an arc-shaped indentation on top that was about three inches wide. Surely that blow had been the cause of death, but what kind of weapon would make such an unusual mark?

I moved the light slowly down the rest of the body, focusing not just on the bones to see if there were any other signs of trauma, which I didn't find, but also on the spaces between and under them. I wanted to see if the victim's clothing was there or if the body had been placed on newspapers or a rug or anything that might provide a clue. But all I saw was dirt, so clearly the clothing had been stripped away. Grace had called that one, too.

The skeleton's shoulders stretched wide, the arm, hand, leg, and foot bones were long and thick, and the pelvis was narrow, leading me to believe the victim had been a good-sized male. As I got to my feet, I thought of my brothers, both of whom were tall. How tragic that someone's brother, son, or father had ended his life right here in the pit of a dank cellar. How long had his family searched before they had given up hope and begun to grieve?

I heard a noise and turned around to see

that Seedy had pulled her leash free and was in the soil near the doorway, digging with abandon.

"Seedy, no! Bad girl!" I gave the bones a wide berth as I hurried toward her. At least she wasn't digging up the body.

I grabbed her leash to tug her away but she strained against it, trying to get at something in the hole she'd dug. I shined my beam down and saw what appeared to be a piece of a brown leather strap about an inch wide and three inches long. Before I could stop her, she snatched it up and turned to hobble away.

"Let me see," I told her, pulling on her leash, but she planted her feet and growled, determined to keep it. Not wanting to engage in a tug of war, I tried telling her what a good dog she was and scratching her under her chin, but she didn't fall for it.

I checked the time. Marco's fifteen minutes were almost up. I had to get back upstairs.

I picked up the dog with the object still clamped in her teeth, brushed off her paws as much as possible, stuck the flashlight in my purse, and headed for the staircase. My hand was on the light switch at the bottom when I heard from above, "What are you doing?"

I glanced up. Marco stood at the top.

"Just checking out the detective's handiwork," I said, climbing the steps. "Have you been down there since they left? They've got the full body uncovered."

"I saw it earlier."

"Did you notice the deep indentation in the skull? It's an odd shape, curved, about three inches long —"

"Let's let the detectives figure that out."

Where was the challenge in that?

Marco crouched in front of Seedy, who was now sitting beside me in the hallway, tail thumping as she gazed up at him. "What do you have in your mouth?"

Seedy dropped the piece of leather at his feet and looked pleased to do so, proving that Marco's charisma worked on females of many species, not just on the human variety.

He picked it up, frowning as he looked it over. "Seems to be part of an old leather strap. Where did she get it?"

"She found it downstairs."

"Where downstairs?" His right eyebrow was raised. He was onto us.

Mimicking Lottie's you're-not-going-to-like-this expression, I said, "In the dirt."

"You let her cross the yellow tape?"

"I didn't *let* her cross the tape. She got

loose and crossed it all by herself when I wasn't looking."

"I hope this doesn't turn out to be evidence, Abby, because if it is —"

"I know," I said with a sigh. "We've tampered with it."

"I don't like getting on the detectives' bad sides." He turned the strap over, clearly as curious as I was. "They can make my PI work a lot harder if they don't trust me."

"Then we'll put it back where Seedy found it, and no one will be the wiser."

I knew he'd nix that. Marco was first and foremost an investigator. In fact, he was so busy examining the piece, my words didn't even register. Whew.

"See the tab at the bottom?" I asked, pointing it out. "It looks as though there might have been a ring attached at one time. Maybe it was a key chain."

"You're right." Marco ran his fingertip over a faint impression on it. "What does this look like to you?"

"A logo of some sort?"

"I'll photograph it so I can blow it up for a closer look." He started toward his office, then came to a sudden halt. I had to put out my hands to avoid colliding with him.

"What's wrong?" I asked.

He shook his head in disbelief. "Old

habits die hard. We have to put this back."

Darn! I'd thought we were on the same page. Now I had to do something fast before that little piece of leather ended up back in the dirt. "I suppose you're right."

"Take the *suppose* out of it," he said, heading for the basement steps. "And then we're going to go have a relaxing dinner."

So sayeth the king of Down the Hatch Land. But this vassal wasn't giving up yet.

As I followed him back downstairs, holding Seedy, I said, "I certainly hope the detectives will realize what a find that is. I just hate to think what will happen if Al Corbison gets his hands on it. Remember how he lost the evidence in that big criminal investigation last summer? Or how he ignored the evidence when I was accused of killing the law professor? That man put me through hell." I took a deep breath and blew it out so Marco would see how that still affected me. "But that's in the past. He must have improved since then."

"We're not investigating this case, Abby," he said over his shoulder.

When had Marco become such a monarch? "You mean *you're* not investigating. I haven't made up my mind about it yet."

He stopped at the bottom of the steps and waited for me. "What?"

I put Seedy down and held out my hand for the strip. "Before you put it back, I want to take a picture with my cell phone. You don't have to be involved."

"Abby, we agreed that we need to spend more time together. We can't do that if we're working on a case."

"That's where you're wrong, Marco. It's when you work at the bar all evening that we're not spending time together. Cut back there if you want to have more time with me. In the meantime, I need something to do in the evenings."

"You know I'm trying to cut back, babe, but Rafe isn't exactly a fast learner."

He looked so sincere that I couldn't help but soften. "I'm not criticizing you, Marco. I know you're trying. I'm just saying that I could investigate this while you're tied up at the bar in the evenings." I held out my hand again. "Ergo, I'll need that for a photograph."

He didn't hand it over. "You're a really stubborn woman — you know that?"

"Like you never knew that about me before." With a smile, I slipped my arms around his waist and hugged him. Too bad he hadn't put the strap in his pocket. I could have slipped it out. "Does this mean you'll help me?"

"No, and we're still putting the evidence back."

"Is that a royal proclamation, King Marco?"

He stepped over the yellow tape and looked around. "Where did Seedy find it?"

I pointed out the hole. With a sigh, I said, "I sure hope Corbison doesn't screw up this investigation, too."

Marco dropped the key chain in the hole.

"I wonder if their lab will detect Seedy's dog drool on it," I said.

He cupped his hand in the dirt, ready to cover the evidence. I had to make one more attempt. "Can't you just see Corbison on a hunt for a maniacal-yet-old killer dog?"

He frowned. I had him thinking.

"That is, if our bones ever become a priority," I added. "I wonder how long leather lasts after it's been chewed by a dog."

Marco got the message. Plucking it out of the hole, he rose and stepped over the tape. "There's no harm in taking a closer look at it."

Eureka! I'd done it. I held out my hand. "I'll hold it for you."

"But all we're going to do, Abby," he said, placing it in my palm, "is take a closer look at it. As soon as I photograph it, I'll put it somewhere safe. Now let's go eat."

I picked Seedy up and headed upstairs first so Marco wouldn't see my triumphant smile. I hated to say that I had tricked him, but, well, as Grace liked to say, the proof is in the pudding.

At the top I said, "I guess it's true about those old habits dying hard."

He gave me a long look as if to say, *You weren't fooling anyone, Sunshine.*

Seedy was chewing on a steak bone under the table and we were finishing our bowls of hearty beef stew when Gert stopped at our booth. "Heads up, lovebirds," she said. "That slick newshound from the *New Chapel News* is asking for you. He's up at the bar talking to Rafe now."

We both turned to look just as Rafe pointed us out to a man around Marco's age. The man was dressed in a beige jacket covered with flap pockets, brown khaki pants, and brown hiking boots, as though he'd just returned from a safari.

"Connor MacKay," I said with a groan. "Is it possible word about the skeleton leaked out already?"

Marco did not look pleased. "Why else would he be here?"

Connor was a crime reporter who'd covered most of the murder cases that Marco and I had helped solve, even giving me a good lead on one case, but only because it had worked to his advantage. Popular with young women in town, he was strikingly handsome, with gorgeous blue eyes, golden brown hair that hung below his collar, and a lanky physique.

"Hey there, you newlyweds," he said, slipping onto the bench beside me. "I heard about the nuptials. Congratulations." He reached across to shake Marco's hand and then turned to give me a hug. I stuck out my hand instead. With a wry grin, Connor shook it. "Have it your way, Freckles. Looks like the best man won anyway."

"What do you want, MacKay?" Marco said. He hated small talk, especially from a man who had once flirted with me to gain confidential information.

"A reliable source told me you've got a skeleton in your closet, I mean basement, so here I am, ready to help you sift through the dirt — or clues. *Hello.* What's that?" He pointed to the leather strap, which we were now calling a key chain, that lay on the table near my plate. "That looks old and dirty and interesting."

"It's just an old key chain," Marco said. "Nothing of interest to you."

"My dog likes to chew on it," I said.

"There's a story for you, Connor. Why don't you write about my rescue dog? She'll make a great human interest piece."

"Right. Let's leave that for the features editor." Connor whipped out a notepad, pen, and minirecorder, and pressed a button on the side of the machine. "You don't mind if I record this interview, do you?"

"There's not going to be an interview, MacKay," Marco said, looking around, as though bored. "I don't have any facts."

"You have at least one," MacKay replied. "There's a skeleton in your basement."

"Then you've got the whole story," Marco said, as I discreetly pulled the key chain toward me and slipped it into my purse.

"You're kidding," Connor said. "That can't be all you know."

"Try me," Marco said.

Connor tapped his pen on the notepad, giving Marco an assessing glance. "Okay. Was any identification found with the bones?"

"Don't know."

"Any signs of a struggle?"

Marco shrugged. "You'd have to ask the cops."

"Male or female?"

"You've got me," Marco said.

Connor sat back with a huff. "You're the

best PI in town and you don't have a clue about a skeleton in your building's basement?"

"It's all in the detectives' hands, MacKay. Abby and I aren't involved."

Connor glanced at me for confirmation, skepticism written all over his face. As Marco has often told me, my face is an open book, but I managed to keep my expression neutral.

"How did the body come to light?" he asked me.

"Ask Marco. I wasn't here when it was uncovered," I said, which was ninety-nine percent true.

Connor glanced across at Marco, who said, "Plumbing problem under the floor."

"So you had the floor ripped up and uncovered the bones?"

Marco shrugged noncommittally.

"Can I see them?" Connor asked.

"Come on, MacKay, it's a crime scene," Marco said. "You know you'll have to ask the detectives for permission."

Connor clicked off the machine, clearly realizing he wasn't going to get any further. "I'll do that then." He tucked his pen and notepad in his shirt pocket and stood up. "You two have a nice evening." At the last second, he gave me a wink, almost as though he knew I had more information to share and he would be back to get it, and then he left.

"If MacKay shows up at Bloomers," Marco said to me, "don't talk to him. I don't want anything in the newspapers until those bones are out of here."

"You know, Marco," I said, "it might not be such a bad thing if the story leaks. Someone out there with a missing relative might come forward and help solve the case."

"They can come forward to the cops, not to us, Abby."

Before I could protest, Marco reached across to take my hands in his. "Sweetheart, think this through. It's pretty clear we're dealing with a murder. So while you're hoping a relative of the missing person steps forward, I'm hoping the killer doesn't. That's why I want those bones gone as soon as possible, and why I don't want you investigating this on your own. Do you see my point?"

"We don't know how old those bones are, Marco. The killer might be long gone."

"When it comes to your safety, babe, I'm not willing to chance it."

"There's always the risk of danger in a murder investigation," I argued, "so how is this case any different from others we've worked on?"

"We investigated those cases because people we cared about were in jeopardy. There's no reason for us to involve ourselves in this case, Abby."

"Imagine the years of agony some poor wife or son or parents have gone through, Marco, when someone they loved didn't come home one day. Wouldn't you like to be the one to finally give them closure?"

"That's what the police are for. We can find something else to do together. I'm sure I'll be getting some routine cases that we can work on."

Routine? Yuck. Routine meant sitting in a parked car for hours watching a doorway, or sitting at the computer looking for paper trails. In my book that equaled boredom. I sighed in frustration. "Then what can I do in the evenings to keep busy?"

"How about this?" Marco said, gazing into my eyes. "Stay here at the bar and be our hostess."

Double yuck. "I'm not good with large groups of people for any length of time, Marco. I'd last about an hour here. You know I'm happiest when I'm arranging flowers or doing something with you, like, oh, I don't know . . . interviewing suspects."

Marco tapped his fingertips on the tabletop, his brow furrowed. Then he turned his head as though listening for something and leaned sideways to look underneath the table. "Here's an investigation for you. Find Seedy."

Wednesday

When Seedy and I arrived at Bloomers the next morning, I could hear Lottie in the workroom singing to a country-and-western song playing on the local radio station, and Grace running water at the back counter in the parlor, preparing beverages for the morning rush. Seedy sniffed the air, which was redolent with the scent of freshly ground coffee beans and just-baked scones from Grace's oven, and tugged on her leash. Did she have a sweet tooth?

"You're going to be a good girl today, right?" I asked the dog, who had eluded us for an hour the night before. It turned out Seedy didn't like crowds either. She'd managed to hobble up the back hallway undetected and slip into Marco's office, where we discovered her hiding under the desk. Our trip to the grocery store hadn't been a picnic, either. The next time we shopped, Seedy was staying home.

Before I could reach the curtain, Lottie

came out carrying containers of roses for the shop's glass-fronted display case. "Morning, sweetie," she said cheerfully, then took a closer look at me and shook her head. "That ol' mattress just isn't gonna cut it, Abby. You look plum worn out again."

"That's because I am worn out. I talked to Marco about the mattress last night, and he said turning it over would solve the problem."

"One can see at a glance that it didn't work," Grace said, gliding like a stealth bomber from the parlor. "Just look at your sallow complexion."

Nothing like making me *more* self-conscious about my appearance. It was bad enough that I was short, busty, and freckle-faced. Now I had bags and sallow skin. "Marco said we have to give the mattress time to reconfigure."

Lottie snorted and Grace *tsk*ed. "And when you saw your reflection in the mirror this morning," Grace asked, "did you tell him that an old, lumpy mattress was not going to reconfigure itself into a new, firm one?"

"I don't want him to think I'm a nag," I said sheepishly. "It's our first week of marriage."

"Yes, it is," Grace said. "And how you

conduct yourself this week will set the tone for the future."

"Don't start sugarcoating things for him, sweetie," Lottie said. "You've gotta be straight with your man. You want him to be straight with you, don't you?"

"You're right," I said. "I just felt awkward criticizing his mattress after I've already complained about the lack of toast, closet space, and bathroom storage."

"But this concerns your health, Abby," Lottie said, putting her arm around my shoulders. "We worry about you, you know."

"I appreciate that," I said.

"You simply must put your foot down," Grace said. "Tell him you refuse to sleep in his bed any longer."

The curtain parted and there stood Marco's mother, a younger version of the famous actress Sophia Loren, glaring at Grace in outrage.

Really bad timing on Grace's part.

I gave Lottie a look that said, *Why didn't you warn me that Francesca was in the shop?*

Sorry, Lottie mouthed. *Forgot.*

"What is this advice you're giving Abby?" Francesca demanded, her ire bringing out her Italian accent. "Telling her to refuse to sleep with my son?"

"Oh, Lordy," Lottie said under her breath.

Classy from head to toe, Francesca was wearing a flowing coral silk blouse and black pants with black patent flats, her thick glossy dark hair falling in waves to her shoulders, gold hoops on her ears.

"You didn't let Grace finish," I said, as Francesca put her arm around my back, clearly intending to shepherd me toward the curtain. She was a stately, voluptuous, tall woman. At five foot two, I didn't stand a chance.

"Bella, disregard everything Grace told you," she said in my ear. "If you are having problems in the bedroom, *I* will help you. Leave the dog here and we'll step into the back for a conversation."

Dear God. She wanted to have *the sex talk* with me. *That* made me dig in my heels. "It's Marco's mattress," I said, turning to face her. "I'm not getting a good night's sleep because it sags in the middle."

She raised one eyebrow, as though she didn't believe me.

"Honest," I said. "Ask Lottie and Grace."

"Mattress," both women said at once, nodding vigorously.

Francesca looked at their earnest expressions and then back at mine. She cupped my face in both hands and stared into my eyes. "Then I will have a talk with my son about the importance of having a firm mattress. 'Marco,' I will say, 'how can you make babies with your wife —' "

"TMI!" Lottie cried, sticking her fingers in her ears as she darted out of the room.

"Francesca," I said, placing my hands over hers and gently pulling them away from my face, "thank you, but that's not necessary. Marco and I will figure it out for ourselves."

If the situation weren't already awkward, Marco decided to put in an appearance, too. The front door was locked, so we all looked around when he tapped on the glass. As I opened it, Seedy let out a happy yip and hobbled over to greet him.

"Hey, little girl," he said, scratching her head. Then he glanced up to find his mother frowning at him, her arms folded beneath her breasts, and me trying to warn him with my eyes.

Clearly puzzled, he said, "What's going on?"

"It's nothing," I said. "Just a little discussion we were having. What's up?"

"Nothing?" Francesca exclaimed. "I wouldn't call problems in the bedroom *nothing.*"

At Marco's astonished expression, Grace went into action. "Francesca, while Abby and Marco sort this matter out privately, would you be a dear and give me your opinion about a new grind of coffee? I'm not sure how it will go over with the public."

Francesca pointed her finger at Marco. "Listen to your wife. We will talk later." Then she turned to follow Grace into the parlor.

"What was that about?" Marco asked me.

"Your mother overheard us discussing the mattress problem and thought it was about something else."

"Like what?"

"Sex."

Marco rolled his eyes. "Glad I missed that discussion, but I thought we resolved the mattress problem."

Lottie's advice popped into my head: *You've gotta be straight with your man.*

"Marco, look at the bags under my eyes and tell me we don't have a problem. I'm not getting a good night's sleep, and turning the mattress didn't help. We're going to have to buy a new one. Soon."

He tilted up my chin and gazed into my eyes. "I'm sorry, babe. You didn't say anything this morning, so I thought you slept okay."

"And I thought you'd notice how tired I looked."

"No, I thought you looked beautiful." He

put his arms around me and drew me close. "Haven't you figured out by now that most guys are clueless?"

"But you've never been like most guys, Marco."

"And now you know I am. You have to tell me these things, Abby. If you don't, you're doomed to eat oatmeal and sleep on a bad mattress. I've never been good at mind reading."

"Then I guess it's my fault for assuming."

"Let's just say it was a learning experience for both of us and let it go at that. How about we go mattress shopping after we grab dinner at the bar this evening?"

I gave him a fierce squeeze. He had totally redeemed himself. "Sounds like a plan, Salvare. So why are you here? Not that I mind."

As though he'd just remembered he had a purpose, he handed me the newspaper tucked under his arm. "I wanted you to see this."

I took the paper from him. "As long as we're sharing things, Marco, I have to say, I miss reading the morning paper at breakfast."

"I'll get it changed."

How easy was that? I unfolded the paper to see a banner headline across the top in large, bold letters: UNIDENTIFIED BONES

BARED IN BAR BASEMENT. A photograph of Down the Hatch accompanied the article below it, written by none other than Connor MacKay.

In a startling discovery, local Down the Hatch bar owner Marco Salvare unearthed a human skeleton while having work done in his basement. "We tore up the floor to fix a plumbing problem and found the bones," Salvare said.

I glanced at Marco. "You didn't say that."
"I know. Read on."

According to former Down the Hatch owner Rusty Miller, who now owns Blazing Saddles Saddlery, the floor was intact for all thirty years that he operated the bar. "The bones must have been down there for a long time, predating me," Miller said. Miller sold the bar to Salvare early last year.

Salvare, a well-known private investigator who has assisted the local PD on solving a number of murder investigations, declined to comment on whether he and his wife, florist Abby Knight, owner of Bloomers Flower Shop, would get involved. When asked to comment, Salvare would only say, "It's in the detectives' hands."

But is it? According to police spokesman Danny Bianco, detectives are working around the clock to find the men responsible for the armed robbery of three local banks. Bianco was unable to estimate when their investigation into the mysterious bones would begin.

Whose body lies in the old bar's basement? Was it a case of murder? No one is talking, not the police or Salvare, leading this reporter to believe that the basement was the scene of a grisly crime. Will Salvare be content leaving his plumbing issues unresolved while waiting on detectives to solve the case, or will he and his wife take matters into their own hands?

If I were a betting man, I'd place my money on the Salvares.

I folded the paper and handed it back. By the grim look on Marco's face, I knew exactly what he was thinking. He wanted to ring Connor MacKay's neck.

Chapter Five

I led my fuming husband into the workroom and had him sit at a stool while I put together an arrangement of yellow roses for a birthday bouquet. "I know you're upset, Marco, but the discovery of a buried body is big news in a small town. Connor wasn't being malicious. He was just doing what reporters always do."

"I was hoping he'd wait until he had more facts."

"Nope, he'll drag this story out for as long as he can. And frankly, now that it's out in the open, maybe we should investigate. Everyone in town will be expecting it."

"Including the murderer, thanks to MacKay." He tossed the paper in the trash can in disgust. "Even if we were going to investigate, Abby, which I'm opposed to, our hands would be tied until the coroner can date the bones. For all we know, that skeleton could have been down there for ninety years."

"In which case the killer would be dead," I said. "No danger to us then. And so what if the bones are ancient? There are ways to investigate old bones."

"Yes, for forensic scientists who have access to DNA analysis, not small town PIs who've never worked on a cold case before."

"There are always dental records that could be checked. You're giving up before you've even started, Marco. Where's your sense of justice? Where's your spirit of adventure?"

He took the snippers out of my hand and pulled me onto his lap. "Being married to you is all the adventure I need," he said, trying to get cuddly.

"But just think about how relieved some family will be to finally learn what happened to their grandpa or great uncle. Won't it feel great to help them?"

Marco grunted, still unconvinced, so I kept talking. "Besides, you don't want that gaping hole in your basement floor for who knows how long, do you?"

With a sigh, he set me on the floor and stood up. "I've got to get back to the bar for a delivery."

"Is that a yes?"

Marco shook his head slowly, as though

he couldn't figure out what to do with me. Finally he said, "If the bones have been down there long enough to satisfy me that the killer is dead, I'll agree to investigate."

"Judging by Rusty Miller's statement, I'd say that's a safe bet."

"Rusty's a terrific guy, Sunshine, but his memory isn't as sharp as it used to be. I'll need more than that to be convinced." He lifted my chin and gazed into my eyes. "Good enough?"

Good but not great. But I nodded anyway and got a kiss as thanks.

Then I caught sight of the old leather key chain lying on my desk beside my *Florists' Review* magazines. I had stuck the strip in my purse and had discovered it only this morning. But I didn't want Marco to remember that I still had it, because I didn't want it put somewhere safe. I wanted to research it myself and surprise him with my sleuthing skills. So I did the first thing that came into my mind. I threw my arms around him to keep him from turning in that direction.

"You are the greatest husband in the world," I said, trying unsuccessfully to back him toward the curtain. "I just wanted you to know that."

"I appreciate that," he said slowly. "What's

going on?"

No fool he.

Lottie poked her head through the curtain. "Heads up, kids. Jillian is here."

Marco instantly unwrapped my arms and headed for the back door. "See you at supper, Sunshine. Bye, Lottie."

The yin and yang of life. One problem ended. One about to begin.

"Lottie," I said in a whisper, "do me a favor and keep Francesca busy. I can't deal with her and Jillian at the same time."

"Not a problem, sweetie. The parlor is full of customers and Francesca is as happy as a clam serving them. And in about fifteen minutes, Gracie is gonna watch the shop while I make deliveries. That'll keep Francesca occupied in the parlor."

"Great. Thanks." I took a steadying breath and prepared myself for the craziness that was my cousin.

Jillian Ophelia Knight Osborne and I were the only two girls on my dad's side of the family, which had made us as close as sisters, especially since we'd had to join forces to combat our villainous brothers. Jillian was younger than me by a year, taller than me by a head, thinner than me by — well, that wasn't important — and wealthier than me by both her parents' money and her new husband's.

Whereas my dad had been a policeman and my mom a kindergarten teacher, Jillian's father was a stockbroker in Chicago making much more than both my parents combined. Jillian's husband, Claymore, the younger brother to the scamp who had dumped me, was a CPA with a highly successful firm in town.

Educated at Harvard, Jillian was now a wardrobe consultant, operating her business out of their roomy three-bedroom apartment in the building where I used to live. Jillian was also newly pregnant and had spent the last several weeks rehearsing for her impending waist expansion, first by strapping a specially designed and weighted ball to her middle, and then by toting around a five pound sack of potatoes wrapped in a baby blanket. The potato experiment had lasted until the surrogate had begun to rot. At that point, I'd left for my honeymoon.

"Hello, hello, you old married woman," Jillian called cheerfully, a stroller preceding her through the curtain, with a small pink bundle strapped into the seat. Beneath the table, Seedy started growling.

She gave me a warm hug, which was fairly unusual for Jillian. She hated to crease her ultrafashionable clothing, which today consisted of a mango silk chiffon bomber jacket over a lacy white tank top with superskinny faded jeans. Her leather purse, which she wore cross-body style, was also mango colored. Her unusual side-zipped booties looked like they had been splashed with silver, gold, orange, and turquoise paint.

"Welcome back, Abs. New Chapel wasn't the same without you."

"Thanks, Jill, but please don't tell me you're doing the potato thing again."

She didn't deny it. Instead, she tossed back her long, copper-hued hair and leaned in to inspect me — it was her mission in life to improve my appearance. With a frown, she said, "You can get rid of that puffiness under your eyes with cold tea bags, you know."

"Thanks for the tip. What brings you to Bloomers?"

"Your honeymoon photos. After the way you gushed about Key West on the phone yesterday, I couldn't wait to see them."

"Don't say that if you don't mean it, because I have a gazillion pictures." I snapped my fingers under the table. "Seedy, stop growling."

She dropped the growls and started barking instead, prompting a small black-and-white doggy face to poke through the fuzzy pink blanket in the stroller. I heard a yip from Seedy, as though to say to me, *Now do you get it?*

Jillian beamed like a proud new parent as she lifted her new pet, a Boston terrier, from the stroller and cradled her like a baby. As was typical with that breed, the dog's black-and-white markings made it look like it was wearing a tuxedo. What was not typical was the lacy pink onesie it sported.

Jillian had spotted the young terrier when I'd taken her and Claymore to the animal shelter to meet Seedy. I had hoped to convince them to adopt Seedy, but the dog's poor physical appearance and ragged condition had turned them off.

"Say hi to your aunt Abby, Princess," Jillian cooed, waving the dog's paw at me.

"I refuse to be an aunt to a dog, Jillian. And seriously, *Princess*? Isn't that your nickname?"

"No," she said, sniffing as though insulted.

Was, too. Her dad had always called her Princess.

"Actually I'm still trying to decide between Princess Sunflower Petal and Marquesa de la Casa Osborne."

"How about just Petal? That's pretty."

"Petal," she said, trying it out. She held the dog to face her. "Hello, Petal." Then she shrugged. "I'll still need something longer when I show her."

"You're going to take her to a dog show?"

"That's generally where people show dogs, Abs. Duh." The terrier wiggled to get free, so Jillian put her over her shoulder as though she were a baby that needed burping. "Where are your photos?"

I pulled out my cell phone and began to scroll through the camera roll. "Here's the hotel where we stayed. It's right on the Gulf of Mexico. And right next to it is Mallory Square, where sunset is celebrated every night."

"Princess, please stop that," Jillian said, shifting the dog back to the crook of her arm. "You're ruining Mommy's jacket. Sorry, Abs. Go on."

"These are photos we took from the parasail. You can see across two islands from that height. I hope you and Claymore get a chance to go parasailing, Jill. What a great experience."

"You know I have a fear of heights, Abs. Princess, would you stop wiggling?"

"I'm no dog expert, Jillian, but I think she wants down. Seedy has some toys she might like."

Jillian put the canine on the floor, but instead of checking out Seedy's toys, Princess began to run around the table as fast as her little legs would carry her, with her pink tongue hanging out, clearly overjoyed by her freedom. Jillian watched for a moment, then, with a sharp sigh, said, "I've got an appointment with Gustav tomorrow morning so we can start training her."

"And Gustav would be?"

"Just the best dog trainer in the entire state. He's Russian, and you know what great trainers they are."

Naturally. Osbornes never settled for anything that was less than the best. For instance, me.

As the terrier whizzed past for the umpteenth go round, Jillian said, "There's a tri-county dog show in two weeks, but Gustav doesn't think Princess will be ready in time. I tried to tell him that she's really smart and learns fast, but I guess he'll just have to see for himself. Okay, now where were we?"

"Here's a photo of Mallory Square, where the sunset celebration happens. You wouldn't believe what a circus it is there, Jillian. I mean an actual circus, with acrobats and sword-swallowers and tightrope walkers and food vendors —"

Seedy began barking. I turned to see her

standing in front of the kitchen doorway staring at something inside. She looked back at me, then back at the doorway, and barked again.

"Seedy, stop it," I commanded. The dog quieted, but sat on her haunches facing the kitchen.

"Anyway," I said, "here's us dancing to Cuban music at El Meson de —"

"What's that noise?" Jillian asked, looking around.

A distinct crunching sound came from the kitchen.

"No!" Jillian cried, her hands to her face. She dashed across the room and through the doorway faster than I'd seen her run in a decade. "Princess, *no*!" she screeched.

She appeared moments later carrying her dog over one arm. "Abs, Princess is on a strict diet now to prepare her to be a show dog. You're going to have to put Seedy's food dish up when we come to visit."

I bit my tongue, and we continued with my photos, while her terrier returned to circling the table, barking now to express her enthusiasm. My nerves fraying rapidly, I was on the verge of grabbing her, when she jumped onto my desk chair and looked around at us. Her eyes twinkled mischievously.

"Isn't that cute?" Jillian asked, as Princess pawed the keyboard on my desk. "I taught her to tap the keys so it looks like she's using the computer. Everyone on Facebook loves the photos of her."

Clearly bored with the computer, Princess put her front paws on my desk and rose up to sniff around my desktop.

"Wait until you see the professional photos I had taken of her," Jillian said proudly.

Oh, joy.

As though she'd completely forgotten about my pictures, Jillian began to dig through her enormous orange-and-blue designer diaper bag. Meanwhile, Princess leaped off the chair and scooted under the table, prompting Seedy to begin growling again.

I glanced at the wall clock and decided I'd had enough. "We'll have to make it another time, Jill. I have a lot of orders to fill."

"Okay," she said, producing a small, leather-covered photo album. "Let me show you just one."

"I really have to get busy."

"See this one?" Jillian asked, tapping a perfectly manicured nail on the photo. "See how regally Princess stands for such a young, untrained dog? Doesn't she just look like a champion?"

Both dogs were growling now and Jillian didn't even seem to notice. As she turned to another page, Seedy came to the edge of the table and barked up at me, as though to say, *Get this mutt out of here!*

"What's wrong, Seedy? Are you frazzled?" I asked, hoping Jillian would pick up on her distress.

Seedy barked again then ducked back under and began to growl.

"I think someone's jealous," Jillian said, closing the album, "because someone else is playing with her toys. Come here, Princess."

The Boston terrier shot out from beneath the table in the direction of the curtain, carrying something in her mouth, with Seedy hobbling in hot pursuit. As though she'd been standing outside eavesdropping, Grace at once stepped into the room, blocking the dog's exit. Princess did an about-face and darted back under the table with Seedy after her, barking madly, and Jillian running around to the opposite side of the room, yelling at me to collar my dog. It was total chaos.

I turned to Grace and gave her a someone-shoot-me-now look.

"Abby, love," Grace said over the noise, "you wanted me to remind you about the appointment you have at ten thirty today to meet with a bride-to-be. Since it's nearly time for her to arrive, I thought it prudent to interrupt."

God bless Grace for coming up with a way to get rid of Jillian.

"Thank you," I said. I dropped down on my hands and knees on one side of the table and Jillian did the same on the other side, while Grace blocked the curtain.

"Princess, put down Seedy's toy and come to Mommy right now!" Jillian demanded. The dogs were engaged in a fierce tug-of-war and paid no attention to her.

"Abby, can you do something, please?" Jillian cried.

Right, like I was a dog whisperer. "Grab Princess's hind legs and pull," I said.

She followed my instructions, causing Princess to let go of the toy and turn to snap at her. Meanwhile, Seedy, the toy hers once again, hobbled over to me and dropped it at my feet.

But it wasn't a toy at all. It was the leather key chain from Marco's basement — covered in dog drool. Talk about tampering with evidence.

Thank God Seedy had rescued it. "Good girl," I whispered, hugging the dog against me, causing her to lick my chin. She was my little hero.

Her plumelike tail thumped against the floor; then she backed up and headed for the safest place she knew — huddled under my desk.

I got to my feet and saw Jillian attempting to buckle her squirming terrier into the stroller. "You really need to train Seedy better, Abs," she said. "The dog simply doesn't play well with others."

My tongue was nearly in shreds by the time Jillian was ready to wheel the stroller through the curtain.

"Oh, one more thing," my cousin said. "Would you do me a huge, huge favor and watch Princess Friday evening? Claymore and I have a function to go to and the pet sitter isn't available."

I glanced at Seedy, shivering beneath my desk. Was there room under it for me?

Chapter Six

Quick, Abby, think of an excuse or you'll have to put up with Princess for an entire evening!

"Um, Jillian, I don't —"

"Have plans? I knew you wouldn't." She threw her arms around me again. "You're a lifesaver, Abs. One of these days you're going to need a sitter for Seedy, and I promise I'll be there for you." She hugged me tight, the knoblike top button of her jacket cutting into my cheek; then she grabbed the stroller handles and launched herself forward. "My place at seven, Friday. Thank you!" she called back, disappearing through the curtain.

I glanced under the desk to see Seedy watching me. Was that pity in her eyes?

Feeling the need for a calming cup of chamomile as well as some motherly wisdom, I sought Grace and Lottie out in the parlor. They were at a white ice-cream table near the back of the room, taking a quick break between rounds of customers. I poured myself a cup of Grace's specialty tea and pulled up a chair.

"Thanks for your help, Grace. That little terrier of Jillian's is a devil, and now I have to watch her on Friday evening."

"And *why* did you agree to that?" Grace asked.

"Because I couldn't think of a reason why I couldn't. Marco will be at the bar."

"If you don't want to watch Jillian's terror," Lottie said, purposely mispronouncing terrier, "you don't have to give her a reason. Next time, just say no."

"She'll ask for reasons," I said, slumping forward.

Lottie shook her head sadly. "You've stood up to kidnappers and killers, but you can't say no to your cousin?"

"It's not that I can't say no," I said. "I just can't lie."

"Sweetie, you can't go wrong if you're honest about your feelings," Lottie said, getting up to pour fresh coffee. "They're your feelings; they can't be argued with. It's just like with the mattress issue. Be straightforward. Tell Jillian you're not up to babysitting her dog."

Grace cleared her throat and straightened her shoulders. "As Confucius said, 'Respect yourself and others will respect you.' "

"Amen to that," Lottie said.

"Well, anyway," I said to Grace, "thanks for helping me get rid of Jillian."

"You're welcome, dear," Grace said, "but you really do need to get ready for that appointment."

During my lunch hour, I took Seedy for a walk around the square to Community Park, the small-town version of New York City's ginormous Central Park. Our park had a band shell and performing stage, a water fountain for kids to play in, benches on the green space ringing the park, and lots of newly planted trees. Seedy was fearful of all the people at first, but once she started sniffing trees, she forgot her fear and began to roll around on the cool grass, having a great time. I saw a few people casting skeptical glances her way, as though they couldn't believe a pitiful sight like her could exist, but others wanted to know all about her. I didn't mind answering because it gave me the opportunity to talk about the plight of rescued animals that needed homes.

As soon as I got back to Bloomers, I took a photo of the leather key chain, uploaded it onto my computer, and enlarged it. Then, while I ate my turkey sandwich, I sketched out what the design on the front looked like — a short pipe sticking out of a circle at a ninety degree angle. There seemed to be a rim around the inside of the circle. Was the circle a wheel?

"Whatcha looking at?" Lottie asked, peering over my shoulder at the image on the monitor.

I held up the key chain. "I'm trying to figure out what this image is. What does it look like to you? I tried to draw it out."

"Looks like a gun," she said, squinting at it.

"It's a cannon," Grace said. Not surprisingly, I hadn't heard her come in. "An old-fashioned military cannon. Cannon Construction has used that logo for decades. If you look closely, you'll see the letter C on the inside of the wheel."

Once she pointed it out, I could see the letter on the monitor's image. It was not as evident on the key chain itself, which had been worn nearly smooth.

"Seedy dug it out of the dirt near the body," I told the women.

"Aha," Grace said. "Your first clue."

"Or not," Lottie said. "It could have been dropped there during the building's construction."

"The building is over ninety years old,

Lottie dear," Grace said. "Cannon Construction Company didn't exist back then. As I recall, Kermit started his business in the late sixties. His son runs it now."

"His name was Kermit?" I asked. "Like the frog?"

"It was an old Irish name long before it was given to a frog," Grace said.

"So," I said, studying the leather strap, "how did a key chain from the late nineteen sixties end up buried beneath the floor of a ninety-year-old building?"

"I'll bet Kermit dropped it there while he was doing some work for Rusty Miller," Lottie said.

"It couldn't have been for Rusty Miller," I said. "According to the interview Rusty gave Connor MacKay that was in today's paper, the floor was intact for the entire thirty years that he owned it. So it would have to have been for the previous owner."

Grace tapped her chin. "I believe Mr. MacKay got that wrong, love — either that or Rusty has a faulty memory. Do ask Gert. She'll know when Rusty took over the place."

"Hey, Gracie," Lottie said, "remember what a big scandal it was when Kermit left his wife and kids to run off with Parthenia Pappas?"

"That's the story I was trying to remember yesterday," Grace said. "Kermit and Parthenia. Midseventies, if I remember correctly."

"Parthenia Pappas?" I asked. "The Duchess?"

"The very same," Grace said.

Parthenia Pappas, who billed herself as the Duchess of Tenth Street, partly due to her regal bearing and Greco-Egyptian descent and partly due to her studio on Tenth Street, was a local celebrity. She worked in multiple art media but had become well-known nationally for her sculpture. My mother was a huge fan and had recently begun taking sculpting lessons from her. I wondered if Mom knew about the Duchess's infamous past.

"What a tragedy it was," Grace said. "Kermit's wife was left with children to raise and a business to run, while Parthenia returned to town years later as a renowned artist and resumed her life as though nothing had happened, with nary a mention of Kermit or what the two of them had been doing."

"And ol' Kermit," Lottie said, "never came back, probably too ashamed, the scalawag."

"Or he was onto another woman," Grace said. "Kermit had quite an eye for the ladies."

"And they had an eye for him," Lottie said. "He was a looker, tall, well built, and a real charmer, too."

I pursed my lips and stared at the key chain, my mind spinning their tidbits of gossip into possibilities. "Was there ever any proof that Kermit actually did leave town, like sightings of him or reports of him contacting his children?"

"Not that I can remember," Grace said. "The *New Chapel News* kept the Cannon scandal alive for months and would revisit it annually, but nothing interesting ever came of it. That's not to say Kermit never contacted family at some point."

"Interesting," I said. "It's as if Kermit vanished into thin air, leaving his key chain behind."

Grace glanced at me with a sly gleam in her eye. "I believe I know where you're going with this."

"Where?" Lottie asked, looking from Grace to me.

"To the basement, dear," Grace said. "She's wondering whether it's Kermit who's buried in the basement. I always felt that there was something peculiar about Kermit abandoning his family. He was an extremely jealous man who watched over his wife as though every chap in town was after her.

He got himself arrested on a number of occasions for battering men who looked at her too long. However, that didn't stop Kermit from going after other women."

"It seems like quite a leap to go from Kermit being a cheating husband to a murder victim just because of a key chain," Lottie said.

"Not just because," I said, "but this key chain is the only link to those bones that I have."

"Might I inquire as to why you have the key chain and not the detectives?" Grace asked.

I was about to explain how I'd ended up with it, but we all knew holding on to what might turn out to be crucial evidence wasn't a good thing to do, so I decided to take Grace's advice and say no.

Her eyes widened in surprise; then she nodded approvingly. "Good for you, love." She looked at Lottie and said with a knowing smile, "She'll tell us eventually."

"Help me out," I said, grabbing my tablet and a pen. "Who besides Kermit might have had one of these key chains?"

"Let me think," Grace said, tapping her chin. "As I recall, it was just Kermit in the company for years until he took on a younger partner. Nice fellow by the name of Henry Greer, who, it's been said, Kermit treated better than his own son. I believe you met Henry once, Abby, when we had a plumbing problem. He owns Greer Plumbing."

"I remember meeting him," I said. "He seems like a nice guy."

"Very conscientious and hardworking," Grace said. "Unlike Kermit, who liked to imbibe a little too much. Toward the end, as I recall, Henry was doing the lion's share of the work due to Kermit's drinking problem."

"I don't remember that," Lottie said.

"You're a lot younger than I am, Lottie, dear," Grace said. "You were probably staging a protest on the university lawn, or burning your bra."

Blushing, Lottie said, "I did do a lot of that, come to think of it."

"Did the business do okay or did Kermit's drinking affect it?" I asked.

"It seemed to do well despite Kermit's drinking," Grace said, "probably because of Henry. After Kermit left, Henry worked for Kermit's wife and continued to do well until he left to start his plumbing company."

I wasn't seeing much in terms of motive for Henry, so I went on. "Other than Kermit and Henry, who else might have had a key chain? Their wives?"

"Henry never married, did he, Gracie?" Lottie asked.

"Never," Grace said. "It's possible that Kermit's wife had one, I suppose. Her name was Lila. She died a few years ago, as I recall."

"How about customers?" I asked. "Would Kermit have handed them out as a promotional item?"

"I would hardly think so," Grace said. "Kermit was as tightfisted as a fellow could be."

"Probably spent his extra money on booze," Lottie said.

"He certainly didn't spend it on his family," Grace said.

"Well, he had at least one key chain made," I said, letting it dangle from my fingers.

"Perhaps Lila had it made as a gift for him," Grace offered, "or perhaps Henry Greer had one made for each of them. Henry was the one who was always trying to promote the business, as much as Kermit would allow, of course."

Lottie looked at Grace in amazement. "How do you know all this?"

"I got to know Kermit's children quite well," Grace said, "especially the oldest,

Douglas, or Doug, as he preferred to be called. I was the high school librarian back then, and Doug spent a lot of time in the library reading books on architecture and construction. I truly believe it was to impress his father so Kermit would take him on as an apprentice after high school, but of course that never happened.

"Very bright young man, Doug was," Grace continued, "and quite close to his mum."

I tapped my pen on the pad of paper. "That narrows the list to Kermit, his wife, Lila, possibly their children, and Henry Greer."

"I would eliminate Kermit's two daughters," Grace said. "They would never have been allowed in a bar, so they wouldn't have had the opportunity to drop a key chain there. I doubt they would have wanted to be around Kermit anyway. No love lost between the children and their father."

"Wouldn't you say the same for Kermit's wife?" Lottie asked.

"I think the poor dear cared for him despite his flaws," Grace said. "I remember numerous occasions when Lila was seen pushing and pulling him to her car, with Kermit drunk as the proverbial skunk and barely able to walk. Unfortunately, there's no way to question her now."

"Am I remembering right that she married Rusty Miller?" Lottie asked.

"Yes, you are," Grace said. "About two years after Kermit's alleged abandonment, Lila got a divorce and married Rusty."

"Hold on," I said, writing furiously. "I'm getting confused. Kermit took on Henry Greer as a partner, and Henry continued to work for Lila after Kermit vanished — until when?"

"I believe until Doug graduated and took over the business," Grace said.

"Do you have any idea why Henry left to open his own company?" I asked.

"Sorry, love. Do you recall hearing anything about that, Lottie?"

"I'm gonna guess that Henry was ready to be his own boss," Lottie said. "Would you want to work for an eighteen-year-old?"

I continued reading my notes. "After Kermit disappeared, Lila got a divorce and married Rusty Miller. Did Rusty own Down the Hatch then?"

"I want to say he did," Grace said, "but please do check with Gert."

"So it's most likely that the key chain belongs to Kermit, his wife, his son, or Henry," I said. "The question is, does it have anything to do with the body we found?"

The bell over the door jingled in the other room, causing both women to head for the curtain, while I sat at my desk musing. What I needed was someone who could tie the key chain to those bones. I didn't know Doug Cannon, but I did recall meeting Henry Greer. Since Bloomers was his customer, I knew he'd make time for me. Hopefully Henry could shed light on the puzzle.

I pulled the black plastic Rolodex file toward me — a relic from Lottie's days as owner — and rolled through it until I got to the *G*s. I found the card for Greer Plumbing and picked up the desk phone to set up an interview. But then I realized I had a dilemma.

I had a partner's feelings to consider now. Would Marco be offended if I didn't confer with him before setting up a meeting? Would he be hurt if I didn't wait for the coroner's report, like he wanted to do? What would I want him to do if our situation was reversed?

This marriage thing was a real game changer.

CHAPTER SEVEN

I was about to put the phone back into its cradle when a little voice of reason in my head whispered, *You could always make an appointment with Henry and then invite Marco to come with you. That would open up a dialogue so you could both discuss your feelings on the matter.*

Excellent advice. I liked that little voice of reason.

"Hello. This is Abby Knight from Bloomers Flower Shop." When would I remember to add *Salvare*? "I'd like to speak to Henry Greer, please."

"He's gone for the day," a man said pleasantly. "If you give me your number, I'd be happy to have him call you tomorrow morning."

"That's okay. I'll call you back." At least I'd have a chance to run it past Marco beforehand. I wrapped the key chain in cellophane, put it in my purse, and plucked the next slip of paper from the spindle.

By four thirty that afternoon, I had cleared away all the orders that had come in and was just about to put finishing touches on an elegant table centerpiece when my niece texted that she was on her way over to see me.

I had made the centerpiece with a rose called Rosa "Joseph's Coat" — a rich orange-red bud that opened to a spray of golden yellow tapering to pinkish orange-red — along with a hybrid tea rose that had creamy white flowers with a sweet rose fragrance, the durable and long-lasting camellia leaf, and the tough leatherleaf fern for my green accents. The Joseph's Coat rose was such a knockout that I liked to keep the rest of the arrangement simple.

"Hey, Auntie A," Tara said cheerfully, stepping through the curtain just as I attached the gift card. She glanced around. "Where's Seedy?"

"Under the table."

Tara dropped her purple backpack on the floor and ducked under the worktable to give the dog a good belly rub, then grabbed a water bottle and her cell phone from her pack and climbed onto a stool.

At thirteen going on fourteen, Tara looked like a young, more slender version of me —

five feet two, green eyes, freckles, and vivid red hair cut in a shoulder-length bob. She had on a faded blue denim jacket over a long white tunic top and dark blue jeggings with brown knee-high boots. The daughter of my brother Jordan and sister-in-law Kathy, Tara was near enough to me in age that she felt more like my younger sister than my niece. Because we were close, when she needed advice she came to me, knowing I would respect her privacy and not blab to her parents.

"What do you think of this?" I asked, turning the arrangement around so she got a three-hundred-sixty-degree view.

"Awesome! Did you have to, like, dip those big roses in paint to get that splattery look?"

"Nope. Mother Nature did that."

"A. Mazing." She leaned forward to bury her nose in one, inhaling deeply and then sighing in pleasure. "I *love* roses. I hope my boyfriend gets me a dozen big fat red ones for Valentine's Day."

"Don't be disappointed if he doesn't. Roses are expensive."

She picked up a loose rose petal and pressed it against her nose to sniff it. "Haydn has money."

"You mean his parents have money."

"He has a job, Aunt Abby."

I hated to sound discouraging, but a paper route, or whatever thirteen-year-olds did for money, wasn't going to go far when it came to a bouquet of expensive flowers, even if I gave him a discount.

She flicked the rose petal into the air and watched it float down. "Why do they cost so much, anyway?"

"It's complicated. Let's just say they are highly prized. In fact, did you know that roses were considered the most sacred flower in ancient Egypt?"

"Like with pharaohs and pyramids and stuff?" Her phone buzzed, prompting her to check her messages as she talked. "So they had roses way back then?"

"Way before then, Tara. Historically, the oldest rose fossil was found in Colorado, dating back thirty-five million years. Thirty. Five. *Million.* Years."

"Huh," she said, texting with her thumbs. Clearly she was fascinated with my florist trivia. With a sigh, she set her phone down. "He's so dreamy."

"Who?"

She rolled her eyes at me. "My boyfriend? Remember back to, oh, about a minute ago, when I said I hoped my boyfriend got me roses for Valentine's Day?"

Ignoring the sarcasm, I said, "Is this someone new?"

"Uh-huh." She took a swig of water, then said coyly, "I really shouldn't say anything else about Haydn."

Translation: *Please ask me about him because I can't tell my parents.*

My inner antennae rose like a periscope. Something about that boy was bothering her.

I pulled the other wooden stool closer and sat on it facing her. Planting one elbow on the table, I propped my chin in my hand and said, "Why shouldn't you say anything else about your boyfriend to your favorite aunt with whom you share everything?"

"With whom?" She burst out laughing. "Are you an English teacher now?"

"Hey," I said. "I try to set a good example. Now answer the question."

Getting serious, she narrowed her eyes, studying me, then suddenly brightened. "Okay." Taking another drink, she capped her bottle and set it aside, then mimicked my posture so we were eyeball to eyeball. "He's tall and has dark hair like Uncle Marco and pale blue eyes and is really smart and popular and plays basketball and writes poetry — how deep is that? — and has his own car and" — she hesitated a second, then blurted — "is seventeen. And he's totally into me."

Mystery solved. Antennae down. Hackles up.

I had to restrain myself from grabbing her shoulders and giving her a hard shake, which I knew would instantly snap those lines of communication. Instead, in a calm, mature voice, I asked, "Don't you think he's kind of old for you?"

Translation: *Are you kidding me?*

"No!" she cried, gazing at me as though I'd just crossed into enemy territory. "Haydn *just* turned seventeen, Aunt Abby, and I'm almost fourteen, so that's only three years difference, and then there's that whole thing about girls being two years older than boys of the same age, so actually I'm almost sixteen, so that makes it like a year between us, and what's the big deal about one stupid year?"

"Tara," I said, "I'm talking about more than just an age difference. You've never dated before — your parents won't even let you date *now* — and this guy's probably had girlfriends and has gone on dates and is, you know, *experienced.*"

"Experienced, like he's had sex? Aunt Abby, Haydn isn't like that. I mean, he writes *poems.* Besides, he's very respectful of me."

"Tara, *all* guys are like that. I don't care how many poems he writes or how respectful he is of you, if you two are alone and start making out, and he wants, well, *more* —"

"Ew!" She gazed at me with a disgusted expression. "Ew!" Then she jumped off the stool and picked up her backpack, angrily stuffing her water bottle and cell phone into pockets. "You don't know me at all." And then she stormed out.

Snap.

I felt something bump against my foot and glanced down to see Seedy gazing up at me as if to say, *You've still got me.*

At five fifteen, I stopped playing FreeCell on my phone in order to watch the weather report on the television mounted above the bar. I was in the last booth at Down the Hatch, waiting for Marco to join me. Seedy lay under the table, gnawing on a rawhide bone. Both of us were damp from the rain that had started just before we left Bloomers. I hadn't had my umbrella with me, but fortunately there were awnings between my shop and the bar.

"Hey, doll," Gert said in her gravelly

voice, "what can I get for you?"

"A glass of that new Australian Shiraz and the answer to a question. When did Rusty Miller become the owner of Down the Hatch?"

"Gee whiz," Gert said, scratching her thinning thatch of graying brown hair, "you're really testing my memory. I want to say Rusty took over the bar in nineteen sixty-nine or seventy."

If Gert was right, then Rusty had owned Down the Hatch a lot longer than thirty years. More like forty-three.

"Let me think about it and get back to you." Gert glanced around to find Marco standing behind her. "Sorry, boss. Didn't see you there. What'll you have to drink?"

"How about the microbrew we got in this morning?"

"You got it," she said, and hurried off.

Marco gave me a kiss, then slid in opposite me. "What is Gert going to get back to you about?"

"Rusty Miller. I asked her what year he took over the bar."

"Abby, if this is about the bones —"

"Yes, Marco, it's about the bones, but would you hear me out before you say anything? Please?"

He gazed at me with brown eyes that at

that moment were telegraphing his disgruntlement. "Go ahead."

I took the wrapped key chain out of my purse and slid it across the table to him. "I put this in my purse yesterday by mistake when Connor came to our table. So since I had it, I enlarged a photo of it and found a Cannon Construction logo on the front. You can just make it out if you look closely."

As he examined it, I said, "Grace told me she remembered that there had been a big scandal in town when Kermit Cannon, the original owner of Cannon Construction, allegedly ran away with Parthenia Pappas. You know who she is, don't you?"

"The artist."

"Right, aka the Duchess of Tenth Street. My mom's taking lessons from her." I paused while Gert set our drinks in front of us.

Marco took a sip of his beer, then said, "Go on."

"Grace has never completely bought the story of them running away together, so that got me to wondering if it might be Kermit in the basement."

Marco seemed a fraction more interested now. "Why doesn't Grace believe the story?"

I filled him in on all the information Grace had given me, watching for signs that Marco was becoming as intrigued as I was. But I didn't see them, so I said, "I want to dig a little deeper to see if I can find a link between the key chain and the bones, and I thought I'd start by talking to Henry Greer, since he was Kermit's partner back then. I want to set the meeting for tomorrow . . . And I'd like you to come with me."

"I thought we agreed to wait until we got a date on those bones before we decided whether to investigate. All I agreed to do was take a closer look at the key chain."

"Actually" — I wiped a drip of wine off the rim of my glass — "what you said was that if the bones were old enough, *you* would agree to investigate. We didn't agree that I *wouldn't* investigate."

"Didn't we have this discussion?"

"Look, Marco, all I plan to do is talk to Henry to see what he remembers about the key chain. I won't go any further than that until we — you and I — talk over what I learn, if there is anything to learn. And if you believe that I'm in danger, I'll stop and wait for the coroner's report. Okay?"

He tapped his fingers on the side of the beer glass, watching me. "Is there anything I can say to dissuade you?"

"No. Is there anything I can say to *persuade* you to come with me?" I reached across to take his hand, that big sturdy hand that I loved. "Because I'd really rather be doing this with you."

He seemed to soften at that. "Sunshine, you know I'd try to lasso the moon if you wanted it, but there's something about the bones that makes me uneasy. You know how you're always talking about your gut feelings? Well, it's like that. It's a strong feeling." He gave my hand a gentle squeeze. "I really don't want you investigating alone, babe."

"But I'm only talking about having a simple conversation with Henry Greer, Marco. You know him, don't you?"

"No, I've never met him. But think about it, Abby. Henry Greer was Kermit's partner, and partnerships are often disputatious. You're talking about meeting with Henry to see what he knows about the key chain, and I'm telling you that you have to consider him a suspect. And you know that any suspect is potentially dangerous."

I sat back, disappointed. "So that's a no?"

Marco sighed deeply, his eyes holding mine. "Are you sure I can't try for that moon instead?"

That was a yes! I clapped silently. "Yay!"

"Let's make this clear," Marco said. "All we're talking about is a conversation with

Greer. Then we'll decide whether to take it any further. But I have to be honest, Sunshine. If I had my way, we'd wait to see what the coroner's report says even before we took this step."

"You two ready to order?" Gert stood at the end of the table with her pencil and tablet in hand.

"Oh, yeah," I said. "I'll have a great big juicy burger topped with goat cheese, Kalamata olives, mustard, and pickles."

"Fries with that?" she asked.

I was in the mood to celebrate, but not to gain weight, and since French fries were my enemy, I decided to skip them. "Coleslaw on the side."

Besides, I knew Marco would order fries. I'd just nip a few of his.

"Abby, try this one," Marco said, patting the thick, quilted mattress next to where he lay.

We were in the bedding store, the only customers there at that early-evening hour, and the middle-aged salesman was hovering, a metal clipboard clasped against his white shirtfront and navy print tie. He'd introduced himself as the manager. The black plastic pin above his shirt pocket read BOB MORRISEY in white letters.

I had Seedy on her leash, but at the moment, she was beneath the bed Marco was testing, peering out fearfully at Bob, who seemed overly eager to sell us something.

"Too firm for me," I said after trying it.

"This isn't too firm," Marco said, pressing his hand into the mattress to demonstrate.

"Too firm for *me.*" I walked up the row, sat on the edge of a mattress with a fluffy pillow top, bounced a little, then lay back on it. "I like this one better."

Marco stretched out on it, too, folding his arms behind his head and closing his eyes. He looked so yummy that two middle-aged women who had just entered the store paused to ogle him.

He sat up. "Not enough support. My back would hurt."

"Hello, young ladies," Bob sang out. "Have a look around and I'll be with you after I help these fine folks find just the right bed."

"Just browsing," one of them called.

Bob dropped them like a hot potato. "Perhaps you'd like a mattress that conforms to each of you," he said to us with a cheerfulness I hadn't seen in anyone since the department store Santa last December. He indicated a bed on the opposite side of the room where the expensive sets were displayed. "It's called the Duality King. Let's go have a look, shall we?"

Marco followed him, but Seedy didn't want to leave her hiding spot, so I had to coax her out and then carry her. By the time I reached the men, Marco had already read the price sign taped to the headboard and was standing with his arms folded, a frown on his face, waiting for me to get up to speed.

"Wow," I said. "That's a lot of money for a mattress."

"My first car didn't cost that much," Marco muttered loud enough for the salesman to hear.

"But it's money well spent," Bob said, lifting his eyebrows to impress that upon us. "You'll both get exactly the kind of rest you need. You'll wake refreshed every morning, ready to face whatever the day brings. Now can you put a price on that?"

I almost expected him to break out in a rendition of "Tomorrow."

Obviously Marco could put a price on it. "I think we'll stick to the beds in the other section," he said, and crossed back to his rock-hard fave.

"Do you have something in between that one" — I pointed to the mattress Marco had stretched out upon again — "and that one?" I pointed to my choice.

Bob gave me a sympathetic smile, as though it pained him that I had to lower myself to an inferior product, then led me to the far end. "This is a medium firm." In a low voice he said, "I really think you'd be happier with the last one."

And he'd be happier with his commission, too.

I set Seedy on the tan linoleum and perched on the medium firm. Not bad, I thought, bouncing. I swung my legs up and lay back. It wasn't as pillowy as the second one, but it also wasn't as hard as the first. Now I felt like Goldilocks. "Marco, try this bed."

He came over and stretched out beside me. "Not as firm as I like."

"It's not as soft as I like, but we have to compromise."

"What kind of price are we talking about?" Marco asked Bob, sitting up.

The salesman's über-cheerful expression instantly faded. "The price is marked on the headboard."

Marco gave him a look that said, *You know you can do better than that.*

"Unfortunately," Bob said with sad eyes, clearly trying to appear aggrieved, "I'm not in a position to lower the price."

"I thought you were the manager," Marco said.

"Well, yes," Bob said slowly, "but it's still not my decision to make."

Marco rolled his eyes. "Then let me talk to the person who *can* make the decision."

I looked around. There was no one else there. Even the two women had left.

The salesman's irritation was obvious as he said, "Wait here. I'll have to make a call."

"You do that," Marco said. "Meanwhile, my wife and I are going up the street to see what kind of sales your competitor is having. Let's go, Abby."

He strode toward the door, not even waiting for me. Annoyed, I grabbed Seedy and followed him outside, where the streetlight's glow reflected on the wet asphalt and the air smelled of fish. At least it wasn't raining.

"Don't you think you could have waited to see what his boss said?" I asked.

"Abby, he's the manager. He can make that decision. I hate it when salespeople play games." Marco opened the passenger door for me. "If he wants our business, he can trot his butt out here with a better deal."

Why had I never seen this stubborn side of Marco before? Did he think the other bedding store would deal with him any differently? Were we fated to wander from town to town looking for a forthright salesman? I sighed in frustration as I slid into the car, imagining weeks, maybe months, of sleepless nights. Marco got behind the wheel and started the engine, but left his door open.

"Sir?" I heard someone shout. "Wait."

I looked out the back window, stunned to see Bob loping toward Marco's side of the car, his metal clipboard still clasped against his shirt. Panting, he said, "Let's go back inside and talk."

"Not unless you've got a better price for me," Marco said, and shut the door.

Seedy, clearly believing she was safe, growled at Bob from the backseat.

The salesman pressed a sheet of paper against the window. "Would this bring you inside?"

Marco studied it for a moment, then rolled down the glass. "Change that fifty-nine on the end to two zeros and maybe."

Bob pretended to ponder the matter, then nodded. "I believe I can do that for you."

"You're starting to make sense now," Marco said. Under his breath, he said to me, "Let's go buy a mattress."

As we stood at the counter waiting for the

credit card to clear, Marco's cell phone rang.

"Salvare," he said quietly, walking away.

"Here's your sales receipt and your warranty information," the salesman said, handing me several papers. "I can get this delivered to you by Saturday afternoon, if you're going to be home."

I'd have to put up with the lumpy mattress for three more nights, but at least the end was in sight. "I'll be there."

I was just tucking the paperwork into my purse when Marco returned. "All done," I said. "The mattress is coming on Saturday."

"Great." He didn't sound great. In fact, he had a furrow between his eyebrows.

"What's wrong?"

"I'll tell you outside."

My heart was in my throat as I picked up Seedy and hurried after him. He didn't say a word until we were in the car, and then he said, "The bones are gone."

"Did the coroner come for them?"

"Not the coroner, Abby. Someone stole them."

Chapter Eight

Marco hit his fist against the steering wheel. "Damn it."

Seedy jumped from the backseat into my lap and hid her head under my arm. "Tell me what happened," I said.

"Rafe saw muddy shoe prints leading from the back door to the basement doorway and followed them downstairs, thinking someone had gone down to get supplies from the storage area. He noticed the overhead bulb was on over the excavation site and went to investigate. That's when he discovered the theft."

"Did it happen just now?"

Marco started the car. "He didn't know, but it had to have been sometime after we left because I walked that hallway. I would have spotted muddy footprints." He smacked the steering wheel again. "I've told Rafe over and over again to make sure that the back door isn't left propped open. I can't tell you how many times I've warned my employees about that, and yet they do it anyway. That's why Rafe *has* to monitor it when I'm not there."

"Why do they prop it open?"

"It gets hot back in the kitchen, so they do it for fresh air. Sometimes they'll leave it ajar because they know they'll be making another trip out to the Dumpster soon, or someone is out for a smoke and leaves it open. Right now I don't really care what the reason is. Someone is to blame and that person is going to get fired."

I was glad I wasn't in Rafe's shoes. Whether he was directly responsible or not, he'd screwed up yet again. "Is there an alarm you can put on the door that will sound an alert when it's left open longer than a minute?"

"Since I can't seem to count on my brother to monitor it, I guess I'll have to look into it." With a heavy sigh he said, "What do I tell the coroner when he comes to collect the bones?"

I wanted to reply, *That he should have collected them as soon as they were discovered so they weren't our problem,* but I knew that in Marco's present mood, the comment would only stir his wrath. Instead, I tried to channel his thoughts away from the angry side.

"How is it possible to get a skeleton out of the basement without being seen?"

"The bones aren't connected. They were probably thrown in a bag and carried out like a load of laundry."

"Still, any of the staff could have come upon the thief leaving the basement," I said. "Who would take that risk?"

"A desperate person, Abby. Do you understand now why I didn't want that newspaper article to come out yet? And why I want the police to handle the investigation? I could choke MacKay for bringing us into it."

Well, *that* diversion didn't work.

"We can forget a DNA analysis now." Marco pulled out his cell phone and handed it to me. "Would you call Sean and ask him if he's free to meet me at the bar in about half an hour?"

I gave him a look that said, *Seriously? Me?*

"Never mind," Marco said. "How about dialing for me?"

I found Reilly in his contacts and hit the CALL button, then handed the phone back.

"Hey, Sean, it's Marco. What's happening?" He listened a few moments, then said, "If you're free, would you meet me at the bar this evening? I need your advice on something. Great. Sure. I just have to drop Abby off at home, so give me about thirty minutes."

I tapped Marco's arm. "You're not leaving me out of this, Salvare."

"Make that fifteen, Sean," Marco amended. "Thanks, man."

With one beer apiece for Sean Reilly and Marco, and a fresh Shiraz for me, we sat at the second to the last booth at Down the Hatch and exchanged several minutes of pleasantries, mostly about our honeymoon.

"So this advice you need" — Reilly took a swig of beer — "does it have anything to do with those bones in the basement?"

"Is the news all over the police station?" I asked.

"Nah. I saw the article in the *New Chapel News*." Leaning toward Marco, Reilly said in a low voice, "Several of the guys down at the station have a bet going that you'll run your own investigation."

I was about to say, *Put your money on us, Reilly,* but decided to let Marco do the talking. As usual, he cut right to the chase. "Someone removed the bones, Sean," he said quietly.

Reilly's eyes grew wide. "When?"

"Between six and seven thirty this evening,

while Abby and I were out."

"That's a busy time here," Reilly said. "Damn, that was ballsy."

"Tell me about it," Marco said.

"Have you called it in?" Reilly asked.

"I have now," Marco said.

Reilly grinned as he pulled a small note-pad and pen from his chest pocket and got ready to take notes. "Proceed."

"My brother discovered the theft when he noticed muddy shoe prints leading from the back door to the basement," Marco said. "Don't even get me started on how someone was able to get inside that door. It's a comedy of errors. And to make the situation even worse, the prints aren't visible anymore, the excavation site has been smoothed over, and the shoe prints on the steps have been obliterated. I questioned my employees about the size of the prints, but no one except Rafe noticed them, and he isn't sure whether they were male or female because they were mashed."

"Why didn't the coroner remove the bones when you first called them in?" Reilly asked.

"Thank you," I said. "That was my question, too."

"I was told that he was busy at an accident scene," Marco said. "He's scheduled to come out tomorrow."

"I'm amazed the detectives didn't close down the whole basement," Reilly said. "You've got a crime scene down there."

"I think they were doing me a favor by not closing it," Marco said. "They cordoned off the excavation site and trusted, I suppose, that I would keep it secure."

Reilly rubbed his face, thinking. "Did they take photos of the bones and collect soil samples?"

"Yes," Marco said. "They haven't sifted the dirt yet though."

"Well," Reilly said slowly, "it's not the best circumstances to conduct an investigation, but at least they have something to go on. Will you show me the hole?"

I tucked Seedy into Marco's office, then followed the men to the basement, where they were already standing at the edge of the concrete. As Marco and I had seen just before Reilly had arrived, the soil was smooth.

Using Marco's flashlight, Reilly crouched down for a closer look. "See this?" He pointed to the dirt. "See these faint ridges? They look like they were made with a tool of some sort, like a trowel."

"Trowels don't have ridges," I said.

"He's not talking about a garden trowel,"

Marco said. "He means the kind used in construction." He glanced around. "There used to be an old one down here, but I don't see it. Maybe the thief used it and took it with him."

Click. The proverbial lightbulb went on in my head. "Marco, when we were down here with the plumber, Seedy dug an old garden trowel out of the dirt."

"You didn't tell me that," Marco said.

"I didn't think anything of it at the time. I dropped it over there with other old garden tools. When you mentioned a trowel just now, it clicked!"

"What clicked?" Reilly asked, as Marco went to find the tool.

"The curved dent in the man's skull. I've dug enough holes in the clay soil of my grandma's garden to know what kind of mark a garden trowel makes. It's an arc, and so was the dent I saw on the top of the skull. It can't be a coincidence that it was buried in the dirt near the body."

"It's fairly unusual for a murder weapon to be left at the crime scene," Reilly said.

"What better place to leave it than under a cement floor?" I asked.

"I don't see it," Marco said, as we joined him by the pile of junk.

I pointed to the other tools. "I laid it right

there. It had the same long wooden handle that these have." I picked through the junk to make sure the trowel hadn't fallen behind them, but it was definitely gone.

Reilly walked back to the hole, studied it for a moment, then turned to Marco. "You asked for my advice, so here it is. If it were my basement, I wouldn't want a big hole in the floor over the winter."

"It'll take that long for the detectives to get over here?" Marco asked.

"All I can tell you is they've got a lot on their hands right now," Reilly said. "Because of the robberies, they've got a backlog of cases piled a foot high on their desks."

"And I'll be at the bottom of the pile even with this new development?" Marco asked.

"Maybe they'll give you some priority," Reilly said, "but it won't be until they catch the robbers. That could be tomorrow or Christmas. I'm just saying, if it were me, I'd do what I could to speed the process along."

I wanted to hug Reilly, but instead I gave Marco a looks-like-we-have-no-choice-now shrug.

"I'll write this up and make sure the coroner gets a copy," Reilly said. "That'll save him a trip."

And Marco the embarrassment.

"Thanks, man," Marco said, clapping him

on the back.

That time I did give Reilly a hug.

"So we're starting the investigation tomorrow morning?" I asked Marco as we drove home. Seedy was in my lap gazing out of the passenger-side window, panting happily. I stroked her fur, waiting for Marco's reply, but got only a heavy sigh as an answer.

"Is that a no?"

"If it wasn't for that damned big hole in the basement floor it would be a *no way,* but I can't leave it open, exposing all that old contaminated soil when I serve food one floor above. The health department would shut me down in a heartbeat. So it's a reluctant yes. But just so you know, I have a lot of misgivings about you being involved, Abby. I'd rather handle the investigation on my own."

"Well, I don't have any misgivings. We're a team now, Marco, and there's no *I* in team. Just so *you* know."

Thursday

Before Lottie or Grace could comment on my tired eyes or somnolence the next morning, I greeted them with, "Morning. New mattress is coming Saturday. I need coffee."

They smiled at me like proud parents.

I put Seedy on the floor and followed

them into the parlor, where Grace poured me a cup of her special brew and offered me a cranberry scone. Although I'd had a piece of toast, in my exhausted state my willpower was weak, so I accepted. Then the three of us sat down at one of the white tables, while Seedy gazed up at me so dejectedly that I offered her a piece of scone.

"I wouldn't spoil her, love," Grace said. "She'll get used to it and will make a nuisance of herself at mealtimes."

"Oh, boy, I know that from the dogs my boys have had," Lottie said. "You don't want to start it, Abby."

"Sorry, Seedy," I said. "That's all you're getting."

The dog tilted her head, as though trying to understand my words. She looked so cute, I had to glance away before I indulged her again. I blamed it on a lack of sleep and drained my coffee cup.

"Any word from the detectives yet?" Grace asked.

"No, and you won't believe what happened. Someone got into the bar's basement yesterday evening and stole the bones, along with a key piece of evidence."

That prompted a barrage of questions, so I filled them in on the details as I poured us all more coffee. "Even Reilly feels that we should investigate," I said. "Marco and I talked about it later and he's finally seeing the wisdom in it, although he's insisting we not let it get around town."

"My lips are sealed," Lottie said, making a zipping motion across her mouth.

"Marco's right about staying mum," Grace said. "It takes a lot of moxie to pull a heist under the very noses of one's employees. That speaks volumes about the person who's willing to chance it. It makes one wonder what else might be chanced to ensure that the killer's identity not come to light."

That was basically what Marco had said, only not as eloquently.

"So where do you begin?" Lottie asked.

"With Henry Greer and the key chain," I said. "We're hoping to meet with him today." I checked the time. "And I need to go set up that appointment right now."

I finished the scone and headed toward the workroom with Seedy at my heels. She went straight for her bed under the table and curled up there, chewing on a rawhide bone that Lottie had brought for her, while I made the call. As Marco and I had decided, I didn't reveal the purpose of our visit. I merely told the man who answered the phone that I wanted to talk to Henry about a business matter and hoped he had time around noon to see me. We set the appointment for one p.m., the soonest Henry was available.

I switched lunch hours with Lottie, and shortly before one o'clock Marco and I made the five-block walk south on Washington Street to an old brick carriage house across the railroad tracks. The weather was nippy for late September, with a stiff breeze, so even though the sun was shining, I wrapped my blue denim jacket tightly around me and stuck close to Marco's side. Seedy was back at Bloomers with Lottie and Grace, happily curled in her bed.

"What's our strategy?" I asked Marco.

"Show Greer the photo and get him to tell us as much as he can about it. As far as he's concerned, we're simply on a fact-finding mission. I'm not going to play connect the dots with him."

"He's bound to put the facts together, Marco. Henry can't be a stupid man and run a successful business."

"Of course he will. That's what I want him to do. When he makes the connection, just follow my lead."

I threaded my fingers through Marco's and gave his hand a happy squeeze. "Team Salvare on the job."

The renovated carriage house served as both office and warehouse for Greer Plumbing. It had solar panels on the clay-tiled roof, both quite uncommon in Northwest Indiana, as well as two hybrid vehicles parked outside with the Greer logo on them. I pointed them out to Marco. "We know one thing about Henry. He's energy-conscious."

A man around Marco's age rose from the reception desk and ushered us to Henry's office in the front corner of the building. The room had a tan ceramic tile floor and narrow windows on the exterior walls, but instead of interior walls, it had partitions made from tall, royal blue metal file cabinets. It contained a modern oak desk with a shiny black granite top, black mesh desk chair, and two lime green folding chairs in front of the desk.

Henry rose as we came in, and walked around the desk to greet us, looking a bit puzzled to see two of us. He was a model-handsome man possibly in his late fifties. He had a slender build, medium height, light brown hair that had gone white at the temples, pale blue eyes, and a warm smile. He wore a blue checkered shirt tucked neatly into dark blue jeans, a navy pullover sweater draped over his shoulders and tied around his neck, a navy belt, and navy canvas shoes.

He had a thick stainless steel watch with a blue face on one wrist and a wide blue rubber band on the other. I could practically feel Jillian shudder. She wasn't a big fan of matchy-matchy, as she called it.

"Marco Salvare," my beloved said, shaking Henry's hand. "We haven't met officially, but your company is handling repair work for me at my bar."

"At last we meet in person," Henry said with a smile. "And this is Abby Knight, as I recall." He had a distinctly formal manner of speaking that sounded almost old-fashioned.

"It's Abby Salvare now," Marco said, looking at me with such a glimmer of pride that a surge of happiness welled up deep inside me. "We were married recently."

It was all I could do not to throw my arms around him and hug him tightly, so I linked arms with him instead. I had to learn to contain my exuberance.

Henry turned his warm smile on me. "I hadn't heard that you'd gotten married. That's wonderful. Congratulations to both of you."

"Thank you," I said demurely, while the child inside me danced.

I glanced at the surroundings as we settled onto the folding chairs. Several sports trophies were displayed on the metal filing cabinets, and a pair of hockey sticks and a blue bicycle helmet hung from hooks on one wall. Henry's desktop was interesting, too. It held a large, ultrathin computer monitor, keyboard, wireless mouse with a bright blue-and-green-plaid mouse pad, a royal blue pen, a two-foot-tall prickly pear cactus in a lime green pot, a neon blue plastic holder for sticky notes, and a square lime green clock. It was still matchy-matchy, but I liked the artistry of it.

Then I looked up and saw three enormous curving spiderwebs suspended from the two-story ceiling, one of them positioned right over my head. And where there were spiderwebs . . . I gave a hard shudder. I wasn't afraid of much, but spiders could make me shriek like a little girl.

Henry leaned forward in his swivel chair, suddenly serious. "I hope you haven't come about the work Stan's doing for you. He's one of my best plumbers."

"You're aware that I had to stop the work," Marco said.

Henry looked perplexed. "The last time I spoke with Stan, he told me about the condition of the pipes, but he didn't seem to think he'd have any trouble fixing it."

"When was that?" Marco asked.

"Tuesday afternoon. I have to apologize for not knowing that there's been a subsequent problem, Mr. Salvare. I've been away for a two-day convention in Chicago and just got back last night. Please tell me what the issue is. My goal is always to satisfy the customer."

Marco folded his arms and sat back. I knew what was coming, so, as per Marco's training, I focused on Henry's face.

"The issue," Marco said, "is that we found human remains beneath the basement floor."

Chapter Nine

Henry's eyes widened and his hand went to his throat. "You found a body?"

"A skeleton," Marco said.

For a moment, all Henry did was sit there shaking his head in disbelief. "I can see now why you stopped the work. Do you have any idea who it is — or should I say was?"

"The detectives haven't identified the remains yet," I said. "We thought maybe you could help with that."

"Me?" Henry appeared surprised but not alarmed. "I'm confused. Shouldn't the police be handling the investigation?"

"We're assisting," Marco said.

He was being rather tight-lipped, so I added, "Marco's a private investigator. We've helped the police a number of times. You've probably read about us in the newspaper."

Henry blinked at me. Okay, so maybe he didn't read newspapers. Before he had a chance to ask any more questions, I took the key chain photo out of my purse and laid it in front of him. "This item was found near the remains. Can you make out the logo on it?"

He leaned over the photo. "My God. I haven't seen one of these in decades."

"Would you identify it for us, please?" Marco asked.

"It's a Cannon Construction key chain. You say it was found near the body?"

"About two feet away," Marco said. "Any idea how it might have gotten there?"

"I suppose Kermit could have dropped it while he was working there," Henry said. "Kermit was the owner of Cannon Construction. I'm assuming keys were discovered with it."

"None found," Marco said, "but the investigation is ongoing."

I took out my notepad and pen, expecting Henry to ask whether we thought the bones were Kermit's, but he merely folded his hands on the desk and looked at us as though waiting for the next question.

"Can you tell us anything else about the key chain?" I asked.

He tilted his head, as though thinking it over. "Not a whole lot, I'm afraid. If I remember correctly Kermit had one, as did his wife and son."

"Did you have one?" Marco asked.

"No, Kermit had them made before I came aboard." Henry studied the photo again. "My goodness, does this bring back memories. Kermit used to stick his finger through the ring and twirl the keys around as he talked. It drove people absolutely bonkers."

"What kind of work was Kermit doing for Down the Hatch?" Marco asked.

"He was hired to install drywall in the basement's main room to cover up the old concrete blocks, put in a cement floor, and make a storage room near the staircase."

"Who had contracted for the work?" Marco asked.

"Rusty Miller," Henry said.

Aha! That was what Grace had said, too. I made a note and put an asterisk beside it.

"Were you working for Kermit at the time?" I asked.

As Henry began to speak, I thought I felt something crawling on my shoulder — a spider? I brushed furiously at my shirt, feeling a shriek coming that would split eardrums.

No, no, no! Stifle it! that little voice in my head cried. *You have to be professional. Don't embarrass Marco.* I clamped down on my tongue, using all my willpower to muffle that scream. I looked at the floor to see if anything had fallen off, but the tile was clear. I glanced at the web hanging above me. Had I imagined it?

Then I realized Henry had stopped talking, and I'd missed his answer. I let out a breath, only then realizing I'd been holding it, and pasted on a smile. "I'm sorry. You were saying?"

"I said we were partners at that time." Henry was watching me curiously.

"Did Cannon Construction put in the cement floor?" Marco asked.

"No, Rusty did," Henry said.

That was a stunner. I wrote: *How could Rusty not remember owning the bar when the basement work was done?* I underlined it and wrote *Fishy* next to it, then subtly showed the notepad to Marco.

"Why didn't Kermit do the floor?" Marco asked.

"It's a long story," Henry said, then sighed sadly, if a tad dramatically.

Unfazed by emotion, Marco said, "Can you give us the condensed version?"

Henry plucked a tissue from the box on his desk and wiped a smudge off the shiny granite top. "The condensed version is that Kermit wasn't getting the job done because of his drinking problem, and then he stopped showing up altogether. Rusty decided to take matters into his own hands, so he laid the cement."

"Weren't you working with Kermit?" I asked.

Henry handed the photo back to me. "I was on another job, a remodel of the New Chapel Savings and Loan's second floor."

"Was it typical to work separately?" I asked.

"Sure, if we had multiple jobs going. There were only two of us back then."

"Just so I'm clear on this," Marco said, "did Rusty fire Kermit?"

"Yes, and then apologized to me later," Henry said. "To be honest, I wasn't aware that Rusty was having problems with Kermit because sometimes I'd go days without seeing Kermit. It wasn't until Kermit's wife, Lila, called me to ask if I knew where her husband was that I learned something was amiss. We both guessed he'd gone on a bender, so I checked with Rusty to see if he knew where Kermit was."

Strange how Rusty hadn't mentioned any of that in the newspaper story. I also noted Henry's *To be honest.* Marco had once told me that it could indicate that a lie was forthcoming.

"Did you talk to Rusty on the phone," Marco asked, "or go see him in person?"

"In person, of course," Henry said. "I was as concerned as Lila was. As soon as I received her call, I went straight to Down the Hatch to find out what had happened. That was when I learned what Kermit had been up to, and frankly, I didn't blame Rusty for being frustrated — I knew he'd needed to get the basement finished to bring the building up to code — but I wished he'd let me know what was going on. I would have put the floor in for him."

"So Rusty never approached you about finishing the basement?" Marco asked.

"Not the floor. Rusty had already taken care of it. Well, I should amend, with Doug Cannon's help."

"Kermit's son was working with his dad?" I asked.

"Oh, no, Kermit never allowed that." Henry paused and gave us an apologetic smile. "I'm sorry. I can see that I'm confusing you. Doug would sometimes ride his bicycle over after school to wherever his dad was working to see if he could help. Not that Kermit ever let him. But that's an entirely different matter. Anyway, as I recall, Doug stopped by to see his dad and found Rusty pouring a new floor, so he helped."

"Did you learn that from Rusty?" Marco asked.

"I believe so," Henry said. "It's been a long time."

"But Rusty did hire you to build the storage room?" Marco asked.

"Correct, plus he had me remodel the kitchen and bathrooms upstairs. But by that time, I was working alone," Henry said.

"Did you ever find out why Kermit didn't show up for that job?" I asked. I loved playing dumb.

Henry studied us quietly, as though taking our measure, then said, "You're young, so you may not be familiar with some of New Chapel's more colorful history, but Kermit abandoned his family and ran off with another woman."

I wasn't good at pretending to be surprised, so I focused on writing it down.

"Would you give us the woman's name?" Marco asked.

"Are you familiar with the artist known as the Duchess of Tenth Street?" Henry gave a sniff of disgust. "It was her."

Feigning ignorance, which I *was* good at, I said, "Parthenia Pappas? She lives in town."

"She came back," Henry said. "Alone."

"Did she ever say anything about Kermit?" I asked. "Where he was, what he was doing?"

Henry's mouth tightened, as though the subject were distasteful. "I wouldn't know. I haven't spoken to her since that time."

"His family must have been worried sick about him," I said.

"I'd use the word *hurt* instead," Henry said. "Especially Doug. You know how a boy wants to look up to his father. Sadly, Kermit left a lot to be desired as a father and a husband."

"Even so," I said, "Kermit's abandonment must have devastated them financially."

Henry rolled the bright blue pen back and forth along the granite. "Not really. They managed well without him. The business was viable enough to provide a good income for all of us. Lila ran it quite successfully until Doug was old enough to step in. At that point I left to form my plumbing company. That was my bigger interest anyway."

Remembering what Grace had said about Kermit treating Henry better than he'd treated his own son, I said, "You don't sound sorry about Kermit's leaving. Weren't you close to him?"

"Not really, but of course I was sorry that he abandoned his family. Absolutely,"

Henry said. "Kermit was a cad to leave them in the lurch. It colors my feelings toward him to this day."

A cad? Who besides Grace used that word anymore? "He left you in the lurch, too, didn't he?"

Henry shrugged. "Let's just say you take the good with the bad in a partnership."

Was that a tickle on my neck? I scrunched my eyes shut and told myself that I was imagining it, but dear God, there it was again — and here came the shriek.

Don't scream, Abby. Do. Not. Scream. Focus! Be a professional not a sissy.

It was all I could do not to open my mouth and let out that shriek. Instead, shuddering hard, I slapped my neck and turned my collar out, giving it a good brushing. But once again, nothing fell to the floor. I cast another fearful glance up at the web but saw no spiders dangling. What I really wanted was to take a closer look at the floor to see if there were any signs of the little fiends, but I didn't want to appear as though I wasn't paying attention.

Marco glanced at me to see if I was ready, then said, "Would you tell us about Kermit's drinking habits?"

Henry gazed at the pen as he rolled it, as though deciding what to say. "I guess the family won't mind me telling you this since it was widely known, but for maybe the last six months before Kermit left town, his drinking had become a major problem. He'd bring whiskey in a thermos and drink steadily all afternoon, then finish up work for the day and hit the bar before going home. He had a large capacity for alcohol, but eventually it got to the point where he wasn't functioning well."

"That must have put quite a burden on you," Marco said.

"To some extent, yes. I had to make up for the work he didn't get done." Henry paused, as though about to say something else, but then he merely smiled and shrugged. "Partnerships don't always work out."

He was certainly cavalier about it. I wrote: *Motive for Henry — Kermit wasn't a good partner. Left him in the lurch.* Since the business had thrived without Kermit, the motive was weak but all I had at that point.

Still caught in his reminiscing, Henry said with a sigh, "Poor Lila. Sometimes she'd call me late at night and ask me to help her get him home from the bar. It wasn't a good scene at all. And Kermit was a mean drunk. The girls were afraid of him."

"Daughters?" I asked.

"Two," Henry said. "Sweet little things. One was in middle school and one in elementary school. Kermit's son, Doug, was very protective of them. He wouldn't let his dad near them when Kermit had been drinking."

"Was Kermit abusive?" I asked.

"No one talked about that much back then," Henry said, "and I never saw any of them sporting bruises, but as we know, there are all kinds of abuse."

I felt something crawling on my right hand and twitched like I'd been bitten. "Damn it!" I shook my hand furiously but nothing was there.

Both men stared at me in surprise. Knowing I should have a better explanation than *I thought I felt a spider,* I said, "I just hate hearing about abuse. But please continue." Then, using the pen to casually scratch my neck, I turned a hostile eye upward, imagining tiny octocreepies dropping down on me like miniature parachutists. But again I saw nothing. I *had* to get a look at the floor.

"Let's just say that Kermit was very heavy-handed with his criticisms," Henry continued, "especially toward the people he loved."

With my hand still tingling from the imagined bite, I wrote hastily: *Kermit was verbally abusive.* Then I "accidently" dropped my pen on the floor so I could see what was beneath me.

No spiders at all. Was I hallucinating them simply because I'd seen the webs? I retrieved my pen just as Henry crossed his ankles beneath the desk, revealing the soles of his neat blue shoes. How odd. Brown mud was caked in the ridges. More mud lay in little piles on the floor, as though it had fallen off the shoes as it dried.

Realizing that it had gone silent above me, I straightened to find the men once again waiting for me. "Sorry," I whispered. "Dropped my pen." I jotted a quick note about his shoes so I'd remember to ask him about them later.

"I never could figure out why Lila stuck with such a bastard of a husband," Henry continued. "But Lila was a faithful wife, a kind and beautiful lady who deserved better. And somehow Doug was able to shrug it off." Henry shook his head sadly. "No accounting for love, is there?"

"Was Kermit critical of you, too?" I asked.

For a split second, I thought Henry was going to cry. Looking down, he said softly, "Kermit was critical of everyone close to him. It was just easier for me to handle than for his kids."

I added to my note: *Inner circle of abuse: Kermit's wife, children, and Henry. The Duchess?* Somehow I couldn't imagine a strong woman like Parthenia Pappas taking abuse from anyone. But then, as Henry had pointed out, love did strange things to a person. I glanced at Marco, trying to imagine him being abusive. Love or not, I'd be out of his life so fast, his skin would peel.

Henry folded his hands on the desktop. "When I look back on it now, I can see that Kermit was an unhappy man. I firmly believe drinking was his means of escape."

Was something on my arm?

I turned my elbow out so I could see the whole arm, but nothing was there. Trying not to interrupt the interview, I scooted my chair closer to Marco's to get out from under the web, but the legs caught on a raised tile and the chair tipped me right into his side.

"Is everything okay?" Henry asked, as Marco righted me.

My cheeks burning from embarrassment, I lifted my chair up and set it down again. "It was rocking. One of the legs was on an uneven tile."

Marco studied me for a moment, then turned back to Henry. "Why was Kermit unhappy?"

"I'm not sure. Depressed, perhaps? You must know people who drink to escape their lives. All I can say for certain is that Kermit was a difficult man. He had an engaging Irish charm but also a wicked temper brought on by dark moods."

I couldn't imagine staying with a man like that. "Was his running off with the Duchess a complete surprise?"

"I was surprised but not shocked," Henry said. "I knew he'd been seeing someone, and by the way, that wasn't the first time he'd cheated on Lila. There had been other women, too."

"Did his wife know?" I asked.

"I'm certain she did," Henry said. "She intimated as much to me after Kermit left. I'm positive Doug knew, too, so he probably told her."

"Did Doug talk to you about it?" Marco asked.

"Not at first," Henry said. "Maybe a month before Kermit left, Doug started pumping me for information about what Kermit did during his lunch hour. I was always honest with him. I told him that sometimes, instead of eating his brown bag lunch, Kermit would vanish and then reappear an hour and a half later with no explanation. I didn't tell Doug that Kermit always came back wearing a big grin and a swagger. And then one day Doug told me he had followed his dad to the Duchess's house. He never said anything to me about what he saw, but I had a strong hunch that he'd caught Kermit in the act."

"When was that?" Marco asked.

Henry pondered the question for a moment. "I'm not sure, but it would have been while I was working on the bank job." With a sigh, he said, "Poor Doug. I used to cringe when Kermit laid into him. I remember the boy leaving the work site practically in tears many times. Sometimes Lila would come down to ream Kermit out afterward, but it never did any good. Kermit was who he was and nothing was ever going to change him."

I wrote: *Kermit abusive to Doug. Doug catches dad cheating? Kermit disappears. Motive for Doug — anger, betrayal?*

"How old was Doug then?" I asked, just as something tickled my ankle.

Ignore it, Abby. It's your imagination again.

No, that was definitely something. I lifted my pant leg and saw a brown spider with short hairy legs and a fat body with a red spot on it crawling up my shin. *That* was not my imagination!

That shriek I'd withheld before came out at full force as I jumped to my feet, slapping the spider as hard as I could with my notepad. It fell to the floor, still alive, and crawled straight toward me. Still shrieking in terror, I stamped my foot on it until it was just a memory. Then I stood there rubbing my arms to stop the shivers, staring at the giant web above me.

Only then did I notice that Marco had risen and Henry had come around his desk. Both were staring at me in surprise.

"Spider," I said in a trembling voice and sank into the chair, shaking like a leaf. This time I tucked my feet beneath me.

Marco shot me a quizzical glance that said, *Are you all right? It was just a spider,* as though I'd gone mental. Well, let him deal with a hairy eight-legged monster on his shin and see how he liked it.

I cleared my throat and went on as if nothing had happened. "So *how* old was Doug?"

Henry resumed his seat. "Doug was fifteen. Big, strapping kid. Took after his dad in height but was bigger built."

"Do you know how the family is doing now?" I asked. I had one eye on the ceiling and one on the floor in case the departed arachnid had avenging siblings. It wasn't easy to take notes.

"I run into Doug every now and then," Henry said. "He still operates the family business. One of his sisters, Sara, moved to New York City. The other one, Rona, lives in Maraville with her family, and Lila married Rusty Miller about two years after Kermit left town. Interesting tidbit: Rusty and Lila were high school sweethearts once upon a time. I always thought it was perfect that they married. She died just a few years ago, God rest her soul."

"Mr. Greer," the receptionist said in a low voice, stepping around the corner of a filing cabinet, "you have an appointment in fifteen minutes. I thought I'd better remind you."

"Thanks, Kevin." Henry picked up a briefcase that had been sitting beside his desk and began putting files into it. "Is there anything else I can answer quickly?"

There certainly was. "I happened to notice the mud caked on your shoes," I began.

But before I could even frame my question, Henry said, "Occupational hazard. I inspect some pretty muddy work sites." He scooted back his chair and stood up. "Anything else?"

"I think that will do it," Marco said.

I glanced at my hubby in surprise. Wasn't he at all curious as to why Henry wasn't asking the obvious question? But he merely gave me a nod toward the door.

Fine. If he wouldn't ask, then I would.

Chapter Ten

Before I could utter a word, Marco put his arm around my shoulders and said, "Let's let him get to his meeting, Abby."

I gave him a questioning glance, and he shook his head, as though to say, *Not now.*

Henry stood up and walked around the desk, his hand stretched toward Marco. "Nice meeting you, Mr. Salvare. Mrs. Salvare. I hope I've helped."

"You've given us a lot of useful information," Marco said. "We appreciate your time."

As soon as we were out of the building, I said, "Why did you stop me? I had questions to ask."

"I know you did, and I didn't want you to ask them."

"Why not? Wait. Are we talking about the same thing — why Henry didn't figure out that we were investigating Kermit's murder?"

"He figured it out, Abby, in the first five minutes. I saw it in his eyes."

"So why didn't he ask?"

"You tell me."

"Ah, a test. Okay, the obvious answer would be that Henry is the murderer."

"Or?"

I pondered it as we waited at the stoplight. "Or . . . maybe it frightened Henry to think that his former partner had been murdered."

"There's another possibility. Henry might know who the murderer is and want to protect him — or her." Marco pointed toward the green light above me. "Are we going to cross the street now or did you want to wait around for the next light?"

I got the hint. I hooked my arm through Marco's and we crossed together. "I could see that as a strong possibility. Henry did seem to like Kermit's wife and children — enough to know what the kids are doing now."

"What's your impression of Henry?" Marco asked.

"Overall he seems like a fussy but decent guy. His reaction to the news that we'd found bones seemed natural, except, as we just discussed, for asking who they belonged to. I didn't buy it when he said he was sorry about Kermit's leaving. His body language said he couldn't have cared less; plus it sounded like the business flourished without him. I also didn't believe him when he said he hadn't known that Kermit wasn't showing up for work. Other than that, Henry didn't really give away much about his own relationship with Kermit except to acknowledge that Kermit was difficult and critical.

"But here's something I found contradictory. Henry clearly didn't like Parthenia Pappas, yet if Kermit was such a lousy husband, father, and partner, and Lila and the kids were better off without him, what was Henry's beef with the Duchess taking Kermit away? It sounds to me like she did the family and Henry a favor."

"See a motive?" Marco asked, as we crossed the railroad tracks.

"Just that Kermit's drinking was dragging the company down. If Henry felt threatened by that, then there's his motive."

"You're on a roll, Sunshine. Keep going."

I thought back over the interview as we waited at the corner by the courthouse for the light to change. "I see a motive for Kermit's son, Doug. Besides taking abuse from his dad, he might have caught his dad cheating on his mom shortly before Kermit's disappearance."

"*If* Henry's information is reliable. Remember, Abby, this happened a long time ago, and memory can be a tricky thing. And don't forget that Henry is a suspect, so everything he says has to be verified."

"Of course. And here's something interesting. Henry struck me as a fastidious guy. His clothing, his desk, his manners, they all seemed neat. But his squeaky clean shoes had mud caked on the soles. I find that odd for someone who's obviously a neat freak. Is it really an occupational hazard or did he track mud from the alley down to your basement?"

"I'm sure he does inspect his work sites, but we don't have prints, so there's no way to know."

"What about Kermit's wife? Do we consider Lila a suspect, too, even though she's dead?"

"We don't rule anyone out yet."

"Then Lila goes on the suspect list. After what Henry told us about Kermit's cheating, I can certainly see what *her* motive would've been."

Marco glanced at me. "Is there a reason you're giving me the stink eye? Is that your subtle way of telling me I'd better not pull a Kermit?"

"Just keep in your head an image of what

I did to the spider."

With a laugh, Marco put his arm around me. "Abby, you're the love of my life. You don't need to worry. You're more than enough woman for me."

"Just so we're clear."

"Gotcha. So you're terrified of spiders, huh? I didn't think you were afraid of anything."

"I don't want to talk about it. I might throw up. Now where were we?"

"There's Rusty."

"Right. Who is another puzzle," I said. "How could Rusty have forgotten that he had work done in his basement when he laid the floor himself?"

"No, Sunshine — I mean, there's Rusty." Marco lifted our hands to point toward a man coming down the courthouse steps. "Let's go see if he has time to talk to us."

Rusty Miller was a legend in New Chapel, at least to the generations that remembered the man who rode his horse into town as though he lived in the Wild West of old. Dressed in full cowboy regalia, Rusty would canter his quarter horse, Dolly, down Lincoln Avenue every Saturday afternoon at exactly one o'clock and tie her up on a bicycle rack outside Down the Hatch, where he would entertain the townsfolk with his stories.

My dad used to bring my brothers and me down to the square to watch Rusty and Dolly ride in. One time Rusty even let me sit on Dolly, with whom I was madly in love. My brothers, however, were too chicken. All it took was one look at the horse's big teeth and they backed away. Sadly, eventually the streets got too busy and Rusty's horse got old, so he switched to a small red Ford pickup truck onto which he had mounted a gigantic pair of bull horns. Even without his horse, he was still a sight to behold.

I saw by the way Rusty was moving down the cement steps that he wasn't as spry as he used to be. He also wore glasses now, and his leathery face was lined with wrinkles, but I had to remind myself that he was, after all, in his midseventies. Yet he still sported the same maroon leather cowboy boots, stiff blue jeans, a red shirt with fringe, a black string tie, and his infamous ten gallon tan cowboy hat with a maroon leather band.

As we approached, Rusty caught sight of us and broke into a wide grin. Doffing his hat, he said, "Well, if it ain't little Miss Abigail Knight. My, but you're a sight for these ol' eyes."

I stared in surprise as he shook my hand. "You remember me?"

"With that purty red hair and those polka dots all over your face, who could forget you? Howdy, Marco. Good to see you stepping out. That ol' bar can suck the life out of a feller, can't it?"

For years I'd thought Rusty was a Texan because he spoke like the cowboys I'd watched on TV, and Texas was where I'd believed all cowboys hailed from. Now I knew that he'd been born and raised in New Chapel. Obviously, he'd talked in his affected manner for so long, he couldn't help it.

"Good to see you, too, man," Marco said, shaking his hand. "How've you been?"

"You'd know if you'd ever come out to my shop," Rusty said with a wink.

"That goes both ways," Marco said.

"I know, I know," he said, "but it ain't easy findin' time these days. With all the renewed interest in Western apparel, my business keeps me hopping. Miss Abigail, there's a pair of boots that are just callin' for you to try them on. Distressed brown leather with blue, yellow, and red daisies stitched onto the shaft . . . They even have pull-up straps to make them easy to slip into. Don't they sound like something a purty young florist would want to wear?"

Yes, they did. "I'd love to see the boots, Rusty. Maybe we can stop by after work one evening. What time do you close?"

"Six o'clock on the nose," Rusty said, tapping his long, crooked proboscis. "Say, is it true what I hear about you two getting hitched?"

"It's true," I said, beaming. I was doing a lot of beaming these days.

"Well, don't that beat all?" Rusty said. "I b'lieve this calls for a drink. Come on. I'm buyin'."

"Thanks," Marco said. He cast me a glance that said, *Perfect.*

With the departure of the lunch crowd, Down the Hatch had nearly emptied out, so we had no problem snagging the last booth. Marco and I slid onto the bench facing the plate glass window in the front and waited while Rusty had a reunion with Gert.

"Golly, how I've missed you, darlin'," he said, lifting her off her feet in a bear hug. "You doin' okay with this greenhorn runnin' the place?"

While they chatted, I did a quick check of the time and saw I had just about fifteen minutes before I needed to be back at Bloomers. "Marco," I said quietly, "I can't stay long. What's our strategy?"

"Just friendly conversation, no note-taking on this one. I'll lead him around to the bone discovery and see what he has to say. If he's talkative and you have to leave, just go. I'll fill you in after work."

"I ordered us some bubbly," Rusty said, sliding onto the opposite bench. "Hope that's all right, but danged shame if it ain't." He guffawed, then glanced around. "Place looks good, Marco. You still have all those ol' photographs up on the wall, I see."

"Everyone loves them, Rusty," Marco said. "I don't dare take them down."

"How's business fer you?"

"We were a little slow until the other day," Marco said, "when that article about the bones made the newspaper."

"I'll bet," Rusty said, nodding, obviously aware of the discovery. "A thing like that is bound to fascinate folks. Police making any headway on who the feller was?"

"It's still too early for results," Marco said. "But as long as we're on the subject, something interesting was found buried near the bones. Abby, do you have that photo with you?"

"Here's our bubbly," Rusty called, as Gert arrived with a bottle of champagne and three flutes.

I waited until Rusty had toasted us and

we'd taken a drink before sliding the photo across. Rusty picked it up and squinted at it, then held it under the overhead light. "Looks like a piece of a leather strap."

"It's a Cannon Construction key chain," I said. "You can just make out the logo on it."

Rusty squinted at the photo again. "Now that you mention it, I can see the little cannon on it." He handed it back as though he had no further interest in the subject, and reached for his champagne. When he picked up his glass, I noticed that his hand was trembling. Had that just started or had I missed it before? "Good stuff," he said, smacking his lips. "Never heard of this brand before. You get a good deal on it?"

"It's Italian sparkling wine," Marco said, "so it's more reasonably priced. Anyway, we talked to Henry Greer today and he identified the key chain as probably belonging to Kermit Cannon."

"Funny guy, that Henry," Rusty said. "Did I ever tell you about the one and only time I ever saw Henry drunk? True story. After Henry's first day on the job, ol' Kermit had a party for him at the bar to celebrate him becoming an official partner. In fact, if you look up on the wall behind the bar" — he turned to point — "you'll see a photo of us standing out front with Henry, who's got a look on his face like a deer in the headlights.

"Well, sir, it soon became as clear as ice that poor Henry didn't know his way around a bottle, because after Kermit finished toasting Henry, the company, everyone in his family, and every person in the bar, Henry was so pickled that he couldn't find his way to the john. Tossed his cookies right in the middle of the crowd."

Rusty was laughing so hard he had to take off his glasses and wipe his eyes. "Henry never darkened our doorstep again. I don't think he ever forgave Kermit for embarrassing him. He always was kind of a fussbudget."

"Henry didn't say anything about that incident," Marco said. He was pretending to study the wine in his glass but I could tell he was watching Rusty like a hawk. "But he did mention that he and Kermit did some work for you downstairs. Do you remember hiring Kermit to do some remodeling work on the basement?"

As though thinking it over, Rusty polished his glasses with his napkin, then put them back on. "Now that you bring it up, I do recall something about it. My memory ain't what it used to be, I'm sorry to say."

His memory had seemed fine for the

interview with Connor MacKay.

Marco continued. "Henry said you got so annoyed with Kermit for not getting the job done that you fired him."

"Now, that ain't quite so," Rusty said with a bit of ire. "I couldn't fire the bastard because he wasn't there *to* fire. Tell you what, though, if he hadn't vamoosed, I sure would've canned his behind. He was tanked up on liquor more often than not."

So Rusty did remember.

"Who finished the job?" Marco asked.

Rusty scratched the back of his head. "I guess that would've been me, come to think of it. When Kermit stopped showing up, I had to put in the new floor to finish off the main room."

"Thinking back," Marco said, leaning against the back of the booth, "when you put your cement down, do you remember the condition of the dirt floor?"

"How do you mean?"

"Did it look freshly turned? Rough? Packed down?"

"Son," Rusty said with a chuckle, "I can't even remember what I ate for breakfast this morning."

"Would Doug Cannon be able to answer that question?" Marco asked.

Rusty's smile stiffened ever so slightly.

"Why would Doug know?"

"Henry told us Doug helped you with it," Marco said.

"Huh." Rusty sat back, looking confused. "Well, considering Henry's a lot younger than me, I guess he'd be remembering right. As I said, it's kind of foggy." Rusty wrinkled his forehead and looked away, as though trying to remember. He took a drink of the sparkling wine, swirled it on his tongue, and swallowed. "Hold on now. The ol' brain is starting to chug."

Then he snapped his fingers. "Of course. How did I forget that? Doug came by one day and saw me putting in the floor and wanted to know why Kermit wasn't doing it. So I explained that I hadn't seen Kermit in a few days, and the kid stepped right up to help. Good boy, that Doug. I never could figure out why that ol' fool Kermit treated Henry better than his own kid."

"That must have been painful for Doug," I said.

"Could you blame him?" Rusty asked, almost angrily.

"Did Doug offer any explanation as to why his dad had stopped showing up for work?" Marco asked.

"No, sir," Rusty said. "It wouldn't have needed explaining. Folks around here knew

Kermit was a notorious drunk. Nothing escapes attention in a small town."

"Did Doug seem angry about it?" Marco asked.

"I wouldn't say he was angry. More worried than anything else," Rusty said. "Kermit would disappear for hours, but he'd never been gone for days."

"Did Doug ever ask you what his dad did during his lunch hours?" Marco asked.

Rusty gave Marco a quizzical glance. "Why would he do a thing like that?"

Instead of answering, Marco pressed on. "Did you ever notice Doug spying on his dad, or following his dad after he left here?"

"Son, I was way too busy running the bar to notice anything of that nature," Rusty said with a smile.

"Did you know Kermit outside of business?" Marco asked.

"Heck, yeah," Rusty said. "We went to high school together, played on the same basketball team . . ." He shook his head. "Now you're really taking me back."

"Were you friends?" Marco asked.

"Like brothers," Rusty said, entwining his first two fingers.

"Did it seem out of character for Kermit to run off with another woman?" Marco asked.

"Wish I could say it was, but the varmint had been cheating on Lila for years. Didn't surprise me in the least that he ran off. I always kinda figured it was a matter of time."

"You married Kermit's wife, didn't you?" I asked.

"Don't sound right when you put it like that," Kermit said. "I married his *former* wife sounds better."

"Did you go to high school with Lila, too?" I asked.

Rusty assessed me, a shrewd look in his eyes. "Been doin' some homework, have you?"

"Lucky guess," I said, feeling my cheeks grow hot.

"Well, you're right. I did." He drained his glass and set it down. "Haven't had bubbly in years, not since I lost my lovely Lila. Forgot how good it tasted. And now I've got to leave you fine people and head on back to the shop."

"Thanks for your time, Rusty," Marco said.

"My pleasure." He scooted off the bench and settled his hat on his head. "Don't be strangers."

As soon as he was out the door, I was on my feet. "I have to get back, Marco. I've got a ton of orders to do."

"I'll walk you down. I want to get your impression of Rusty while it's still fresh."

"I wish I could've taken notes," I said, stepping outside as Marco held the door for me. "He gave us a lot of information. So here goes from memory. First thing I noticed was that he didn't seem shocked when he found out what was in the photo, but I noticed his hand trembling afterward."

"I caught that, but was it nervousness or an old age tremor?"

I hooked my arm through Marco's as we walked down Franklin. "I couldn't tell and forgot to look for it later. Rusty also tried to deflect the subject of Kermit working for him by telling us the drunken Henry story. And did you catch the fake smile when I asked Rusty if he and Kermit had been close?"

"If it hadn't been for that, I might have bought the *like brothers* response."

"The only time Rusty seemed the least bit out of joint was when he learned that Henry had told us he'd fired Kermit. He didn't like that at all. And wasn't it amazing how suddenly his memory became clear?"

"I caught that. He also seemed defensive of Doug," Marco said.

"I thought so, too. Henry and Rusty both

remembered Doug as being worried about his dad's absence and agreed that it was in character for Kermit to run off with another woman. And also that Kermit's drinking problem was well-known."

"Anything else about Rusty?"

"Not really, except that I was having a hard time believing he'd forgotten about the basement work. Sure memory can fade with age, but Kermit's disappearance was a major event. And then Rusty married Kermit's wife. So why was he pretending not to remember?"

"For the same three reasons that you gave for Henry," Marco said.

"I just can't imagine Rusty killing anyone, Marco."

"That's because you're looking at him as an old cowboy. This murder happened close to forty years ago, Sunshine. Rusty would have been in his prime. Have you ever seen the photos of him at the bar? He was a big guy. As much as I don't want to admit it, I think we're going to have to consider Rusty a suspect. We'll need to verify everything he told us with Doug Cannon and Henry Greer."

I glanced at Marco in surprise. "Does that mean we're going to keep investigating?"

"If I say yes, will you wait until we're

home before you throw your arms around me and whoop?"

"To get you to say yes, you bet I will."

"Man, you cave easily." And with that, he swept me up in his arms and carried me the last ten feet to Bloomers's door, where he gave me a kiss and set me down. "See you at five."

I stood out front and watched Marco stride confidently up the sidewalk. How had I gotten so lucky?

Inside, Lottie was ringing up a customer at the front counter and Grace was serving tea and scones to three women in the parlor, so I headed straight for the workroom. As soon as I stepped through the curtain, Seedy gave a yip and came out from under the table to greet me, wagging her bushy tail as hard as she could. I crouched down to cuddle her and got a few licks on the chin as my reward.

Lottie came into the room and headed toward the walk-in coolers. "We sold out of the carnations and daisies. Don't that beat all? It isn't even a holiday."

"Look at this, Lottie. Seedy saw you and isn't ducking for cover. She must be getting to know you."

"She's my little buddy, aren't you, Seedy?" Lottie gave her a scratch under the chin then disappeared inside the cooler, reappearing in a minute with containers of flowers. "How did the interview go?"

"Better than I thought. We met with Henry Greer and then we ran into Rusty Miller. He insisted on buying us a bottle of champagne to celebrate the wedding, so we got to ask him a few questions, too."

"Two birds with one stone." Grace sailed through the curtain with fresh slips of paper to put on the spindle and a doggy biscuit for Seedy, who wagged her tail in delight. We were making progress.

"You've been a good girl today, haven't you, love?" Grace asked her.

Seedy took the biscuit to her bed, where I could hear her crunching it.

"We're all ears, love," Grace said to me. "Tell us about your interviews."

As I prepped flowers for the next order, I filled the women in on our conversation with Henry, but had to put Rusty's story on hold when more customers came in. It wasn't until after three o'clock that they were both able to rejoin me in the workroom.

"Here's a nice cuppa," Grace said, setting down a cup of tea on the table nearby. "Now do tell us about your talk with Rusty."

"We didn't get to talk to him at length," I

said as I snipped rose stems for a bouquet. "At first he claimed his memory wasn't good, and then he tried to change the subject, but he finally did offer a little information."

I gave them the finer points of our conversation, then ended it with, "After we interview Doug Cannon, I'm sure we'll need a trip to the saddle shop for a longer talk with Rusty."

"I take it that means you plan to investigate?" Grace asked. "Didn't I say our Abby would prevail, Lottie, dear?"

"Didn't I agree?" Lottie replied.

"Is Rusty a suspect then?" Grace asked me.

"We have to consider him one," I said. "Rusty not only owned Down the Hatch when Kermit went missing, *he* put in the floor that covered the body, which we wouldn't have known if Henry hadn't mentioned it."

"But isn't Henry a suspect, too?" Grace said doubtfully. "And isn't it possible that Henry is trying to turn the spotlight on someone else?"

I tore off a big piece of floral wrap and laid it under the pot. "That's what suspects usually do, Grace. But actually Henry was pointing more in Parthenia Pappas's direction."

"I know you and Marco have to do what you have to do," Lottie said, "but be gentle with Rusty. I've always had a soft spot in my heart for him, and since he lost his wife, the poor old guy just hasn't been the same."

"Rusty took his wife's death hard," Grace said, sweeping pieces of fern fronds off the table and into the trash can. "Most people thought he was a confirmed bachelor until he surprised everyone by marrying Lila. It was shortly after Lila's death that he began looking to sell Down the Hatch."

The bell over the door jingled, and then I heard a familiar, "Yoo-hoo!"

"It appears your mum has arrived," Grace said, and sailed out to greet her.

"I hope she's not mad at me," I told Lottie as I snipped lily stems. "I haven't had an opportunity to talk to her since we uncovered the bones."

"Well, she's bound to have read about it in the paper," Lottie said, "so she might be a little put out. Hey, now there's someone who might be able to help you find out more about Kermit Cannon. Your mom's got an inside track with Parthenia Pappas."

"At least I know she's not bringing in a new piece of art, and *that's* a relief."

Lottie gave me a puzzled glance as she handed me a greeting card to put on the arrangement. "What makes you think she doesn't have art for you?"

"It's not Monday."

"You weren't here this past Monday, remember? You came back on Tuesday."

Relief gone.

Chapter Eleven

On weekdays my mom was just an average, mild-mannered kindergarten teacher. She dressed in conservative clothing, wore her honey brown hair in a simple layered bob, cooked healthy meals for my dad, did volunteer work at the animal shelter, and cared for her llama, Taz.

The weekend mom was a different story. That was when Maureen "Mad Mo" Knight appeared dressed in her paint-splattered artist smock, frayed jeans, and fuzzy blue socks, clumps of clay caught in her hair and a plucky gleam in her light brown eyes. Weekends were Mom's creative time, when she would produce works of — something — that she then brought down to Bloomers on Monday for us to sell, believing she was helping to improve our bottom line.

The bottom line was, however, that each one of Mom's works of — something — was like having two nightmares in the same night: There was the actual piece, and then there was having to sell it.

Once, Mom made the Mad Mo version of a strawberry pot, which one would think would be harmless enough until one saw hers. Painted in four different neon colors, its spouts placed at all the wrong angles, its sides uneven, the pot was so ugly that I told Mom it sold, then hid it in the basement and later actually used it as a weapon to take down a killer.

I was never sure if it had been the sight of that horrendous pot sailing toward him or the hard thunk on the head that had done the job, but what had it mattered? Now I could say with all honesty that my mother's artwork knocked people out.

Parting the curtain, Mom paused to gaze at me as though I were a cute little bunny. "There's my beautiful daughter."

She didn't seem angry, but something was definitely up. Mom never called me beautiful. One, I wasn't. Two, she didn't believe in labeling children. She claimed it ruined them.

She put a large Macy's shopping bag on the floor and gave me a hug. "My precious little girl — married. I still can't believe it."

Hearing a soft yip from under the table, Mom bent down to look. "Hello, Seedy! Are you happy your mommy's back home? Come here, girl." She clucked her tongue, which worked on her llama but not on Seedy, so she straightened and hugged me again. "How does it feel to be Mrs. Salvare?"

"Mom, you've asked me that five times, and my answer hasn't changed. Please don't call me Mrs. Salvare. It makes me feel like Marco's mom."

"Speaking of whom," Mom said, sliding onto a stool as I attached the card to the arrangement, "I hear Francesca is helping out here."

"Just three mornings a week."

"Still, I remember how you've complained before about her crowding your space, and I know how much you like your privacy. Don't you think you could get along without her?"

Was my mom jealous of Marco's mom?

"If we didn't need Francesca, she wouldn't be working here, trust me, Mom. But I left it up to Lottie and Grace, and they said they needed the extra hands."

Mom's smile faded. "Oh. I see. Then I suppose if we look on the bright side, that means business is good." She slid off the stool and walked over to the Macy's bag. "But I'll bet you wouldn't mind it being even better."

Cue the drummer. It was time for the big reveal.

Mom lifted her piece out of the bag just as Lottie came through the curtain. Lottie uttered a stunned, "Oh!" then clapped her hand over her mouth. Mom didn't notice, thankfully. She was too busy arranging her latest clay sculpture on the table in front of me.

Oh! didn't begin to cover it. *Oh, dear God,* maybe.

A giant peanut loomed before me. Standing a good two feet tall, it had a woman's face carved into a peanut shell–shaped body, long wire arms that cradled a smaller peanut, long wire legs, and wire feet with tiny red beads on the ends that clearly represented toes. Peanut Woman stood on a base that looked like the top half of a peanut shell. The smaller peanut was gazing up rapturously at the larger one, its thin wire arms reaching up as though to touch the larger one's face.

"Ta-da!" Mom said, holding out her arms. "My latest creation. I call it *Nutter and Child.*"

Lottie backed out through the curtain, her hand still over her mouth. I thought I heard muffled snickers as she hustled away.

"Nice work," I said. Telling the truth was out of the question.

Mom gently tucked a lock of my hair behind my ear. "Mother and child. I was thinking of us when I made it, Abigail. You were always my special girl, you know."

Being the only girl could have explained that. Was this sudden emphasis on mothers and daughters due to Francesca's presence at Bloomers? "Thanks, Mom. How did you come up with a peanut theme?"

"The Duchess said I should take my inspiration from what's around me, so as I sat on the sofa one evening trying to come up with a new idea, your dad was eating peanuts and making a mess of the shells."

There was no accounting for inspiration. "And what did the Duchess have to say about your — creation?"

"She thought it was brilliant, and, coming from her, that means a lot."

Brilliant? Was I missing something or did the Duchess simply want to keep a paying student?

Mom smoothed her thumb over an imperfection in the clay. "How do you think we should price it?"

The other half of the nightmare! "Did the Duchess have any suggestions?"

"Not really. She said it would depend on

the market."

Supermarket, perhaps. What were peanuts going for per pound these days? "I'll have to research it."

"I don't want to leave it here in your way," Mom said. "Where should I set it?"

On fire? "Just put it on the counter over there by my desk."

She placed it on the counter and adjusted it twice before she found the right angle. "I can't wait for you to see my next project."

"You've already started another one? What was Dad eating this time?"

"It wasn't your father who inspired me. It was a walk I took at the new skateboard park, and that's all I'm going to tell you."

That was more than I wanted to know. What I really wanted was info about Parthenia. To get it, though, I had to risk Mom's ire. "Did you see the article in the paper about the bones Marco and I found?"

"Your father read it to me," she said. "That's his new hobby — reading the news out loud. I think he wants to drive me crazy. But what a horrible discovery that must have been for both of you, Abigail, and how comforting to have a husband there for support." She paused to flick a piece of green foam off the table. "Was Marco's mother lucky enough to hear the news from her child or did she have to rely on the newspaper, too?"

Yep, Mom was irked. "I'm sorry I haven't called. Things have been crazy lately."

At that, she softened and came over to hug me again. "You don't need to apologize, honey. I do remember what's like to be a new bride."

"Thanks, Mom."

She took a seat on a stool while I went to the cooler to pull stems for the next order. "Have you and Marco decided whether you're going to investigate?"

I stepped out of the cooler with an armful of white spider mums, orange carnations, and yellow roses. "We're going to investigate, but you have to keep it a secret. We don't want it to get around town."

Mom pursed her lips the way she always did when she wasn't pleased with what she was hearing. "You never need to worry about me letting anything out, Abigail. Have you mentioned the need for secrecy to Francesca, too?"

"Not yet. We made our decision just a few hours ago."

"Perhaps you should tell Francesca when she comes in to help you tomorrow."

Oh, boy. Mom was not going to let that go. I decided to ignore it. As I prepped the blossoms I asked, "How are you enjoying your lessons with the Duchess?"

"I love them, Abigail. Parthenia is so worldly and knows so much about the creative process that it's an honor to work with her."

"She seems so exotic. Do you know anything about her background?"

Mom perked up. This was her chance to show just how helpful she could be. "I know that she was born in Alexandria, Egypt, of Greek parents; speaks fluent Greek, Arabic, and French; and has won many awards for her sculpture. I know she is living above her studio on Tenth Street and uses olive oil to keep her skin soft and her hair shiny. Let me think what else."

"Was she ever married? Did she have children?"

"I believe that's a no on both counts." Mom reached over to retuck the lock of hair that did not want to stay behind my ear. She wasn't above spitting on her fingers to accomplish that, so I had to keep one eye on her. "Parthenia never mentions having any children, and a mother will always talk about her children. I know I talk about my beautiful daughter the florist all the time."

That was a switch. She used to talk about me as the daughter who couldn't make it through law school.

Mom hopped off the stool and wandered over to my desk, where she flipped through the slips of paper on the spindle. "You don't seem that busy today. I see only a dozen or so orders waiting."

"I've made several dozen arrangements already, and we were very busy this morning."

She peered over my shoulder as I snipped spider mum stems and inserted them in the wet foam. "But are you so busy that you need Francesca?"

"If business dies down, I promise Francesca won't be here."

"Oh, good — for you, I mean. I know you like to work undisturbed." She patted my arm, causing my snippers to bob. I wondered if she was aware of the irony.

"Has the Duchess ever mentioned the scandal she and Kermit Cannon caused?" I asked.

"That happened a very long time ago, Abigail. Where did you hear about it?"

"Someone at the bar mentioned it." Did she need to know that someone was me?

"Parthenia has never brought that subject up, and I certainly wouldn't ask her about it. How embarrassing it has to be for her. I'm sure she'd rather forget the whole thing ever happened."

"She can't be too embarrassed about it, Mom. She did come back to town."

"That's true." Mom resumed meandering around the workroom.

"Do you remember hearing about it? You were probably what — a teenager?"

"I was fourteen, about Tara's age, and I do remember my parents talking about it — when they thought I wasn't listening." She had a slight grin on her face as she picked through my containers of silk flowers, as though she had been quite the little eavesdropper.

She pulled out a silk bird of paradise blossom. "Would you mind if I borrowed this?"

"You can have it. Did you ever hear what happened to Kermit Cannon?"

"No, although there was some buzz at one point that he deserted Parthenia and went to Mexico because he found out she was pregnant. But looking back on it now, I'm fairly certain that was just idle gossip."

Gossip or not, it was new information. "What makes you think it was just gossip?"

"What I said before about a mother always talking about her children. There have been many occasions when Parthenia could have mentioned a son or daughter, or at her age, grandchildren, but she never has. I realize that doesn't mean she didn't have any children. Being a mother, it's just a strong feeling I have. You'll understand, too, when you're a mom. That wouldn't be anytime soon, would it?"

"No," I said, giving her a scowl. "Do you remember when that gossip about Parthenia began? Was it right after she left town?"

"Not right after. Maybe three months later. Someone talked to someone who claimed to have seen Parthenia at an art show down in Columbus, Indiana, and thought she looked pregnant. I overheard my mother and some of her friends talking about it at one of their coffee klatches."

My mother, a sneaky teen! I was seeing her in a whole new light. "Did you overhear anything else about Parthenia?"

She fixed me with a shrewd gaze. "You're awfully interested in the Duchess all of a sudden."

"I just find her an interesting person." Or a person of interest, depending on one's viewpoint.

Mom's cell phone rang, so she dug through her purse to get it. "It's your dad," she said, checking the screen. "He's probably wondering where I am. Hello, Jeff. I'm heading home right now. I stopped at Bloomers to drop off my sculpture. Abigail loves it, by the way."

Right. The way I loved diving into an icy-cold lake. Once the shock wore off, I swam like hell for the shore.

Mom kissed me on the cheek. "I know I usually wait until Monday, but I'm so excited about my new project that I'll be back Saturday morning with another surprise for you."

I'd have a surprise for her, too. I wasn't scheduled to work on Saturday.

At five fifteen, I set the alarm and locked the front door. Then Seedy and I crossed the street to the courthouse lawn so she could take care of her business before we headed toward Down the Hatch. I was standing at the corner waiting for the light to change when a bright red Mustang screeched to a halt. The Mustang's bass was turned up full blast, causing the car to rock, the air to vibrate, and Seedy to scrunch her body low to the ground and put her head down, as though she were trying to muffle the sound.

Annoyed, I stuck my fingers in my ears and glared at the two teens inside. It was a boy and a girl who were kissing so passionately over the console that they were oblivious to me. So I yelled as loud as I could, "Hey! Idiots! Turn it down!"

The pair broke their lip-lock, and the passenger turned toward me to glare back. But then her eyes widened and her mouth dropped open.

Coincidentally, I had the same look on my face.

It was Tara.

Chapter Twelve

The light changed, the Mustang took off, and so did I, straight for Down the Hatch, practically dragging Seedy on her leash. "Marco," I said breathlessly, bursting into his office, "Tara . . . in a Mustang . . . kissing a boy . . . driving too fast!"

"Abby," he said, rising, "catch your breath and start over."

As Marco came around the desk to pick up Seedy, who had sensed my distress and was crouched at my feet whining, I gulped in a lungful of air and pointed toward the doorway. "I just saw Tara in a car smooching with an older boy who nearly blew through the stoplight. I know she saw me, so she has to be scared — and she should be! When her parents hear about this, they'll ground her for a year."

"But they're not going to hear it from you, are they?"

"What? Yes! Marco, this is *Tara,* an innocent young girl with no dating experience. She doesn't understand the dangers of teenage boys, especially the older teens. I *have* to let my brother know. It's my familial duty."

"Abby, Tara's not stupid. From what you told me earlier, she knows she's in the wrong to be out with him. Now that you've seen her with this boy, maybe she'll stop."

"And if she doesn't? Come on, Marco, you were a teenager once. You know how potent those hormones are."

"Sunshine, think about what would happen to your relationship with Tara if you ratted her out."

I felt all the steam leave my body. Hadn't I told myself the same thing? But what was I going to do? I didn't want to be the family snitch, the aunt my niece couldn't trust. Yet at the same time, I was concerned.

"Let's have some food and talk about a possible solution," Marco said. "I'll get a big steak bone for Seedy and let her chill out in here. She's still trembling."

I ran my hand down her scrawny little body. "I'm sorry, Seedy. I forget how sensitive you are."

She gave my face a lick. All was forgiven. If only it were that easy for humans.

The bar was busy, so we didn't get our

favorite booth at the back, but at least we had one. We ordered green salads and bowls of beef stew and were discussing Tara's situation when my phone beeped to signal a text message.

"Speak of the devil-child," I said, and showed Marco her message: *Pls don't tell M & D. I wn't do it agn.*

Marco read it. "I take it M and D are Mom and Dad? Interesting that she doesn't say *what* she's promising not to do again. Ride in the boy's car? Kiss him? See him?"

"I'll text back and ask."

"You're better off having a face-to-face, Abby. Then you can lay down some ground rules."

"And act like her parents? She'll just sneak around me, too."

Marco leaned back and sipped his beer. "Tough one."

"What did your mom do to protect your sisters?" I asked.

"You don't want to do that."

"Tell me."

"If *Mama* suspected anything was going on, she'd send my older brother, Rico, and me to spy on that sister, and if she was sneaking around, we were told to deliver a message to the boy."

"And that message was?"

"Touch one hair on that girl's head and we'll snap you in half like a twig."

"Did it work?"

"Do you really think I'd spy on one of my siblings? But yes, it did work, only because *Mama* told the girls what her instructions were, and they believed her."

While Marco ate, I pondered his story. "Okay, what if we invite Tara and her boyfriend for ice cream after school? Then I'll find a way to get Tara to slip off to the ladies' room with me, and you can threaten to snap the boy like a twig if he hurts her in any way."

"Yeah, right. And the next day he'll show up with his dad and a cop. Who is this boy anyway? Not the police chief's son, I hope."

"All I know is that he's got a fancy Mustang and his first name is Haydn." I began tapping the keypad on my phone. "I'll find out his last name right now."

"It's not that important. I was just curious."

"So am I." I set the phone down and resumed eating. When I hadn't heard anything by the end of our meal, I texted her again and got a one word reply: *Busy.*

"Just leave her alone for now," Marco said. "She can't ignore you forever, and I'm sure she got the message that you're concerned."

Still fuming, I said, "She'd better have gotten the message."

"Let the rest of that steam out of your ears so you can hear me. I've got a jammed day tomorrow, so I'd like to go see Doug Cannon first thing in the morning. Seven o'clock is a good time to catch construction people before they get busy. Are you up for it?"

"Hey, I'm a team player, Marco."

"Good." Marco paused, then arched his eyebrow devilishly, telling me his thoughts had gone in a different direction. "Speaking of playing, what do you say we set a playdate for, oh, say eleven o'clock tonight?"

I gave him a skeptical glance. "You're not talking about doing surveillance work, are you?"

He picked up my hand, turned it over, and pressed a light kiss on my wrist. "What do you think?"

Friday

Why had I promised Marco to be up early again? Oh, right. The interview with Doug Cannon. And why had we gotten to sleep so late? Oh, right.

I showered, dressed, dabbed on a little makeup, had coffee, and ate toast with almond butter and honey, all without speaking a word. When I was tired, and it was still dark outside, I didn't converse much, because at such times, cheerful things did not tend to come out of my mouth.

"Ready?" Marco asked, as I clumped out of the bathroom after brushing my teeth.

He stood at the apartment door looking his usual hunky self, in black leather and blue jeans and black boots, holding Seedy's leash in one hand, a thermal mug in the other, studying my face for signs of coming to life.

He held out the travel mug. "I've even got coffee to go for you."

"Thanks," I rasped, not having used my voice yet. "That was sweet of you."

"I'm a sweet kind of guy."

My first smile of the day.

We drove separately to Bloomers, got Seedy set up, then took Marco's car and headed to Cannon Construction. By that time, I had finished my coffee, the sun was up, and I was on the case with my teammate. The day was looking bright once again.

"Let's talk about our meeting with Doug," Marco said. "Unless he got a call from Henry, he won't be aware of the key chain's existence. We need to make sure he believes that the detectives have it, which I should have done with Henry. I don't want a repeat of the bone theft."

"Got it. You do want me to take notes, right?"

"Yes, just proceed as we normally do."

Marco drove through the open gate of the cyclone fence that surrounded Cannon Construction and pulled into a parking space in front of the two-story gray frame building. We entered the building through a heavy glass door imprinted with the Cannon logo into a very small, windowless, gray-walled reception room. It had two white vinyl chairs in one corner, a small Formica-topped reception counter at the back, and a doorway behind it.

When no one appeared to greet us, I tapped a bell on the counter, and a few moments later a man with salt-and-pepper hair stuck his head around the corner. "Yes?"

"We're here to see Doug Cannon," Marco said.

The man stepped all the way out. He was an imposing guy — tall, very sturdily built and good-looking — in his late forties or early fifties. He was wearing a long-sleeved tan work shirt and brown work pants. He didn't smile but said pleasantly enough, "I'm Doug Cannon. What can I do for you?"

Marco flipped open his wallet to reveal his PI license as he introduced us. Then he said, "I don't know if you saw the article in the newspaper, but a skeleton was discovered in the basement of my bar, Down the Hatch, along with an item that may have belonged to your father. If you have time, we'd like to get your take on it."

At the mention of Kermit, something flickered in Doug's eyes. Was it anger? Fear? But he spoke calmly. "Rusty said you might be stopping by. Come on back to my office."

So it had been Rusty, not Henry, who'd contacted him. Interesting.

We followed him through the doorway, up a short hall, and into an office paneled in light wood. The room was outfitted with an oak desk that appeared to be quite old, a worn brown leather desk chair, a few wooden shelves on a side wall that held stacks of magazines, files, and blueprints, and two plain oak chairs.

"Have a seat," Doug said. He settled himself at his desk, his hands folded serenely on top, watching me as I took out a notepad and pen. Shifting his attention to Marco, he said, "Is it safe to assume that your investigation is centering around the bones being Kermit's?"

"It's one avenue," Marco said. "We've chosen to investigate it first."

"Because of the key chain?" Doug asked.

"Mainly, yes." Marco didn't elaborate.

Doug steepled his fingers under his chin. "I have to be honest with you. I think you're on the wrong avenue."

Marco didn't reply, just gazed at him coolly.

Doug waited a moment, then said, "Has a DNA analysis been done on the bones?"

"A DNA analysis takes four to six weeks," Marco said, "and investigators would like to get this wrapped up quickly."

The investigators being *us,* he meant. He made no mention of the bone theft, or that there couldn't be a DNA analysis.

"Have you been brought in on the case by the detectives?" Doug asked.

I had a feeling Doug already knew the answer — it was probably something he'd asked Rusty — but clearly he was trying to make a point.

"We're working in conjunction with the police," Marco said. "If you'd like, I'll give you the name of a sergeant on the force who can verify that."

"Not necessary," Doug said. "I just want to establish that this visit is not part of an official police investigation and any information I give you is completely voluntary."

"That's right," Marco said. "However, any

information we receive will be turned over to the police."

Doug thought about that for a moment, then said, "May I see the key chain?"

"We don't have it," I said, pulling the photo out of my purse. "All we have is a picture."

I handed it across the desk, and Doug sat back to study it.

"What can you tell us about it?" Marco asked.

His expression blank, Doug handed it back. "There were three of these at one time. My parents and I each had one, but I don't know where any of them are. Did you find keys, too?"

"No, but the detectives haven't finished examining the site," Marco said.

That got no reaction. Doug seemed almost uninterested.

"Can you speculate as to how this key chain may have gotten buried in my bar's basement?" Marco asked.

"I'm sure Kermit dropped it while he was working down there."

Interesting that he referred to his dad by his first name. I made a note of it, then asked, "Did he have a habit of losing his keys?"

"When drunk, yes," Doug said unblinkingly.

"We understand that your father put up the walls in the basement's main room but didn't lay the floor," Marco said.

"That's correct. Rusty Miller and I laid the floor."

"Did you help Rusty prepare the dirt beforehand?" Marco asked. "Smooth it out, that kind of thing? I'm sure you know that process better than I do."

"No, I didn't do anything to the dirt. I stopped by when Rusty was ready to pour the cement and offered my help."

"Did Rusty tell you he had fired your dad?" I asked, just as my phone started to ring. I glanced at the screen in case it was an emergency, saw Jillian's name, and quickly muted it. Jillian's emergencies tended to be of a personal nature, such as a bad hair day or a broken fingernail. If it were a true emergency, her husband would be calling.

"I'm not sure he used those exact words," Doug said. "I just remember Rusty being frustrated because his work wasn't getting done. That was why I offered to help. I felt some responsibility for his predicament because Kermit had caused it."

"By not showing up?" I asked.

"That and by drinking on the job. I couldn't blame Rusty for not wanting Kermit back. He and Kermit had been friends for a very long time, so I'm sure it wasn't easy for him to, in effect, fire him, knowing it would end their friendship."

"How long had your dad had a drinking problem?" I asked.

"He'd always been a drinker," Doug said, "but that last six months or so, the drinking got out of hand."

"Did he ever mistreat you or any of your family?" Marco asked.

"Kermit had a mean streak that came out in full force when he drank. We tried to steer clear of him at those times, but he never raised a hand to any of us."

Doug was so calm, it was eerie.

"Would you say he was verbally abusive?" I asked.

"I guess that would be the modern term for it," Doug said. "Mom would refer to it as one of his black moods."

"Was your mom subjected to his black moods, too?" I asked.

"Of course. She took the brunt of it until I got older. Then I'd try to defuse the situation whenever I could."

"How did you defuse it?" Marco asked. "Did you have to get physical with him?"

"No. All I had to do was step in front of my mother. Kermit knew I'd protect her."

It had to help that Doug was big for his age. Even now, he was an imposing presence.

"Did you know your dad was seeing Parthenia Pappas?" Marco asked.

Still with that unnatural calmness, he said, "Yes, I did."

"Have you ever asked Parthenia what became of your dad?" I asked.

"We don't speak. It's too awkward. But I don't harbor any ill will toward her. She was a beautiful young woman and my father was a charming man when he wanted to be. Parthenia probably had no idea what Kermit was really like. She saw the side he wanted her to see."

"Did you ever hear the rumor that she was carrying your dad's child?" I asked.

I'd forgotten to mention that to Marco, so my question brought raised eyebrows from him. I gave him a shrug to say I was sorry.

Doug, however, gazed at me as though I'd just asked about the weather. "Yes."

"Do you know if the rumor was true?" I asked.

"It was true. That's why Parthenia wanted to leave town."

The gossips had been right. I scribbled it

down as Marco continued. "How did you find out?"

Doug looked down for a moment, as though composing his thoughts. "I'm not proud of this, but I followed Kermit to Parthenia's house and eavesdropped. They were discussing what to do about it."

"Would you mind sharing what you heard?" Marco asked.

"What I heard," Doug said in an emotionless voice, "was Parthenia urging Kermit to divorce my mother and make a fresh start with her and the baby."

I had a sudden image of Doug as a teenager, standing outside, listening to that conversation, and I couldn't help but put myself in his shoes. "You must have been shocked."

"It wasn't a good time," was all Doug said.

"Did you confront your dad?" I asked.

"No point in it. He would have just denied everything."

If I'd heard my dad's lover urging him to leave my mom, I would have confronted them both.

"What was your father's response to Parthenia?" Marco asked.

In that same eerily calm voice, Doug said, "He kept saying he didn't know what to do, and that infuriated her so much that she struck him in the face and screamed obscenities at him."

I shook my head in wonder at the scene he'd described. The man was simply too composed.

"Then you never heard them making plans to leave?" Marco asked.

"No, I didn't hang around that long. I'd heard enough."

"Do you think they would have stayed in town and continued their affair if she hadn't been pregnant?" Marco asked.

"That's rather a moot point, wouldn't you say?" Doug asked with a weird half smile.

"Did your mom know about your dad's affair?" I asked.

"She knew. She's the one who sent me to spy on Kermit, but I always claimed I couldn't find him, trying to protect her. But she knew in here." Doug tapped his chest. "She used to say a woman sensed those things."

"I don't know how your mom felt," I said, "but I would have wanted to wring his neck."

Marco draped his arm across the back of my chair and gave me a slight tap, as though to say, *Go easy.*

Doug thought for a moment, then said in an indifferent tone, "She was hurt, of course, but my mother loved that bastard no matter what he did. But she always saw the good in people. She was determined that Kermit would come to his senses and go back to her."

Doug's unnatural composure was unsettling, to say the least.

"What kind of relationship did your dad and Henry have?" Marco asked.

"Good at first," Doug said, "but it deteriorated over time due to Kermit's drinking."

"What was Henry's reaction when he learned that your dad had disappeared?" Marco asked.

"I wasn't there, so I can't answer that. I'm sure Henry was concerned. Everyone was."

Did Doug include himself in *everyone*? By his aloof expression, it was impossible to tell.

"Were the police called in to investigate?" Marco asked.

That seemed to strike him as amusing. "Kermit left town with his lover. That's not something you call the police for."

"Even after Parthenia returned alone?" I asked.

"That happened three decades later," Doug said. "We assumed Kermit was long gone."

"But didn't you want to know what happened to him?" I asked.

"Not particularly."

That was cold. "It doesn't sound like you cared for your dad," I said.

"When you get pushed away often enough," Doug said, "that happens."

"I understand you visited your dad while he was working at Down the Hatch," Marco said, as I flipped the notepad to a clean page.

"On occasion," Doug replied.

"What was the occasion?" Marco asked.

Looking down at his folded hands, Doug said, "I was always hoping he'd let me help, but Kermit preferred to work alone."

His words held such poignancy that I expected to see tears in his eyes when he looked up, but instead his gaze was flat, detached.

"Was Henry ever present on those occasions?" Marco asked.

"Henry was on another project at the New Chapel Savings and Loan."

"Were you and Henry close?" I asked.

"No," Doug said. "For years, I thought Kermit preferred Henry over me, but then I came to realize that Kermit preferred himself over everyone."

"Did it surprise you that your dad ran off with Parthenia?" Marco asked.

"It shouldn't have," Doug replied, "and yet it did. I thought he loved my mom too much to leave her. If any man looked at her twice, he got insanely jealous. Obviously, I was wrong."

Remembering what Grace had told me, I asked, "Did your dad ever get into any fights over your mom?"

"My mother had to bond Kermit out of jail twice in my memory. He claimed he was defending her honor, which was nonsense. No one would have said anything bad about Mom."

"Then you don't think your dad would have willingly abandoned her?" I asked.

"I think he would have under the right kind of coercion," Doug said.

"Are you speaking of Parthenia?" I asked.

Doug gave me a wry look that said, *Who else?*

"Were you and Rusty close?" Marco asked.

That got a genuine smile. "Not at first, but we became close over the years. Rusty always treated me like his own son, and I really respect him for that, and also for how he took care of my mother. He would have done anything for her."

Doug seemed about to say more, but then stopped.

At a knock behind me, I swiveled for a look and saw a teenage boy stick his head around the doorframe. "Dad? Could I see you for a minute?"

He was tall and good-looking, like his dad, and I guessed he was around eighteen years old, with short brown hair parted on one side and striking blue eyes. He seemed vaguely familiar.

"Sorry to interrupt," he said to us. Then he saw me and his eyes widened as though he recognized me.

"Can it wait five minutes, Haydn?" Doug asked. "I think we're about done here."

Chapter Thirteen

Haydn? Could there be *two* teenage Haydns in town or was Tara's secret boyfriend Kermit Cannon's fast-driving, hot-lipped grandson? I glanced back at the doorway to get a better look at the culprit, but he'd ducked out. I turned toward Marco, my eyes wide, and he nodded to indicate he'd caught it.

"Sorry," Doug said, glancing at his watch, "but I'm going to have to cut this short."

That was probably a good thing, because I was having a hard time focusing on the interview now. What I really wanted to do was tell Doug to call off his son. Marco must have sensed the direction of my thoughts because he gently squeezed my shoulder.

"I have just a couple more questions, and then I'll wrap it up," Marco said. "I'd like to verify a few things that Henry mentioned, such as that after your father left, business improved and things were generally better. Is that an accurate statement?"

"Yes, I'd say so," Doug said.

Marco gave me a tap to remind me to write it down.

I put the pen to the paper, then stopped. Write what down? *Okay, focus, Abby. This is important, too.* Oh, right. What Henry said.

"Did you spy on your father until the time he disappeared?" Marco asked.

"Once I knew what he was doing, there was no point in it." Doug let out a breath, almost as though he'd been holding it for some time. "Frankly, it made me sick. My mother didn't deserve to be treated like that."

Finally, a spark of emotion. "But she did end up happily married to Rusty for many years," I said. "That must have helped ease your mind."

"Definitely." Doug opened a drawer, took out his cell phone, and slipped it into his chest pocket. "When I stop to analyze it, Kermit's disappearance worked out well for everyone, despite his almost bankrupting the company."

They'd been near bankruptcy? Why hadn't Henry mentioned that?

"Would you mind telling us how that came about?" Marco asked.

"Kermit emptied the Cannon Construction checking account before he left," Doug said.

"How much did he take?" Marco asked.

"Over ten thousand dollars. It doesn't sound like much now, does it?"

"If we find out that it is your father who was buried in the bar's basement," Marco said, "what do you suppose became of the money?"

"I'd ask Parthenia Pappas that question," Doug said.

"Should we be looking at her as a murder suspect?" Marco asked.

"I can't tell you your business," Doug said, "and as I said earlier, I don't think murder is the right avenue. But if you're determined to continue on, then I would recommend that you take a close look at Parthenia. Remember, I saw her strike Kermit. I wouldn't doubt for a moment that she could kill someone."

Marco waited to make sure I got it all down. Then he said, "With bankruptcy looming, how did the business continue to function?"

"Through hard work and bill collection," Doug said. "Kermit was terrible when it came to billing customers, so once my mom sent out all the past due notices, enough money came in to keep Cannon up and running. And of course Henry was doing a lot of work."

"Did you ever talk to Rusty about how Kermit treated you and your mom?" Marco asked.

"I did, but only because Rusty brought it up. My mother's motto was to never air your dirty laundry in public."

"Had Rusty witnessed something that prompted his question?" I asked.

"Not that I was aware of," Doug said. "He must have suspected my father's abuse though — or maybe he heard it from someone else."

"Did you admit to Rusty that Kermit was abusive?" I asked.

With a straight face, Doug said, "I had no reason to lie to him."

I wondered if Doug had taken some small satisfaction in ratting out his dad. Maybe he'd even hoped Rusty would do something to stop it. "Did Rusty ever talk to your dad about his behavior?" I asked.

"Not that I'm aware. I doubt that Rusty would have interfered." Doug rose, signaling an end to the conversation.

Marco stood up and reached across the desk for a handshake. "Thanks for taking time to see us."

"I'd like to be kept abreast of any developments in the case, if you wouldn't mind," Doug said.

"We'll try to keep you in the loop," Marco said.

I didn't see Haydn on our way out, but I did see the Mustang in the parking lot, so I knew I was right about his identity.

"Do you know how much I wanted to grab Haydn and give him a hard shake?" I asked, as Marco opened the car door for me.

"I could feel the heat bouncing off your head." He shut the door and went around to his side to get in.

"Maybe we should wait until he comes out," I said. "We could have a little talk with him."

"Not on your life. Did you see Haydn's face when he saw you? He knew exactly who you were, Abby. Tara is a mini you, remember? The last thing we want is for his dad to know of your connection to Tara and put her in jeopardy."

"How would we put her in jeopardy? Did you pick up on something about Doug Cannon that I didn't?"

"I shouldn't have used the word jeopardy," Marco said, as we pulled out of the parking lot. "All I'm saying is that we need to ensure that there is absolutely no possibility of Tara being put into an awkward position."

"Being in an awkward position is a lot different than being in jeopardy."

"Bear with me here, Sunshine. You know I've been leery of taking this case all along, and talking to Doug just reinforced it. His reactions were not normal. He's got something bottled up inside that put me on edge. That's why I want Tara out of the picture."

Marco must have realized how much he was frightening me. He reached for my hand and held it. "Look, sweetheart, I don't mean to alarm you, but this isn't just a puzzle to be solved, as much as you'd like to believe it is. If those bones did indeed belong to Kermit, then the case isn't that old and the killer is walking around town a free man — or woman — who's running scared right now. And a scared killer is nothing to mess around with. As you pointed out, Tara's too young to be seeing a seventeen-year-old boy anyway. Wouldn't you rather err on the side of caution?"

"How do we know Haydn won't tell his dad who I am?"

"Because he'd have to admit to seeing a thirteen-year-old, and I doubt he'd want to do that."

"You're right. I'll text her right now and

invite her out for ice cream after school. She *loves* ice cream. She'll get my message as soon as school is over. In fact, I'll tell her that I'll be waiting outside the school to pick her up."

"Now you've got it. I'll rearrange my day so I can go with you. With the two of us there, she'll get the importance."

I sent Tara a text, then put away my phone as we approached the town square. "Done. Do you still think I shouldn't tell my brother and sister-in-law?"

"Let's see if we can handle this without involving them."

"I just wish I knew how to get through to Tara. I don't want to frighten her, but that's probably what I'll have to do."

"Let's not bring in the murder case unless it becomes absolutely necessary. If we have to, then we'll use a little psychology on her, but to start with, how about just coming from the heart about the boy being too old for her?"

"I tried that before and she shut me out. You remember what it's like, Marco. Teens always think they know better when it comes to love. And besides, they hate any display of emotion from adults. What I need to do is play it icy cool. I'll be Cool Aunt Abby, the person who saved Tara from certain calamity."

My phone dinged. "Speaking of calamity," I said, reading the message on the screen, "Jillian just texted a reminder that I'm dog-sitting for her this evening. That was probably why she phoned earlier."

"Why don't you pay Tara to do it?"

"Hey! Great idea."

"I'm full of great ideas. Meeting for lunch is also a great idea. If you're game, we can slip in time for a little extra something."

"That sounds like another excellent idea, Salvare. Your place or — your place?"

"How about the Duchess's art gallery on Tenth Street?"

"That's not quite what I was picturing."

"I'll bring sandwiches for the ride."

"Still not what I, um . . . bacon, turkey, and Swiss cheese?"

"I know how to take care of you, babe."

"You're on."

"Okay, very quickly," Marco said. "What did you think of Doug?"

"I agree with you about his reactions. He seemed freakishly calm, especially when he talked about finding his dad with Parthenia, and then the temper tantrum he saw her have. He watched her strike his dad, Marco. I would have been either frightened or so furious I would have pounded on the window to make her stop, but it was as though Doug has dissociated himself from those memories. And he always referred to his dad by his first name, but not his mom. I know some people do that to their parents, but it sounds weird."

Marco turned on the windshield wipers, as a mist had begun to fall. "The only people I've ever heard do that are the ones who have issues with a parent, which he obviously did."

"But Doug did seem to appreciate Rusty. The reason I asked him if he had told Rusty about the abuse is because I wondered if Doug had hoped Rusty would do something about it."

"I know you don't like to hear this, but it's still possible that Rusty did do something about it. As I've told you before, everyone has a breaking point, especially when it comes to defending someone they care about. That also applies to Doug being protective of his mother, by the way. Did you get a reading on Doug's feelings toward Henry?"

"He seemed ambivalent about Henry. Did you notice that Henry's version of Doug spying on his dad differed from Doug's? Henry made it seem like it happened on numerous occasions, but Doug wanted us to believe it was just the one time. And I don't understand why Henry failed to mention that Kermit had cleaned out the checking account. You'd think that would have been the first thing to come up when you asked about the business."

"Did you make a note of that? We're going to have to revisit the subject with Henry."

"Noted with asterisks. I also thought Doug's comment about Parthenia's coercion was interesting. He was definitely pointing us in her direction."

"Maybe for a good reason."

As Marco stopped in front of Bloomers to let me out, I saw Grace standing at the door. I knew something was up, because as soon as she saw me, she came out to meet me.

"Did your cousin reach you?" she asked, as I got out of the car. "She's been calling here for the past hour. She sounded quite panic-stricken and said it was a royal emergency."

"A royal emergency?"

"I believe that was the word Jillian used. She was talking so fast, I couldn't be sure."

"I got a text from Jillian in the middle of our interview, but she didn't say anything about an emergency. She was reminding me that I'm dog-sitting this evening."

"You don't suppose that was the reason for all those calls, do you?" Grace asked.

"Probably, but I'd better check in with her just to be sure."

Grace pointed toward the big bay window. "Do you see who's watching you?"

I glanced at the window on the left side of the door and there sat Seedy wagging her tail. "Has she been in the window the whole time?"

"Indeed she has. I believe she's been waiting for you. She didn't hide from the customers, either."

"She's making progress."

I stepped inside Bloomers and crouched down to cuddle Seedy, who was so excited to see me that she wouldn't stop licking my face. I finally had to stand up.

Lottie was working with a customer, so when the phone rang, Grace answered it at the cashier's counter. "Bloomers Flower Shop. How may I help you?" She listened, then pointed to me and mouthed, *Jillian.*

"I'll take it in the back," I said, and gave Lottie a wave as I hurried through the curtain.

"What's up?" I asked my cousin.

"I just wanted to make sure you remembered about tonight. I tried your cell phone but you didn't answer."

"I was busy, but I saw your text. What is the *royal* reference?"

"Didn't I tell you what name I decided on? It's Her Royal Majesty Princess Moon Petal Osborne."

Dear God. "Is that firm?"

"Yes. Well . . . yes. Anyway, be at my apartment at seven o'clock."

"I thought you were bringing Her Royal whatever to my apartment."

"You'll never remember to put Seedy's food up. Love you, wittle cuz. Bye."

"Dog-sitting tonight, are we?" Grace asked blithely, wearing a know-it-all expression as she brought me a cup of tea. "Didn't take our advice, did we?"

"I'm not going to think about tonight," I said, as Lottie joined us. "I'm going to focus on having a great day. We've already had a very informative interview with Kermit's son, which I will fill you in on next, and we're going to see the Duchess over my lunch hour."

"That should prove interesting," Grace said. "The woman is quite the eccentric."

"And look, sweetie," Lottie said, pointing to my desk. "We have fifty orders waiting on the spindle."

"We're out of our slump!" I put down my

cup to give Lottie and Grace hugs. "After that kind of news, what's an hour or two of watching Jillian's spoiled pooch? If that's the worst that can happen today, nothing can faze me."

"Well, actually," Grace said, "with this being Friday morning and all . . ."

"It's TGIF," I said. "Even better."

"I don't think that's what Grace meant," Lottie said.

"Bella!" I heard from behind me. "You're here at last!"

Ah! It was a Francesca morning. I downed the tea and held it out for a refill just as Grace lifted the pot to pour more. With that many orders waiting, it was still a good day no matter who invaded my space.

"I'm making my famous Italian beef roast this Sunday," Francesca said, chucking me under the chin. "You will adore it. We'll dine at four o'clock. Lottie, Grace, you're welcome, too. The more the merrier."

"I would love to," Grace said, "but my Richard and I have a long-standing invitation with another couple for dinner and bowling. Thank you so much for asking, though."

"Four teenage boys?" Lottie asked. "I'm just gonna say no and spare everyone the hassle. But thanks anyway."

Francesca looked at me and smiled. "I know you can come. I've already spoken to my son this morning. He said you have no plans for Sunday dinner."

Bless his little Italian heart.

The bell over the door jingled, and I peeked through the curtain to see Connor MacKay step inside. First Francesca and now Connor? Was I being tested?

"Whatever do you suppose he wants?" Grace asked, peering through with me.

I was fairly certain Connor had gotten word about the bone theft and had come to mine me for information, but I didn't want Francesca to know about the theft, so I said, "You know reporters, Grace. They're always looking for local interest stories to fill out the news."

"Anyone here?" Connor called.

"Lottie, would you handle him?" I asked.

The words were barely out of my mouth when Francesca said, "I will take care of him."

As Francesca marched into the shop, I glanced at Lottie and Grace in alarm. I couldn't allow her to talk to the media. There was no telling what she'd say. I darted through the curtain with Lottie and Grace right behind me.

"Connor!" I called. "What a coincidence.

I've been hoping to get a little publicity for Bloomers."

I whispered to Francesca as I passed her, "I'll handle this." Then I hooked my arm through Connor's and led him outside.

"Talk about my lucky day," he said.

Dragging him away from the windows, I said, "I don't have any information, so save your questions for the police."

"Don't get your freckles in a lather," he said with his easy grin. "I just wanted to find out if your bone thief left any clues behind."

"Like I'd tell you. How did you hear?"

"Like I'd tell you," he teased. "Come on, Abby. It was raining Wednesday night. The thief came through the alley. There must have been muddy prints. Were they work boots? Running shoes? Flip-flops?"

"You can stop guessing, MacKay. The prints were too sloppy to be of any use."

"And no one saw a thing? I'm amazed the perp slipped past Marco . . . unless he was too focused on his lovely bride to notice."

"They only say *perp* on TV, MacKay, and besides, we weren't even there, so obviously, your source isn't as good as you thought." I caught movement out of the corner of my eye and glanced to my right to see Seedy pawing at the glass in the big bay window, trying to catch my attention. She yipped when she saw me looking at her.

Connor noticed Seedy and said with a smirk, "What is that? Your mascot?"

"Yes, she's a rescue dog and she's very smart. Do you have a problem with that?"

He held up his hands. "Hey, I'm sorry. I didn't mean to offend you. So how's your investigation coming? Talk to Rusty yet? Or the Duchess? No? Or you don't want to say?"

"As we've told you before, MacKay, we're not investigating, the police are."

"You're cute when you're telling a lie."

"I get that all the time."

"I don't think you realize the untapped potential here," he said, pressing his fingertips against his chest. "I'm good at hunting for clues, too. And I can get people to reveal things like you wouldn't believe."

"Good for you. Good-bye, MacKay."

As I turned to walk away, he stepped in front of me. "No, seriously, Abby. Let's at least do an information swap."

"Right. Like you have information for us."

"I'll bet I know something about Kermit Cannon that you don't."

"Like what?"

"Not so fast, freckles. You tell me something first."

I studied him for a moment. If he really did have useful information, I'd be foolish to pass it up. "Okay, I'll tell you this. I noticed an arc-shaped indentation on the skull."

Connor whipped out a small notepad and scribbled it down. "Okay. And?"

"And now it's your turn."

"That's all you've got for me?"

"That's it."

"Well, just for the record, I feel cheated, but a deal is a deal. I went back through old police records and found three arrest reports for a Mr. Kermit Cannon. One in particular was especially noteworthy."

"Why?"

"Because of the reason for his arrest. Are you ready for this? Seems one Kermit Cannon got into a fistfight with one Rusty Miller."

I was all attention now. "Go ahead."

"Apparently Kermit didn't like the way Rusty was flirting with his wife." Connor's eyes were sparkling with excitement now. "Here's the best part. Kermit claimed the fight started because Rusty was trying to steal Lila away from him."

Kermit was jealous of Rusty? So was the reverse true, as well?

"Ah! Look at those green eyes light up,"

Connor said. "You liked that, didn't you?" He put his arm around me. "I'm telling you, freckles, you, me, and Salvare could be quite a powerhouse if we joined forces."

"I wouldn't let Marco see you with your arm around me, MacKay."

Connor stepped back. "Fair enough. But do talk to your hubby about my proposal and get back to me."

"I'll do that." When Seedy grew wings.

I waited until Connor had crossed the street to phone Marco to relay the news. "Considering that Rusty and Lila were high school sweethearts, and combining that with what Connor found out, it sounds like there could have been a long-standing rivalry between the two men," I said.

"We'll have to put it toward a motive for Rusty," Marco said.

"I really hate to do that, Marco, but I get your point."

"It's vital that we remain impartial, Abby. But I'm surprised MacKay gave you that information without asking for something in return."

"He wanted something all right — for the three of us to work as a team."

"I'm assuming he came to see you because he'd heard about the bone theft from his police source. You didn't give him any information, did you?"

"None." Or had I? Thinking back, I did remember mentioning that the prints were sloppy. But Connor would have known that from the police report. "No information."

My spindle was so full that in the next four hours Lottie and I put together over forty arrangements. We were floral machines. And because we were so busy in the back, Francesca was kept occupied up front. So in a way, even Marco's mom improved my day.

Although I wasn't exactly looking forward to my dog-sitting duties, the only real cloud on the horizon was my forthcoming talk with Tara. Since Marco had impressed upon me the importance of her not seeing Haydn, I kept picturing a crazed Doug holding her prisoner until we swore to drop our investigation long enough for him to escape to Mexico. That was just the way my mind worked. I'd always been cursed with an overactive imagination.

I didn't discuss Tara with Lottie and Grace, however. I informed them only about our interview with Doug and let it go at that.

At noon, Marco, Seedy, and I made the trip to Tenth Street, located about a mile inside the northern edge of the New Chapel town limits. Parthenia's studio was housed in a small, two-story white frame building with black trim that had once been a grocery store. According to my mom's information, Parthenia's gallery and workshop took up the main floor, and she lived on the second floor in an apartment she'd designed herself.

"What's our strategy?" I asked Marco, as we parked at the curb in front.

"From what I could gather, the Duchess is exceedingly egotistical, so we're going to have to lay on the charm if we want her cooperation."

"Then it's all yours, Marco. I know what the Salvare magic does to women."

"I don't know about that," he said, trying to appear modest.

"Yes, you do. I'll just stand back and let you do your thing. And on a side note, would you check with me before accepting your mom's dinner invitations, please?"

"I didn't think it'd be nice to turn her down after all the help she's giving you."

I poked him gently in the ribs. "Marriage, Salvare. It's all about communication and teamwork."

"Gotcha."

I put Seedy on her leash and we walked toward the black-framed glass door. We passed a bike rack with one bike in it that was decorated with glossy black-and-white polka dots. Next to the door was a large plate glass window where Parthenia displayed a dozen of her sculptures. A hand-lettered sign in the window said: INQUIRE ABOUT ART CLASSES WITHIN.

There was an OPEN sign on the door, so we entered to the soft tinkling of wind chimes. Since no one was in the shop, we wandered around looking at the artwork. Seedy stuck close to me. Unfamiliar environments made her nervous.

"The Duchess likes black and white," I whispered to Marco, pointing out a row of tall, glossy clocks sitting on a long console against one wall. Some were in black-and-white stripes, some in checks, some in plaids, and all of their bodies curved into an elongated S shape, appearing as though they were swaying in the breeze. "I'll bet that bike out front is hers, too."

In the center of the room, a glass dining room table held an assortment of dining plates and platters. They, too, were in black-and-white patterns and curved into a soft S shape. A small sign in the middle said: CUSTOM ORDERS AVAILABLE IN SETS OF EIGHT OR TWELVE.

Staggered white shelving filled the black

wall at the rear of the shop, with each shelf holding sculptures in different themes, such as waterbirds, tropical flowers, cats, and dogs. All of her sculptures had a distinctly Egyptian look to them. The bases they sat on were even edged in hieroglyphics.

"Did you see the prices on these things?" my practical hubby asked, showing me the handwritten sticker on the bottom of a cat sculpture.

"But aren't they beautiful?" If only Parthenia's talent would rub off on my mom.

"I guess there's a reason why she's won so many accolades." He pointed to the other side of the room, where, above the glass-topped cashier's stand, her framed awards were hung. On that wall, too, were oil paintings in a variety of sizes, all of Grecian and Egyptian architecture. Clearly, the Duchess was proficient in a wide variety of media.

"Yia sas," a rich voice sang out.

I turned to see Parthenia Pappas swish majestically into the room. A purple, pink, and blue madras, floor-length, silk caftan swayed about her curvy form, held close to her body by a blue scarf tied around her waist. A striking woman around Grace's age, she was tall and solidly built, and had the slightly slanted dark eyes and darker Mediterranean coloring that showed her

Greco-Egyptian ancestry. Her snowy white hair was swept back on one side and held in place with a large, glossy purple-and-white-striped barrette that made Lottie's little pink ones look like they belonged to a doll.

I remembered learning from a former Greek neighbor that Parthenia's words meant *hello,* so I returned her greeting with a *"Yia sou."*

She didn't seem to hear me. She had come to a full stop and was staring at Seedy in amazement. "What is it?" she demanded. "Boy or girl?"

"A girl," I said. "Her name is —"

"Come, come," she said to Seedy, reaching into her pocket as she bent over and held out her hand. "Here's a treat for you. Come to the Duchess, little marvel. Do not be shy."

Seedy immediately backed behind me and pressed her face against my pants, trying to hide. Parthenia straightened and looked down her nose at me. "How will this dog sit for me if she does not trust me?"

"We're not here to have her painted," I said.

"Good. She is much too unique for a painting. She must be sculpted in my finest clay. I've never seen such a hideously beautiful animal. Come, come!" She tried coaxing

Seedy out again, but my hideous marvel merely pressed harder against me.

Obviously wanting to get the interview started, Marco stepped forward and showed her his PI license. "I'm Marco Salvare, and this is my wife, Abby. We're investigating a case you may have read about in the newspapers — a skeleton that was buried in the basement of Down the Hatch Bar and Grill."

"If you are not here for an appointment, I have no time for you," she said with a dismissive wave of her hand.

"We'll take up only ten minutes," Marco said, bestowing upon her his most earnest expression, guaranteed to melt the heart of even the coldest female. "I promise."

"Pah!" she said with a curl of her lip. "Your charm has no effect on me. 'Once burned, twice shy' is my motto. Now, go!"

I'd never seen a woman who was impervious to Marco's magnetism. I glanced at him in surprise, and he merely raised his eyebrows. He was flummoxed, as Grace liked to say, but in true Salvare spirit, he wouldn't go down without a fight. "We think the remains may be those of Kermit Cannon. I understand you and he —"

"You understand *nothing,*" she cried dramatically. "If you did, you would see that

I am leaving this room right now."

Without waiting to see what we were going to do, Parthenia stormed toward the door in the back. For once Marco seemed at a loss for words, so I had to think of something quickly or we were sunk.

"Would you like to sculpt Seedy?" I called out.

Parthenia stopped shy of the doorway and swung toward me, a look of disbelief on her face. "Did you just ask me if I would sculpt *seedily*?"

"No, *Seedy,*" I said. "That's my dog's name. Would you like to sculpt her?"

"What a terrible name." The Duchess had a scornful look on her face, but she was listening.

I handed Marco the leash and walked toward her, holding out my hand. "Abby Knight Salvare. You know my mother, Maureen Knight. She takes lessons from you."

"I know who Maureen is."

"Then you should also know that she can't say enough about your talent. And after seeing your work here?" I paused to sweep my arm around in a wide gesture. "I understand why. And that's why I'd be thrilled and honored if you'd sculpt my little See— um, marvel."

And the little S'marvel, being the intuitive

dog that she was, began to tug Marco toward me, hobbling on three legs, her long pointed ears straight up, her plumy tail wagging anxiously.

Chapter Fourteen

Parthenia tapped her chin as though weighing her options. "You will let me sculpt her?"

"Yes," I said, nodding excitedly — until an image of the Egyptian cat's price tag flashed in my mind. "You're not expecting us to buy it, are you?"

That earned me a frown of displeasure. "Don't be a peasant. This is my sculpture to do with as I see fit. And in exchange I will answer ten minutes' worth of questions. That *is* your offer, is it not?"

"Yes. Absolutely."

She narrowed her eyes at me, then at Marco, and finally at the dog, whom she began to circle. Seedy was still tugging on her leash trying to reach me but, wisely, Marco wasn't letting her because he knew she'd hide again.

"Will we start today? Now?" Parthenia demanded. "This minute?"

"That would be great," I said.

"Endaksi," she said, which I was pretty sure meant *Okay.* "You will ask your questions while I take photographs and sketch her. Then you will bring this animal, who shall have a proper name, back to sit for me tomorrow."

"But tomorrow's Saturday," I said.

"Does an artist create only from Monday until Friday?" she cried. "No. We create all the time, every minute. What am I doing while I'm talking to you? I am sculpting you in my head. Unfortunately, I don't do freckles. Now let us begin."

"We can't make it tomorrow," I said. "We have a full day."

She frowned at me, thinking. "I suppose I could see you at noon on Monday."

"That would work," I said.

The Duchess marched grandly from the room. Marco picked up Seedy and we trooped through the doorway behind her like obedient subjects. Just inside I paused to whisper to Marco, "Looks like I'm handling this one. What's my strategy?"

"You know what information we need, so let your instincts guide you. She seems to trust you. Give me your pen and pad. I'll take notes."

Parthenia's workroom took up the back half of the building and had large, multipaned windows on three walls, allowing in a lot of natural light. Through the back window I saw that she had a nice-sized garden bordered by railroad ties, though the plants were long gone now. "Do you grow flowers?" I asked.

"Flowers and vegetables," she said proudly. "The flowers are nourishment for my mind, the vegetables are fuel for my body, and this," she said with a sweeping gesture that took in her entire studio, "is sustenance for my soul."

I glanced around the room and saw free-standing wooden shelves filled with sculptures in varying stages of development, a pottery wheel, a drafting table, an easel, a stack of blank canvases, and a slate-topped worktable positioned close to the north wall of windows. An incense burner in the center of the table emitted a thin trail of smoke, the aroma of patchouli hanging heavily in the air. Most of the floor was draped in tan drop cloths that were crusted with dried clay and splattered with all colors of paint.

"Place her here," the Duchess said, tapping one end of her worktable. She removed the incense burner, took a small camera from the drawer beneath the table, and prepared to photograph Seedy, who sat on the table looking at me with her head tilted, as though to say, *What are we doing here?*

"Good girl," I said, and stroked her head until Parthenia gave me the okay. Then I stepped back, and she began to shoot. Seedy kept her gaze on me, as though the Duchess frightened her. Marco leaned against the wall nearby, the notepad at his side.

"Now," Parthenia said, putting away the camera, "I must sketch her. You may ask questions while I work."

Seedy started toward me, so Marco stepped up to keep her on the table, talking to her softly and rubbing her head while I took over the interview.

"As we mentioned before," I said, "a skeleton was found in the basement of Down the Hatch Bar and Grill, and we're trying to identify it."

"I have heard my students discussing it."

I took out the photo and showed it to her. "This is a key chain that was found near the bones. Do you recognize it?"

She glanced at it, then returned to sketching. "I have never seen it before."

"It's a Cannon Construction key chain."

Her hand slowed briefly, but that was her only reaction. "And?"

"And that leads us to believe the bones may be Kermit Cannon's," I said.

At that she stopped. "You truly believe

Kermit is buried in that basement?"

"We believe he might be," I said. "If it's true, then he was most likely murdered."

She studied me for a long moment, her eyes narrowed, as though she was having a hard time absorbing the information. Then she said, almost to herself, "That would explain a lot."

"What would it explain?" I asked.

She waved her hand. "What does it matter now?"

It mattered a lot, but I didn't want to press her for details just yet. "We're waiting for the police to investigate, but that may take weeks, so we're trying to find out as much about Kermit's disappearance as possible."

Parthenia's pencil scratched against the paper as my marvel dog's features took shape. "And you are here to see me because you have heard the old rumors?"

"Yes." I glanced at Marco, who was watching from the other side of the table. He gave me an encouraging nod. "So what we need to know," I said, "is whether Kermit actually did leave town with you. And" — I knew the next question could be touchy, so I paused for a breath — "whether you were carrying his child."

She sketched for a moment before she spoke, and then it was in a sarcastic voice.

"If I tell you the truth, will you believe me? No. That is what the rumors have done to my reputation. And I have no proof to offer you."

I rushed to assure her. "Really, Parthenia, those rumors —"

"Duchess," she cut in, "if you please."

"I'm sorry, Duchess. Anyway, those rumors are so old, Marco and I hadn't even heard them until we started investigating. Your reputation now is that of a highly acclaimed and very successful artist. So we have no reason not to believe you, and we'd really like to hear your story."

She huffed, but it wasn't an angry huff. "Very well. To answer your questions, it is *not* true that I was carrying Kermit's child. I would never be so stupid. As for the other, I did *not* leave with Kermit. We were supposed to meet at my apartment before dawn but he never showed up. I waited hours and finally left without him."

"Where were the two of you going?" I asked.

"South, wherever the wind led us."

"Without Kermit, where did it lead you?"

"Nowhere for a long time. I was adrift, lost, disoriented, no family to turn to, no friends . . . I finally took a room in a small artists' colony and stayed there for many years."

"Where was the artists' colony?" I asked.

"Does it matter? A small town in southern Indiana."

Seedy began to whine. She was tired of sitting on the table, and Marco had stopped petting her to take notes.

"Not long now, my darling," Parthenia cooed, her hand flying across her paper.

Not long? We'd just begun! "Did you try to find out what happened to Kermit?"

The Duchess put down her pencil to fix me with her piercing gaze. "From whom? His wife? His children? Who would tell me? *Me?* The woman people said had broken his marriage?"

She let that sink in for a moment, then went on. "What was I to do but assume Kermit had chosen to remain with them? So I made my way alone — heartsick, my spirit crushed — but as you see, I rebounded, resolved to rebuild my life, and determined that no man would make a fool of Parthenia Eugenie Pappas ever again!"

Her initials spelled PEP, and she was certainly full of that. I was a little intimidated by her, but I had to admire her spirit. "Did you ever meet Kermit's children?" I asked.

"Pah! Silly question. What man would introduce his children to his mistress?"

Good point. "Did you know that Kermit's son, Doug, spied on you?"

"Oh, I knew all right. I saw the boy following along after us on two occasions, and then I saw his face at my window several times after that. I warned Kermit not to come back to my house during the day, but he was a reckless man. He feared nothing, not even his children finding out."

Her gaze wandered to the window, and in a melancholy voice, she said, "It made me wonder if he wouldn't treat me the same way he treated them."

"Whose idea was it to leave town?" I asked.

"Mine. I knew I couldn't live any longer under such a cloud, and believed, foolishly, that Kermit loved me. So why not leave town together and make a new life for ourselves?" She tapped her head. "Do you see the thinking of a young, smitten woman? Love can solve everything." She shrugged. "I knew no better, sadly."

"Was Kermit ready to leave his family or did you have to convince him?" I asked.

That earned me a fierce scowl. "Of course I did not have to convince him! I could not keep Kermit away from me. I was young and beautiful and fiery . . . Oh, how he loved my fire. My passion! Unlike that mouse he was married to. Pah!"

She shuddered. "I will never forget the look on Kermit's son's face as he stared through my window. Such hatred. Such contempt. When we made eye contact, he didn't even look away. It frightened me, and I am not a woman who frightens easily. That was another reason I wanted us to leave. But Kermit didn't seem to care."

"When you say it was a reason to leave — do you mean that you felt you were in danger?"

"Yes, for myself as well as for Kermit."

In the background, Marco flipped the page and continued writing.

"Wasn't his son just a teenager?" I asked.

"And do teenagers not commit horrible crimes? Do they not shoot up classrooms for lesser reasons?"

She made a good case for it. "And what about Henry Greer?"

"I heard through Kermit that Henry was quite unhappy. He wanted to split up the partnership."

I glanced at Marco to make sure he caught that. "How close was that to when you had planned to leave?"

She paused to think. "Perhaps a week —

two — it's hard to remember now."

"Did Kermit say why Henry felt that way?"

" 'Henry wants to run things,' Kermit said to me, but he wouldn't tell me why. Me, I believe it had to do with Kermit's drinking. I knew his work was suffering from it because I overheard Rusty Miller complaining about that very subject. But when I questioned Kermit, he pushed me away. He had everything under control. That was his answer always. 'Everything is under control, my Duchess. Don't worry.' Pah!"

"What were Rusty's complaints?" I asked.

"Rusty complained that Kermit was showing up late in the mornings and drinking in the afternoons," Parthenia said. "He was angry, naturally, because the work wasn't being completed."

"How did you happen to overhear them?" I asked.

Seedy whined again and tried to climb off the table. Marco put down the notepad to hold her.

"Two minutes, my sweet," Parthenia called. "How did I hear this? At the time, I worked for the Lincoln Avenue Furniture Company, which had been hired to refurnish the second floor of the New Chapel Savings and Loan. One day I went upstairs to draw a design plan and saw Rusty talking to Henry while he was doing remodeling work there. Naturally, I did not show myself. I knew what everyone thought of me and didn't want to be subjected to their scorn.

"I hid myself in another room and listened as Rusty complained about Kermit to Henry. I told Kermit about it later and said I didn't blame Henry for wanting to split, but Kermit just laughed it off. He said Henry was too much of a girl to strike out on his own."

"That's what he called Henry?" I asked.

"Yes. A girl." She lifted one eyebrow. "To his face, also."

Ouch. That Kermit must have been a real prize. Whatever had Parthenia seen in him? "Do you think Henry's frustration made him a danger, too?"

She pursed her lips. "Partly." She finished her sketch, held it up to study it, and proclaimed it done. Rising, she said, "I would say our ten minutes are over, yes?"

"Oh, no!" I exclaimed, startling her. "You have to explain your answer. Do you think there was more to it than frustration?"

Parthenia put her hands on her hips and looked at Marco for the first time since we'd entered her workroom. "What would you do if someone called you a girl?"

Marco gave me a look that said, *Is she serious?*

"I don't think anyone would call Marco a girl, Duchess," I said. "He's way too male."

"So you would laugh it off, eh?" she asked him.

"Something like that," my macho man replied.

"Because you are secure in your manhood, yes?" Parthenia asked.

"Sure," Marco said.

She moved up to Seedy and held out the treat she had offered before. "I will say no more."

"Are you saying Henry wasn't secure in his manhood?" I asked.

She waved me away. "No more!"

As I tried to ferret out her meaning, Seedy sniffed her palm, ate the treat, and wagged her tail for more.

"You," Parthenia said to Marco, as she gave Seedy another treat, "have behaved like a gentleman. Perhaps I was mistaken about you. I am mistrustful when it comes to men."

"Thank you for letting my wife interview you," Marco said.

The Duchess gave him a regal nod. "And you," she said, turning to point at me, "will bring this raggedy dog back Monday at noon. Agreed?"

"Agreed," I said. *"Efharistó." Thank you* was another Greek word I had learned.

She went to her drafting table and sat down. *"Yia sas,"* she called over her shoulder. Good-bye. She was done.

"She was quite a character," Marco said as we headed back to Bloomers.

"I liked Parthenia, though. She has spirit. It takes a lot to make a fresh start and then really do something with your life."

"The question is," Marco said, "did she do something with Kermit's life?"

"I don't know. She seemed genuinely surprised to hear about the possibility of Kermit being buried in the basement. Did you understand what she meant about Henry not being secure in his manhood? Was she hinting that he might be gay?"

"That's how I read it."

"So if Kermit was constantly drunk on the job and not getting the work done, and the business was suffering, and Kermit was being abusive, would him calling Henry a girl be enough to make Henry snap?"

"I could pose almost the same scenario with Doug and ask, would catching Kermit with Parthenia be enough to make Doug snap? And here's another one. Would Kermit not showing up at the assigned time be enough to make Parthenia go looking for him with murder on her mind?"

"Of the three suspects, I could see her situation being the most unstable," I said. "What if Kermit didn't show up, and she went to the bar to find him? Maybe he told her he wasn't leaving and she grabbed something close at hand and hit him with it."

Marco pulled the notepad out of his shirt pocket and handed it to me. "Take a look at my notes and see if I got everything."

I flipped it open and found the page where Marco had scribbled, literally, his notes. "What does this first one say? 'Diclnt recog K C'? Oh wait. That's *didn't.* She didn't recognize Kansas City?"

"The key chain. Are you making fun of my handwriting?"

"Of course I am. Okay, on the second line, I can make out that Parthenia verified Doug's statement that it was her idea to leave town but denied that she was pungent — make that pregnant. I can't tell what it says after that."

Marco waited until he was at a stop sign, then looked it over. "It says I need to find out where the artists' colony was so I can check hospital records to see if there's any indication of her giving birth."

I read over the rest silently. "I wonder why she was afraid to come right out and say that Henry was gay."

"Maybe she doesn't know. And remember, this is only her version of things. If she's our murderer, then she has to point a finger at someone. In this case, she pointed at two someones."

I closed the notebook and handed it back. "What's our next step?"

"Talk to Tara. Then tomorrow morning I'll see what I can dig up on those birth records. After that, we'll visit Rusty at his saddle shop. He has some explaining to do."

CHAPTER FIFTEEN

At three o'clock, Marco and I were parked in the loading zone in front of the huge, sprawling one-story structure that served as both a middle school and high school, waiting for Tara to appear. Five minutes earlier, I'd gotten a text from her in reply to my earlier one. It had said: *Why?*

It's a surprise, I'd texted back.

Fine was her answer, followed by a frowning face. She probably figured she'd be in for a lecture.

"You weren't serious about ice cream, were you?" Tara asked as she climbed into the backseat of the Prius. "*Yogurt,* Aunt Abby. *Frozen yogurt* is cool. Ice cream isn't."

"Hey, Tara," Marco said, reaching out a hand so my niece could slap his palm. "Where are we going for this cool frozen yogurt?"

"To Yog-earth," she said, as we pulled out of the school parking lot.

"Is Yog-earth by the shopping mall?" Marco asked.

"That's the one."

Through my side-view mirror, I saw Tara pull out a tube of lipstick and apply it with the aid of a small mirror from her purse. I shot Marco a disgruntled look and pointed to my lips so he got the message. Tara had always shunned lipstick, or makeup of any sort, for that matter.

"So Auntie A," Tara said. "You're not angry with me about, you know, *yesterday,* are you?"

Be cool, Abby. "We just wanted to hang out with our favorite niece for a while and catch up on what's new."

"Awesome. That's what I told Haydn because he was like, 'Oh, man, you are so in for it if you go,' and I'm like, 'No, way. My auntie A is way too cool.' He didn't believe me, so I told him to meet us there so he could see for himself."

"Haydn's going to be there?" I asked, swiveling to glare at her.

"Uh-huh." She didn't see me. She was checking her phone messages.

It was Marco's turn for the disgruntled look. He pulled into a driveway, turned the car around, and headed in the opposite direction.

"Hey!" Tara called. "Where are we going?"
"To the ice-cream parlor," he said.

Tara slouched onto the blue bench opposite us in the booth at the iScream Ice Cream parlor and crossed her arms, refusing to look at either one of us. "This is so uncool," she muttered, scowling.

"Tara," Marco said, leaning forward, trying to catch her eye, "do you know why we're here?"

She shrugged.

"Tell me why," he said.

"Because I'm seeing Haydn."

"Because you're sneaking out to see Haydn," I corrected, "and you know your parents wouldn't approve."

She shrugged again, twisting the white paper cover from a straw into a knot.

"Let me tell you about a boy named Dennis," I said.

Tara heaved a very long, very bored sigh. "Do you have to?"

"I'll go get our ice cream." Marco rose and reached for his wallet. "What flavor do you ladies want?"

"I'll have double dark chocolate," I said, "in a sugar cone."

Tara scowled at her fingernails. "I *hate* ice cream."

"Chocolate for Tara," I told Marco.

"Wait!" she cried, and when he stopped, she said, "Strawberry. With fudge on top. In a cup." Then she sank against the seat and glared at me.

Not a great way to start.

As soon as Marco was out of earshot, Tara said, "You tricked me!"

"You tricked me first. We invited *you,* not Haydn. You had no business telling him to meet us there, knowing how I feel about your seeing him."

"See! You *are* angry!" she cried, pointing at me.

"Damned right," I said, making her gasp. "You know what would happen if your parents found out about yesterday afternoon?"

She sat up, her eyes wide. "You won't tell them, will you? Promise me you won't tell them! *Pleeeeeee-ase?*"

"Promise me you won't sneak out to see Haydn anymore. And I'm talking about the cross-your-heart-and-hope-to-die promise."

"But he's so amazing!" she whined, flopping against the seat back. "Why are you being so mean?"

"Tara, give me your hands."

At her wary look, I said, "Just give them to me. I'm not going to spit on them."

"We'll look creepy if we hold hands."

"Okay, then look right here in my eyes. What do you see?"

"Green eyes."

"Who else has green eyes? And red hair? And freckles?"

"I know where you're going with this, and I'm not playing."

"Tara, you're like me in more than just looks. I snuck out with a boy, too, when I was your age, and I'm really lucky I didn't get into trouble. You know what stopped me? My dad being a cop. Yep, your grandpa warned me that he had his buddies keeping their eyes on me. So every time I saw a cop car, I knew I'd better be behaving. I didn't like it — no, make that I *hated* it — but it kept me out of trouble."

"All I did was ride in Haydn's car. What's so wrong with that?"

"Today you're taking a ride with him. Tomorrow you'll go see his frog collection in his bedroom."

She made a face, half annoyed, half amused. "He doesn't have a frog collection."

"Okay, then any kind of collection. You're like my little sister, Tara. I don't want to rat you out to your parents, but if anything bad happens to you because of Haydn, I'll blame myself for not telling them what you were doing."

"You don't have to get all emotional on me, Aunt Abby. Nothing's going to happen. I'm way too smart for that."

She wasn't getting it. I telegraphed that message to Marco as he handed out the ice cream. He gave me a subtle nod to let me know he was on top of it.

Tara picked up a plastic spoon and stabbed it into the cup, making a big show of how much she disdained the dessert. But she started eating it anyway.

"Have you told her yet?" Marco asked me in a low voice.

"Not yet."

Tara looked up suspiciously. "Told me about what?"

We both turned to study her; then I said to Marco, "I don't think she's ready."

"Yes, I am," Tara said, sitting upright.

Marco and I looked at each other; then Marco shrugged. "I think it's time to tell her, but it's your call."

I studied Tara for a moment longer, making her squirm with curiosity. Finally I said, "If I trust you with this, will you swear to keep it a secret? I mean swear right here in front of us?"

Tara's gaze narrowed. "This is a trick to

get me to stop seeing Haydn, isn't it?"

"I wish it was a trick, Tara," Marco said. "But this is real and it's risky."

Her eyes wide now, she nodded mutely.

"We're investigating a murder," I told her quietly.

"I knew that," Tara said with a glare in my direction.

"You don't know everything," Marco said. "Our investigation took a dangerous turn two days ago. I can't tell you any more than that at this point, but what I can tell you is that until we give you the all clear, you need to stay away from Haydn."

She sat back with a grin. "I knew it was a trick!"

"Tara, look at me," Marco said, then waited until she did. "Does it look like I'm in the mood to play tricks on you?"

"No."

"Have you forgotten about being kidnapped last winter?" he asked. "Do you remember that Abby was the target, but because you two look so much alike, the killers got you instead?"

"Yes." She shuddered. "But I don't see how Haydn could be dangerous, other than, you know, the sex thing, which, for the record, I am totally not going to do. He isn't going to kidnap me or anything." She suddenly looked worried. "Is he? Did you hear something?"

"You have to trust us, Tara," I said, reaching for her hands. That time, she gave them to me. "We can't tell you if Haydn is connected to this case until we investigate more, so to keep you safe, we need to insist you stay away from him. We don't want anything to happen to you. Will you promise?"

"I can't stay away from him at school. What if I see him in the hallway?"

"You know what I mean," I said.

"What if I say no?"

"Then I'll tell your parents what you were up to yesterday and you'll get grounded for two months," I said.

She pulled her hands back and resumed eating with a scowl. When she had finished, she said, "Okay, fine. I promise."

"Great!" I said.

"But," she said, "only if I can help you investigate him."

"No," Marco said. "Absolutely not. We're trying to keep you out of harm's way, not put you into it."

She pointed at me accusingly. "*You* said you wouldn't know if Haydn was involved until you investigated more. Well, who would be better able to investigate him than me?"

She had a point. Marco, however, wasn't buying it. "I can't allow it."

Tara studied him, a stubborn gleam in her eyes that I knew all too well. "Fine. But you have to promise to keep me in the loop."

"As soon as it's safe for you to know more, we'll gladly do that," Marco said.

"Awesome."

That had been way too easy. If I knew my niece, she would not be able to keep her nose out of it. I also knew not to tell Marco that. There wasn't anything he could do anyway, and he'd only worry. I'd have to keep tabs on Tara myself.

She pulled out her cell phone. "Now what do I tell Haydn? He's probably still waiting at Yog-earth."

"How about telling him that your parents found out and grounded you?" Marco asked.

"How geeky would that look? I'll blame it on you instead, Aunt Abby."

"Whatever it takes," I said.

She texted something, then sat back with a snicker. "You horked all over the passenger seat of the car, so we're taking you home. You might be pregnant."

I slipped on my jacket and got ready to

leave. "Like I said, whatever it takes."

Tara glanced at me suspiciously. "You're not, are you?"

"No," I said, and smiled at Marco. "That's a long way off."

He put his arms around both of us. "Yes, it is. I'm still getting used to having one other person in the apartment. And a dog."

"Good," Tara said. "One pregnant aunt is all I can handle."

"Speaking of pregnant aunts," I said, "Jillian asked me to watch Princess tonight."

Tara covered her mouth to hide her laugh. "At least you're not babysitting a sack of rotten potatoes."

"So," I said, "how much would it take for you to watch Princess tonight instead?"

"More than you can afford to pay," she replied.

At seven o'clock that evening, I returned to my former apartment building with Seedy in tow and a tension headache looming. I knocked on the door to Jillian's posh three-bedroom apartment on the second floor, and Princess immediately began to bark. Seedy looked up at me as if to say, *Seriously?* then did an about-face and started back toward the elevator.

I swept her up and carried her back just

as my cousin swung open the door. As usual, she looked like a fashion plate, wearing a chic little black dress with black opals dangling from her earlobes, her copper hair swept up in a gorgeous chignon, yet she also looked more frazzled than I'd ever seen her, as if she hadn't slept in days.

"Princess, stop it," she cooed over her shoulder, stepping back to let us in.

Princess ran up to sniff my ankles, but Seedy growled at her, so she backed away, turned around, and trotted into the living room.

"Are you okay?" I asked. "You look exhausted."

She gave me a weary smile. "You know how little ones get days and nights mixed up."

"Newborn babies do that, Jillian, not dogs."

As though she hadn't heard, she said, "I fed Princess earlier, and Claymore just walked her, so she should be set until we get home." She gave me a hug, then said, "Oh, Johann may need more aspirin when he wakes up. Let's go, Claymore."

Fastidious Claymore was the younger brother of Pryce Osborne II, the heel who had dumped me two months before we were to be married because I'd been kicked out of law school. At the time, I thought my life was over, yet if neither of those things had happened, I wouldn't have met Marco or bought a flower shop. Dog-sitting might have been the highlight of my day.

Like Pryce, Claymore was exceedingly well groomed and wore only tailor-made suits. Unlike Pryce, Claymore was very kindhearted and coddled Jillian to the extreme. Now he came into the kitchen with Jillian's black pashmina over his arm. "You might need this, darling."

"Who's Johann?" I asked, as he draped the shawl across her bare shoulders.

"Just the best German dog trainer in the greater Chicagoland area," Jillian said.

"What happened to Gustav?" I asked.

"He fired us," Claymore said with a shrug. "He said someone wasn't being co-operative." I wondered if Johann meant Princess or Jillian. "Text if you have any questions."

"Wait," I said. "You're leaving me with your German trainer?"

"Johann came down with the most horrific migraine while he was working with Princess," Claymore said, "so he took an aspirin and lay down on the sofa. He said covering his eyes with a cold cloth eased the pain, but then he fell asleep."

"He'll be up soon." Jillian patted my shoulder. "Thanks, cuz. You're the best."

Best what? Sucker? The door shut behind them and I turned to find Seedy sitting on her haunches in the doorway to the living room, watching something. She looked over her shoulder at me as if to say, *Seriously, what were you thinking?*

I entered Jillian's expensively decorated living room and saw a stocky blond man in a black athletic outfit lying on the leather sofa, a washcloth covering his eyes. Seedy hung back, too fearful of the man to enter the room, while Princess dropped what I thought was a chew toy at my feet. The toy, I discovered when I bent down, was a baby's rattle.

"Let's take this to the kitchen," I whispered, but apparently that wasn't what Princess had in mind, because she snatched it out from under my hand and ran around the room rattling it like crazy. The noise caused Johann to stir and then moan as he sat up.

He took the cloth off his face and squinted at me. "Yillian?" he rasped.

Obviously the pain had affected his vision. "I'm her cousin Abby. Jillian and Claymore had a function to go to."

"Yillian is gone?" He pressed his hands

together in prayer. *"Gott sei Dank!"* Then he fell back against the sofa holding his head and moaning. *"Ach, mein Kopf!"* I believed that was German for, *Oh, my head!*

"Would you like more aspirin?" I asked.

"Nuzzing vill make dis pain go avay," he exclaimed, "but to leave dis place and never return."

Puzzled, I sat on the love seat adjacent to the sofa and put my elbows on my knees. "Aren't you used to working with misbehaving dogs?"

"*Ja, ja!* Dat is vat I am trained to do! I vork vit dogs. Your cousin believes dis dog is her *Junge,* her baby! 'Should I burp her after I feed her, Johann? Do you tink she has colic, Johann? Don't you tink she should wear a baby bonnet ven ve go out, Johann?' " He grabbed the sides of his hair. "How can I vork vit a dog who is treated like a baby? How?"

He jumped up, then staggered back, groaning in pain. Clasping his head in both hands, he shuffled toward the door, sending Seedy scattering for cover. "*Fertig!* Done. You may tell Fräulein Yillian that I vill send her my final bill tomorrow."

The door slammed behind him, provoking Princess to go on a barking rampage. I pressed my fingers against my temples.

Where did Yillian keep those aspirin?

At ten thirty that evening, my cell phone rang, and I grabbed it as though it were my lifeline. "How's it going, babe?" Marco asked. "Sorry about the background noise. It's jammed here, and a football game is on TV."

"I can barely hear you," I yelled. "Princess won't stop barking, Marco. Every time the furnace kicks on, she barks. Every time the refrigerator kicks on, she barks. If someone rings a doorbell on TV, she barks. I've tried petting her, I've tried feeding her treats — just let Jillian scold me for that! — I've tried playing soothing music, and nothing works. Even Seedy wants to help. She keeps trying to back her into the bathroom."

"I'm sorry, Abby. Can you lock her in another room?"

"Tried it. She scratched up the door. I am never dog-sitting again. Ever. If I ever even think about saying yes, stuff something in my mouth. Seriously, Marco, if Jillian doesn't come home soon, I'm going to muzzle this little cretin with duct tape."

I heard the sound of a key in the door, which started another round of furious barking.

"Marco, it's Jill. I'll talk to you later."

I tried to catch Princess before she got to

the door, but it was too late. She ran up to my cousin and pawed at her legs, wanting to be held. Jillian scooped up the dog before she did damage to her long black skirt and in a gooey-sweet voice said, "Did you miss Mummy?"

Princess licked her face and made her laugh. I turned to look for Seedy but didn't see her.

"Was she a good girl?" Jillian asked.

"Jill, your dog has a barking problem. Everything sets her off."

Jillian straightened to stare at me in surprise. "Really? Johann said he would break her of that habit."

"Well, he didn't. She barked at every sound."

The furnace kicked on and Princess began her high-pitched barking. "Princess, stop," Jillian called. The dog ignored her and ran toward the heat register.

"Isn't there a command you can use?" I called over the noise.

"Yes," she called back. "It's *Princess, stop*!" She walked toward her only to have Princess take off running, her tongue lolling from the side of her mouth as she circled the room. "Princess, stop!" she kept saying, following the dog.

I joined in the chase, the dog leading us

into a spare bedroom, where she ran under the bed. Before I could get down on my knees, I heard a growl and then a yelp, and then out backed Seedy, dragging Princess by the tag on her gemstone-encrusted collar.

Jillian picked up her dog and held her beneath her front legs so they were face-to-face. "You are a bad girl! Just wait until I tell Daddy. I'm so sorry, Abs. I don't know what to say."

"Wait until you tell Daddy what?" Claymore asked.

"Abby said she's been barking all evening," Jillian said. "Johann may not work out."

I was about to deliver Johann's message when Claymore handed me an 8 × 10 yellow envelope. "This was on the table under the mailboxes. Someone sent it to your old address."

I tore open the 8 × 10 mailer and pulled out a color photo of a young woman with flowing black hair. She wore an aqua blue tunic top, a long, colorful skirt, and cork-soled sandals. She was standing behind a cloth-covered table at what appeared to be an art fair, and on the table in front of her were sculptures of birds, flowers, dogs, and cats. A sign pinned to the front of the table said: DESIGNS BY THENIA. Could she be a young Parthenia Pappas?

Judging by the clothing of the people in the picture, it appeared to have been taken in the midseventies. I flipped the photo over and sure enough, in the upper left-hand corner someone had printed: *Columbus, IN, October 1976.* I turned it over again and studied the woman's face. It had to be the Duchess. And that wasn't all that the photo showed.

Jillian peered over my shoulder. "Who's the pregnant hippie?"

Chapter Sixteen

As soon as I was back home, I called Marco. "Can you talk now?"

"Hey, Buttercup. Hold on while I get to my office. It sounds quiet there. Are you home?"

"Yes, but that's not why I called. Someone sent an envelope to my old address with a photo inside of what appears to be a pregnant Parthenia at an art fair in Columbus, with a date on the back of October 1976. If this really is Parthenia, Marco, she lied to us."

"If that's Parthenia, Abby, then someone from her past is making sure we know the truth, either to point us toward the real killer or to point us away from himself."

"Who else would it be but one of our suspects? We haven't talked to anyone else about her. But which one of them would have possessed such a photo?"

"The likeliest person would have been Lila

Cannon, who may have hired a private investigator to find Kermit. Doug was only fifteen, so I doubt he would have had the presence of mind or the funds to do that. Henry probably didn't care where Kermit was, and Rusty wouldn't have either, unless he wanted to find Kermit so Lila could divorce him."

"But why not just come forward with the photo?"

"It's worth taking the photo to our suspects and asking." At a loud cheer in the background, Marco said, "The Bears are winning. In about a minute, I won't be able to hear you, Sunshine, so let's talk later."

Saturday

Later hadn't worked for me. Because of my evening with Princess, I was fast asleep when Marco got home. Then, after spending a restless night on the sagging mattress, I didn't sleep well until after Marco got up. So when I finally opened my eyes it was nine a.m., and the apartment was empty. In the kitchen I found a note that said, *Took Seedy to park. Coffee ready to brew. If you want to talk to Rusty, we can go when I get back. Luv you lots, M.*

Love you lots, too, M, I thought, as I poured myself coffee. Marco had put the newspaper on the table, still rolled up, so I sat at his small kitchen table and opened it. The banner headline announced that another armed robbery had occurred, this time at a convenience store in town. Great, I thought. That would push the cold case investigation even further behind.

Then I noticed a smaller headline below the fold: BAR'S BONES STOLEN.

My stomach knotted as I read the article. Connor had quoted as fact my answers to what he'd asked me about, with no credit given to his police source. Marco was not going to be happy about that. I folded the paper and stuck it in the recycling bin. I'd have to tell him about the article, but I'd make sure he was in a good mood first.

By the time Marco and Seedy returned, I had showered and dressed and was ready to go. "Thanks for the coffee," I said, giving him a kiss, "and for letting me sleep in."

"I even brought the paper in for you."

I put my arms around Marco's waist and smiled at him. "Like you pointed out before, Salvare, you're just a sweet kind of guy, and you get a kiss for that. Oh, and there was a small article in the paper this morning about the bone theft. Time to go!" And then I kissed him.

Naturally Marco had to read the article

before we left, and, as I'd predicted, he wasn't pleased that Connor had attributed the information to me. "As long as you give him something, Abby, he'll keep coming back for more, so please don't say anything else about our investigation. Let me decide what to tell him. I've had more experience at this than you."

I might have argued his autocratic position if I hadn't known he was right. And he had said please.

Seedy pawed at the front door, gave a yip, and looked back at us. Her leash was on, and she knew that meant we were going out. "She's a smart dog, Marco. You should have seen her drag Princess out from under the bed. By the way, did I tell you that both of Jillian's trainers fired them? I'll tell you all about it on our way to Rusty's."

Marco rolled his eyes. "I can hardly wait."

Blazing Saddles Saddlery was located on the county highway just outside New Chapel's eastern boundary. It reminded me of shops I'd seen in old Westerns, a low one-story wood-sided building with a false front and a hitching post near the door. Inside were all manner of Western and English riding outfits, more styles of Western boots than I'd ever seen, racks of belts, a wall of riding hats, a room devoted to saddles and riding equipment, a glass display case stuffed with silver and turquoise jewelry, and in the center of the floor, a life-sized horse wearing a turquoise warm-up coat.

I stared around in awe. "I feel like a kid in a toy store."

"I'll see if Rusty is here," Marco said, and strode toward the young woman behind the counter. In fact, all the employees seemed to be young women. Clearly, like Kermit, Rusty had an eye for the ladies.

With Seedy on her leash, I walked around the large space taking everything in. I came to the boot section and perused the aisles until I found the tan leather ones with stitched flowers on them. I had to admit, they were knockouts. "What do you think, Seedy?"

Hearing her name, she looked up at me and tilted her head, then turned and wagged her tail as Marco came around the corner. "Rusty's here," he said. "He's coming out shortly."

"What do you think of these boots?" I asked.

"Nice, but I've never seen you wear anything Western style."

I held one up, trying to envision it on my foot. Then I turned it upside down and checked the price. With a sigh, I put it back. "Too expensive."

"Who says it's too expensive?" Rusty asked, causing Seedy to scamper behind me. Rusty peered around me for a look at her. "Well, if that don't beat all. A three-legged doggy."

Seedy hid her face against my jeans, crouched low to the ground, and tucked her tail beneath her. "She's afraid of men," I said.

"Hey there, pup, I won't hurt you." Rusty clapped Marco on the back. "Let's see if we can find Miss Abigail a pair of boots that fit. What size are you, darlin'?"

"Six and a half."

"Tiny feet, big heart . . . or something like that. Let me go pull a seven. I have a feeling you might need a bigger size in these boots." As he ambled off with his arthritic gait, he turned to say, "Chairs are against the wall. Might as well have a seat, Marco. You know how these little gals are once they start shopping for shoes."

"Actually, we came to talk to you about our investigation," Marco said.

"You're not in a big rush, are you?" Rusty called back. "Settle down. We've got time."

He returned with two boxes of the boots, one in my size and one in size seven, so I handed Seedy's leash to Marco so I could try them on. As Rusty had predicted, the seven was more comfortable.

"Didn't I say so?" Rusty asked. "Now, let's talk price." He leaned close to whisper something to Marco, then said, "Ain't that an offer you can't refuse?"

"That's quite a discount," Marco said.

"What is it?" I asked.

"Now, never you mind," Rusty said. "Let's just say it'll be your weddin' present."

I glanced at Marco wide-eyed. Would it be wrong to accept a gift from a suspect?

"Ring it up," Marco said.

Apparently not.

After paying for the boots, which Rusty gave to us at cost, we sat at a table in the break room with glasses of his homemade sarsaparilla. He even set out a bowl of water for Seedy. I took her off her leash so she could reach it, but she wouldn't budge from my side.

The break room had three round wooden tables painted red, a sink set in a bright red laminate countertop, refrigerator, microwave, and black cabinets, with a shade-covered window in the rear wall. A door on the side wall stood ajar and I could just make out rows of shelves inside stocked with boot boxes.

"So," Rusty said, opening the conversation, "someone stole those ol' bones out from under you, did they? Or so the newspaper said this morning."

Marco glanced at me and I could see the disgruntled look in his eyes. Darn that Connor! "Yes, unfortunately," was all he said.

"Who do you think did it?" Rusty asked.

"Someone who's running scared," Marco said, then leaned down to pet Seedy, who had ventured out from beneath the table and was staring up at him, her long ears facing forward, as though on alert. She cast a nervous glance in Rusty's direction, then slid her face under Marco's hand.

Rusty took a drink of his tea. "Got any suspects?"

"A few names have come up," Marco said. "Nothing serious yet."

"You still think those bones have something to do with Kermit?" Rusty asked.

"We do," Marco said, "but our information about him is still somewhat sketchy. All right if we pick your brain?"

"Go ahead and shoot," Rusty said, as I took out the notepad and pen, "but I think you're wasting your time chasing your Kermit theory. He took off with his girlfriend, plain and simple."

"Then how would you explain the bones?"

Marco asked.

"My guess is that a couple of itinerants slipped down those basement steps with flasks of whiskey one night and got into a drunken brawl," Rusty said. "You know how easy it is to forget that back door is propped open — or at least it was for my crew. So maybe one did the other in, then got scared and buried him in the dirt. That floor was just sitting there open for weeks."

Marco couldn't hide his skepticism — or maybe he didn't want to. "Did you have a problem with itinerants?"

"Not regular-like, but every so often we did. A few of 'em were always drunk and lookin' to make trouble. I'd chase 'em out with my shotgun and that'd be the end of it for a while."

"Wouldn't you have noticed that the dirt was disturbed?" I asked.

"Maybe, maybe not." Rusty shrugged. "I didn't pay much attention to the hole in the floor until Kermit stopped showing up, and I knew I had to do something about it."

Marco propped his chin on his hand and thought about that for a moment. "Let's say you're right about the itinerants. Digging a hole takes time. Wouldn't you or one of your staff have caught the murderer in the act?"

"Depends on whether we found him before closing or if he stayed the night," Rusty said. "You'd be surprised how easy it is for someone to hide down there."

Marco nodded, a frown on his face, as though he were adding up the times the back door had been left propped open on his watch. "It would still take a shovel to dig a deep enough hole."

"Kermit's tools were just layin' around, Marco, where he left 'em. How do you think he dug up that floor in the first place? He broke up the concrete with a sledgehammer and then shoveled it off to the side. You asked me about his key chain before. I'd bet that's when it dropped out of his pocket." Rusty paused. "You never found the keys, did you?"

"No, but we haven't sifted the dirt yet," Marco replied.

"Bet you won't find 'em," Rusty said. "He probably fished 'em out of the dirt and didn't bother with the leather, especially if it broke apart."

Marco pondered some more. "So you don't think there's a chance that it was Kermit buried in the basement?"

"No, sir," Rusty said.

I had one eye on Seedy, who'd grown brave enough to venture out and was now sniffing along the perimeter of the room. She stopped at the storage room door to peer cautiously inside, her ears flat and her tail down, as though she expected something sinister to pop out at her.

"Don't you think it's odd that Kermit never had any contact with his kids?" I asked.

"Miss Abigail, you'd have to know Kermit to understand. Life was all about him. If Kermit was having a good time, he didn't much care about anyone else."

Marco said, "Do you remember asking Doug whether his dad was abusive?"

Rusty scratched his forehead. "No, I really don't, Marco, but, as I told you before, my memory ain't what it used to be. If Doug says I asked, then I probably did. I can tell you that Kermit had a terrible temper."

"Did you ever talk to Kermit about it?" I asked.

Rusty seemed surprised that I'd ask. "About how he treated his family? No, ma'am. It wasn't any of my beeswax."

"Did Lila ever try to find Kermit?" I asked.

"Yes, she did," Rusty said. "She hired a gumshoe."

"A detective?" I asked.

"Former detective," Rusty said. "Ol' Pete

Morgan. Retired from the force and became a private eye. He died back in the nineties." Rusty leaned back and got a faraway look in his eyes. I had a feeling a story was coming.

"Yeah, good ol' Pete. His grandson is deputy prosecutor now. You might know Greg, Miss Abigail, seeing as how you worked for Attorney Hammond and all."

I knew the extremely handsome Greg Morgan very well. I'd had a major crush on him in high school. Sadly, he'd had a crush on himself, too; also on women's breasts, and I hadn't had any to speak of. Then I went away to college and returned with a whole new profile, literally. His interest in me changed drastically after that. But so had my taste in men.

"Can you elaborate as to why Lila hired the detective?" Marco asked.

"What can I tell you, Marco? She thought that woman — what's she callin' herself these days, a duchess? — was conniving."

Seedy suddenly appeared beside my chair with something in her mouth. She dropped it and looked up at me, wagging her tail. I bent down to see what it was and found a worn, dirty garden glove. I gave her a pat on the head, then edged the glove under my chair with my shoe. I'd have to put it back when we were finished.

"In what respect was she conniving?" Marco asked.

Rusty scratched his head. "I don't know if I should be telling you this, but Kermit cleaned out the company's bank account before he took off, and Lila was sure that woman talked him into it. She couldn't accept that Kermit would do that to his family — ruin his business and all. Luckily, she had Henry. That young feller knew just what to do to keep that company afloat."

"Did Lila suspect foul play at all or did she just want to locate her husband?" Marco asked.

"As I said before, she didn't talk about it much. My wife was a gentle, kindhearted soul, and for her to speak out against someone, well, it took a lot to push her to that point. But I can tell you that folks around town were leery of that Duchess woman back then, calling her a Gypsy because of her foreign ways. Now they treat her like a movie star." Rusty shook his head.

"Do you know if Lila ever located the Duchess?" I asked.

"Can't tell you that, Miss Abigail. Like I said, Lila didn't care to discuss the past with me. And her kids were very careful not to bring up their papa around her, knowing how his leaving had wounded her and all.

Lord, how they did worship their mama. Would've done anything for her."

I wrote down his last comment and underlined it. Would that have included murdering their own father?

"So you're not aware of Lila receiving any photos from Pete Morgan?" Marco asked.

"No, sir."

"Was any attempt made at a later time to find Kermit?" Marco asked.

"Lila tried again before we got married. Said she didn't want to be a bigamist." Rusty laughed. "She'd joke about that from time to time, saying, 'What would we do, Rusty, if Kermit suddenly showed up?' And I said, 'First thing we'd do is check to see if he was a ghost.' "

"So you believed Kermit was dead?" Marco asked.

That caught Rusty by surprise. He scratched his head again. "Well, you got me there, Marco. I guess I did think so."

"Any particular reason?" Marco asked.

"None that comes to mind. Maybe because it had been so long since anyone had heard from him." Rusty took a long drink of tea, then wiped his mouth with the back of his hand and got up. "Can I get either of you a refill?"

"None for me, thanks," Marco said.

"I'm fine," I said, and took a drink. I didn't much care for the taste and set it back down.

While Rusty had his back to us, Marco tapped my notepad, as if to ask whether I got that last interesting bit of information. I pointed out my note to him: *Rusty believes Kermit left town/was ghost. Can't explain contradiction.*

"Did Doug ever tell you that he'd spied on Kermit and caught him with the Duchess?" Marco asked, when Rusty returned to the table.

His cheerful demeanor slipping a little, Rusty replied, "After a fashion. Doug had been helping me with the basement after his pappy left, and he'd drop little bits of information here and there, so I pieced together what had happened. I took him under my wing and did what I could to make up for Kermit's absence, and I think he really appreciated it. I feel good about that."

"How much do you think that experience affected Doug?" Marco asked.

"It surely broke that boy's heart to see his pappy with another woman. No matter what happens, a boy still wants to be able to look up to his father. And then, of course, seeing his mama's pain affected him, too."

"Lila was your high school sweetheart," I said. "Finding out that Kermit was cheating on her must have affected you, too."

He sipped his tea for a moment, then said, "I didn't like to hear about it, naturally. But there wasn't anything I could do."

Seedy dropped another glove at my foot and wagged her tail happily. Clearly, she was pleased with herself for inventing a new game. I snapped my fingers to try to get her to come to me, but she hobbled off again.

"Do you think Doug would have been angry enough to take action against Kermit?" Marco asked.

"Are you askin' me whether Doug coulda done his pappy in?" Rusty asked. "No, sir. He was a kid, Marco, a nice kid who stepped up to help me when his pappy let me down. If you ask me, I'd take a long look at that Duchess woman. Always struck me as shady that she came back alone — and a success to boot. Why don't you ask her where she got her seed money?"

"I'll do that," Marco said. "I know you're not going to like it, Rusty, but I have to ask you the same question. Where did you get the money to remodel your basement?"

Rusty gave him a puzzled glance. "Why shouldn't I like it? I've got nothing to hide. But I know how you fellers work. You've got to suspect everyone. So let me put your mind at ease. I saved a long time to have that work done and have my old bank records to prove it."

"Thank you. Then let's move on," Marco said. "Abby, would you show Rusty the photo we received yesterday?"

I pulled it out of my purse and handed it to Rusty. He brought it close to his face, squinting to see it. "Am I supposed to recognize these people?"

"Just the woman behind the table," I said. "It was taken in nineteen seventy-six. Do you remember anyone who looked like that?"

Rusty blinked a few times, then took another look. "Is that what's-her-name? Duchess?"

"That's who we think it is," Marco said. "That photo was taken in the fall of the year Kermit supposedly left town."

"Looks to me like she's got a bun in the oven." Rusty looked at the back of the photo, frowned as though doing some calculating in his head, then handed it back. "So she was carrying Kermit's child after all," he said, more to himself than to us.

"Someone obviously wanted us to know that the Duchess was pregnant," I said.

"Can I ask how you came by that photo?"

Rusty asked.

"It was dropped off anonymously," Marco said. "I'm going to venture a guess that Pete Morgan took this photo when he was working for your wife, but obviously he wouldn't be dropping it off now. That means someone who had access to Lila's belongings might have. Any idea who that could be?"

Rusty gave Marco a skeptical look. "Are you askin' if I did it?"

Marco replied with a flicker of a grin. "Did you?"

"Son, if I had something that I thought would help you, I'd give it to you."

"Fair enough," Marco said. "Maybe you can help with this. You said Kermit seemed to favor Henry over Doug, yet when we talked to Henry, he said he wasn't close to Kermit."

"Let me tell you something," Rusty said, crossing one booted foot over his other knee. "When someone is hurt by someone else, he has to make up a story in his head to take away the pain. I know Henry was close to Kermit at first because that was how Kermit operated. He'd charm the socks off you, then later on show his true self. Henry was always a gentle person. If Kermit hurt him, then Henry probably told himself that it didn't matter 'cause he wasn't close to him anyway. See what I'm saying?"

"You're saying that Henry was close to Kermit at the beginning," I said, reading from my notes, "but later on, Kermit pushed him away?"

"That's what I'm saying," Rusty said with a smile. He stabbed a finger at me. "She's a keeper, that one is, Marco."

"Thank you," I said, smiling at my groom. "I think I'll keep Marco, too."

"Ah, how I miss my Lila," Rusty said, a look of intense sadness crossing his leathery features. He turned away and sat for a moment staring out the window, then wiped his eyes with his thumbs and said, "I hope you two will be as happy as we were. Now don't mind the musings of a maudlin old man. Get on with your questions."

"Are you sure?" Marco asked. "We can stop at any time."

"Let's get this over with once and for all," Rusty said.

"Did you ever witness Kermit being verbally abusive toward Henry?" Marco asked.

"You mean laying into him? Can't say that I did but I wouldn't be surprised if he had. Kermit would lay into a judge if one crossed him. Got himself into some nasty fistfights because of that mouth of his. He even fought with the officers as they hauled him off to the slammer. He had a wicked temper, ol' Kermit did."

"Is it true that you and Kermit got into a fistfight?" I asked.

Rusty chuckled. "Lordy, I haven't thought of that in years. Since you asked, here's what happened. Kermit was at my bar drinking after work, and being that he was already on his way to drunk, he took offense when I suggested he get home to his wife. Accused me of trying to steal her away. He socked me in the nose, that bastard did, so I let him have it in the jaw. Someone called the cops and they took him away."

I wrote it down. That satisfied me.

"Think back to when you were having problems getting your basement finished," Marco said. "Did you ever let Henry know what was going on?"

"I'm sure I did," Rusty said, looking perplexed. "Can't really remember how that came about, though."

"Do you recall going to see him at the savings and loan?" Marco asked.

Rusty scratched the back of his head. It seemed to be his gesture of concentration. "I guess I could be talked into it. Did Henry say I did? Because if he did, then I guess it's so."

I really wanted to believe that Rusty's memory was foggy, but I also wondered if it wasn't a convenient excuse.

One of Rusty's employees stuck her head around the corner and whispered, "It's almost time for my lunch. Do you want me to wait? The store's empty."

"I'll be done in a few minutes, darlin'," Rusty replied. "Right, Marco?"

"I think so," Marco said.

"How's your mama been?" Rusty asked him.

"Excuse me," I said. "I need to get Seedy."

I picked up the gloves and headed through the doorway into the storage room. It was a large room that had deep shelves filled with store merchandise from the floor to the ceiling on all four walls, with one center aisle that had shelves on both sides as well. I didn't see my dog at first, but then I heard her scratching at something and located her in a back corner under a window, sniffing among rusty old garden tools in a big tin bucket that was partially tucked under the lowest shelf. A spiderweb stretched from the rim of the bucket to the wall, and more webbing clung to Seedy's nose. Obviously the bucket had been undisturbed for some time.

I snapped the leash onto her collar, wiped

the sticky web off her nose, and dropped both gloves inside the bucket. That was when I took a closer look at the wooden-handled tools. They were identical to the ones I'd seen in the bar's basement.

Coincidence?

Chapter Seventeen

"Did you find your dog?" Rusty called from the other room.

I heard him scrape back his chair and knew he would be heading my way, so I pulled out my cell phone and snapped a photo of the tools, then picked up Seedy just as Rusty appeared.

"Seedy was looking for a place to do her business, weren't you, bad girl?" I said to the dog, who tilted her head as though puzzled by my scolding tone. Gliding past Rusty, I said, "Marco, I need to take Seedy outside. I'll meet you by the car."

I made a quick exit from the store and walked over to a tree to set Seedy down, where she actually did do her business. Marco appeared a few minutes later, so I tugged on the dog's leash and we jogged to the car.

"Is Seedy okay?" Marco asked, as we buckled ourselves into our seats.

"Look at this," I said, and showed him the photo on my phone. "These tools are exactly like the ones at the bar, Marco, down to the same brand name carved into the wooden handles."

Marco studied the photo then turned on the engine.

"Why are you frowning?" I asked.

"I don't like what we're finding, Abby. In addition to your discovery, some of the comments Rusty made aren't sitting well with me, like his ghost reference, which contradicted his earlier statement. And his itinerant theory. I've never had a problem with itinerants getting into the basement."

"Do you think times were different back then?"

"Maybe. I can check police records, but that may take some time."

"You know who might be able to help us with that? My dad."

Marco gave me his irresistible grin, the corners of his mouth curving up just a little. "We're on the same wavelength, Mrs. Salvare."

Mrs. Salvare. Hmm. It didn't sound so bad coming from Marco.

"It's almost noon," he said. "Do you want to stop for lunch somewhere? Then we can drop by to see your dad."

"Not gonna happen, *Mr.* Salvare. Our new mattress is supposed to be delivered between noon and three p.m., and there's no way I'm going to miss that baby."

He patted my knee. "And there's no way I'd let you miss that, baby."

After a quick sandwich at home, Marco headed to Down the Hatch, leaving Seedy and me to wait for the new mattress. So as soon as I finished my own lunch, I called my dad to see what he knew about Rusty, Kermit, and the Duchess.

My father, Jeffrey Knight, had been a New Chapel policeman for almost twenty years when he was hit in the upper leg by a felon's bullet while chasing drug dealers during a sting operation. He was rushed into surgery, but an unfortunate surgical mistake caused him to be paralyzed from the waist down. He had regained enough feeling in his legs that he was able to use crutches to maneuver stairs, but otherwise he was confined to a wheelchair.

His Irish zest for life, however, had not been dimmed. He refused to look back and instead concentrated on his blessings. He was my role model and my earliest hero.

"Hey, Abracadabra!" he called jovially, using the name he'd dubbed me due to my ability to disappear at chore time. "Good to hear your voice, honey. Of course I'll help."

"Thanks, Dad. Just don't tell Mom I'm inquiring about the Duchess."

"I haven't lived with her all these years for nothing, Ab. Your mother practically worships the woman. How about I just won't mention you called? Now, what I remember about Rusty is that he had a couple of run-ins with homeless men trying to camp out in his basement. We advised him to keep a better watch on his back door and the problem stopped. I don't remember it being a big concern, though, and I don't think he ever had us arrest anyone."

I was relieved that Rusty's story was confirmed. I hated to think that he had lied to us.

"As for the Duchess, back then there were some in town who called her a Gypsy because of the way she dressed and talked. As far as I know, she wasn't, but she did have a volatile temper. We had to pull her in once for threatening one of her neighbors with a knife, a man she said was harassing her. The man said she was nuts."

That sounded like Parthenia.

"Kermit was a strange, self-absorbed man," Dad said, "charming one moment, brooding and angry the next. We arrested him on several occasions for getting into fights. He was what you'd call an abject drunk, a miserable, unpleasant man."

I made notes while Dad told a few more Kermit tales. Then I flipped the notebook closed and capped my pen. "Great stuff, Dad. Thanks for your help."

With nothing to do after that, I rearranged the books on Marco's bookshelves in his living room by color, then headed for the kitchen to move the dishes in the cabinets and the utensils in the drawers. On the way, I had a sudden flash of Francesca rearranging my tool drawer and decided to play fetch with Seedy instead. When we both grew bored, she napped and I surfed the Internet for new ideas for floral arrangements.

It wasn't until five minutes before three that the doorbell rang at last, sending Seedy running for cover. Unfortunately, her shelter was the bed, and having strange men dismantling it over her did not help her nerves. She backed into a corner and growled and snapped at them until I had to drag her out and put her in the bathroom to calm her down.

Half an hour later, I had a brand-new mattress, and the deliverymen had extra twenty dollar bills in their pockets to haul away the old one. I let Seedy out of the bathroom, then remade the bed and stretched out on it to see how it felt.

It seemed as though I had just lain down when I heard "Abby?"

I opened my eyes to see Marco standing above me. "I was going to ask how the mattress is, but I guess you answered that question. It's almost dinnertime."

I yawned and stretched. "That's the first good rest I've had since we started our honeymoon."

"Something every groom wants to hear," he said dryly, stretching out beside me.

Seedy began to make her little yipping noise, so Marco reached down and lifted her to the bed. "Just this once," he said. "We're not going to make a habit of it."

"I guess I should go make us some supper," I said.

Marco rolled over to face me, propped on his elbow. "Want to see a movie tonight after we talk to your dad, Sleeping Beauty?"

"I already talked to my dad, Prince Charming."

"Isn't Prince Charming from the Cinderella story?"

"Would you rather be called Prince Phillip or Prince Charming?"

"If we're sticking with the fairy-tale

theme," he murmured in my ear, "I'd rather be the Big Bad Wolf."

It amazed me how fast he could change directions. Never able to resist his strong sexual magnetism, I snuggled closer. "You're straying into dangerous territory, Mr. Salvare."

"I live for danger, Mrs. Salvare," he said huskily, then kissed me with a passion that ignited all kinds of fires.

The flames were doused, however, when Seedy pawed my shoulder and whined, as if to say, *Let me in!*

Marco sighed and picked her up, bringing her between us. "Nothing like a dog to get you back on track. Just remember, Seedy, this is a onetime deal."

Seedy lay down, panting happily.

"What were we talking about?" I asked. "Oh, right. Dad said Rusty did call the cops on several occasions about itinerants sleeping in his basement, and he remembered people referring to the Duchess as a Gypsy. He also recalled having to haul her down to the police station for threatening a man with a knife. He described her as volatile."

"That puts a different spin on things, doesn't it?"

"Yes, it does. For instance, what would a volatile person do to a man who left her pregnant and in the lurch? And do you remember what was outside her back window? A garden. And where there's a garden there are usually garden tools."

"But there's the glitch, Abby. Presupposing that the murder weapon is in fact a trowel, would she bring her garden tools to meet Kermit?"

"You're right. If she were going to take them, they'd be packed in a box."

"So back to my original question. Do you want to see a movie?"

"I'd love to see a movie, Marco. It's been ages since we took a Saturday off. But do you trust Rafe to handle the bar?"

"I left my brother a whole sheet of instructions. I made it so simple a five-year-old could follow it. So what I'm saying is that it's Saturday night, and I'd like to take my bride out for a movie date. Does my bride accept?"

"She would like to, except what do we do with Seedy?"

Hearing her name, Seedy's large tufted ears came forward and she looked at me expectantly. "What do we do with you, Seedy?"

Marco stroked her head. "She should be fine alone for a few hours, Abby."

"But I feel so bad leaving her all alone.

She hasn't been alone since we brought her home. How about if I ask Tara to watch her at her house? Then Seedy can play with Tara's puppy."

"Sounds like a plan." Marco lifted the dog's chin and gazed into her eyes. "Does it sound like a plan to you?"

Seedy gave her little yip, then started playing with him, pouncing like a cat and then backing away, her whole body wriggling in excitement. I watched the two of them for a moment, remembering what a sad little creature she'd been when I'd first laid eyes on her. How she was blossoming under our love. It was such a warm feeling that I almost hated to leave them.

I called Tara, who told me she was going to a sleepover and wouldn't be able to help.

"What about Jillian?" Marco asked. "She owes you."

"Good thinking." I phoned Jillian next, but she and Claymore were going to Chicago with another couple to see a play. Her brother was going to watch Princess for her.

"Seedy will be fine here alone, Abby," Marco said. "We'll take her outside before we go. What trouble can she get into in a few hours' time?"

Within ten minutes of the movie's conclusion, Marco's phone vibrated. He held it down by his foot to discreetly check the screen, then whispered, "It's Reilly."

"Can't you call him in ten minutes?" I whispered back. "If it's really important, he'll call again."

Marco slid his phone into his pocket and stretched out his long legs. But when his phone vibrated a minute later, and Reilly's name popped up again, he left the theater. I was torn between wanting to stay for the ending and wanting to know what was going on, so I walked up the aisle and watched the last scene from just inside the door. Before the credits began, I hurried into the lobby and saw Marco waiting by the exit.

"Trouble at the bar," he said, shepherding me to the parking lot. "A brawl started and the cops were called. It got messy. I've tried to reach Rafe three times, but he hasn't answered."

"Is Reilly there now?"

"Yes. He says it's over and the troublemakers have fled, but my staff is shaken. They closed the bar for the evening." Marco sighed. "So much for my list of instructions."

I didn't envy Rafe. As the manager, the onus would be on him.

Marco didn't say much on the way there,

and I could see by the look on his face that he was tense, so I stayed quiet. My phone vibrated, so I checked the screen and saw my mom's name. I let it go to voice mail.

Instead of trying to find a parking space, Marco pulled into the alley and parked just outside of the bar's rear entrance. Using his key, he opened the door, and we went inside.

"Hey, Marco," Reilly said, as we came up the hallway and into the main room. He was sitting in a booth talking to Gert and taking notes. Rafe and Chris, another bartender, were sweeping up broken glass near the front door, and Mary, the other waitress, was mopping the floor behind the bar.

"Is everyone okay?" Marco asked.

"We're fine," Gert said. "I've handled a few of these in my lifetime. No biggie."

"Rafe?" Marco asked.

"Yeah, we're fine," Rafe said in a subdued voice, keeping his gaze on the floor.

"Are you done with me, Sarge?" Gert asked. "I need to help with the cleanup."

"We're done," Reilly said.

Gert patted the bench that she'd just vacated and said to me, "Sit here, hon, and take a load off."

As I sat down, Reilly said jokingly, "Trouble at the bar and you weren't at the center of it? Who would've thought it possible?"

"Gosh, I've missed you, Reilly," I said. "We really should do this more often."

"How did the brawl start?" Marco asked, directing his question to his brother.

Rafe paused his sweeping to give Marco a deer-in-the-headlights stare.

"Two college-aged kids caused a dustup," Gert said. "One of them was wearing a New Chapel U sweatshirt. I didn't see how it began, but Mary waited on them."

Mary, an attractive, friendly, thirty-six-year-old divorced woman, said, "I don't know for sure, Marco, but it seemed to me that they came in wanting to start something. It just felt staged, the way they were all friendly with me at first, and then after they got their beers, they started talking loudly and making obscene remarks about women."

"Directed toward you?" Marco asked.

"No, just to women in general. The things they were saying got some guys on the stools around them riled up and they started arguing, and pretty soon some punches were thrown and threats were made and then it was like an explosion of fists. It got crazy."

"I heard some of the things those two guys were saying," Chris chimed in. "And with smiles on their faces, too. I agree with Mary. I think they came in here purposely to cause a fight."

"I heard them making racial jokes," Gert said. "I told them to knock it off or take a hike."

"Did you alert Rafe as to what was going on?" Marco asked.

All three of the employees shot Rafe an uncomfortable glance. Then Gert said, "It all happened so fast, Marco, no one had a chance to react."

It was easy to see that they were covering for Rafe.

Marco waited for his brother to say something, but when he didn't, Marco didn't press him. "What's the damage report?"

"Nothing major," Gert said. "Broken bottles and some glasses, sticky floors and stools, probably some customers with bruises."

"Thank goodness my insurance is up-to-date," Marco said. "All right, everyone, thanks for cleaning up. As soon as you're done, you can go home."

Rafe said in a sheepish voice, "Do you want me to stay behind?"

"No, I don't," Marco replied, his chilly glance making it clear he was in no mood to deal with Rafe tonight. He slid in beside me and said to Reilly, "Who called you?"

"Your brother," Reilly said. "It was about over when we got here, and the two instigators were long gone. I did get statements from a couple of your customers, and someone even had the presence of mind to take photographs, so I'll write up a report and put out an alert in case the idiots show their faces around town."

Marco ran his fingers through his hair, shaking his head as though he couldn't believe the brawl had happened. He shot me a look of exasperation, so I put my arm around his shoulders and said, "At least the damage was minimal, Marco. It could have been a lot worse."

"But what was their purpose?" Marco asked. "Just to start a fight?"

Rafe stopped at the booth, a dustpan full of glass shards in his hand, and said guiltily, "I guess I should tell you now, Marco, that after the cops came I went to the storage room to get the brooms and found the back door open."

"Damn it, Rafe," Marco said through gritted teeth.

"It's not my fault," Rafe said. "I checked on it earlier and it was shut tight, honest."

Marco looked at his other employees and all nodded in agreement.

"What about the cooks?" Marco asked.

"I asked," Rafe said. "They said they hadn't been out to the bins yet. It was too early."

"Someone must have opened it from this side," Reilly said.

"Who would have done a stupid thing like that?" Gert asked.

Marco was out of the booth so fast, Reilly and I stared at each other in surprise. I saw him head up the hallway and knew immediately where he was going.

Reilly and I followed him to the basement. Marco had already turned on the light over the hole and was standing at the edge. The yellow tape was still intact, but the dirt looked like it had been raked with some kind of tool.

"I'll be damned," Reilly said, and took out his cell phone to snap photos.

"Someone was paid to start that fight," Marco said. "He propped the back door open to let someone else get down here."

"It has to be the same thief who took the bones," I said. "I'll bet he was looking for something he left behind."

"Hello?"

Hearing a familiar voice, I turned toward the stairway just as Connor MacKay stepped into the basement, smiling broadly.

"Hey, it's a party and I wasn't invited. I hear there was trouble tonight."

"Nothing to see here, MacKay," Reilly said, stepping across the yellow tape to reach him.

"This little hole proving to be a trouble magnet?" Connor asked.

"Out," Reilly said, backing him toward the steps.

Connor pointed to me, mimed talking on a phone, and mouthed, *Call me.*

"Don't hold your breath," I said.

"Wait, Reilly," Marco said. "MacKay, do you want a statement?"

"Are you kidding me?" Straightening his khaki shirt, Connor took a minirecorder out of his pocket and clicked it on. "Fire when ready."

"What are you doing?" I whispered.

"I want this to end, Abby. I'm not going to put my staff in jeopardy any longer."

Another reference to jeopardy. I wished Marco would stop using that word.

Marco gave Connor a brief rundown of the break-in, then concluded with "A surveillance camera is being installed today on both the main and the basement level. There will not be a repeat occurrence." He said to Connor, "Print that in your paper tomorrow."

"But you're still on the hunt for the killer, right?" Connor asked.

"Still?" Marco asked. "I never said I was in the first place."

"Move it along, MacKay," Reilly said. "I'll make sure he finds his way out, Marco."

"Thanks, Sean." Marco glanced at me. "Are you getting the picture now, Abby? We have a desperate person on the loose who's not above hiring accomplices and breaking in on a crowded Saturday night. I don't know if that person found what he or she was looking for, but I want you to take a break and let me handle it from here on out."

"No, Marco. I won't do that. Being a team means we're in it together."

"Abby, please listen." He cupped my face and gazed into my eyes. "Do you understand that the thought of something happening to you tears me up inside?"

"I understand, and I'll be as careful as I know how, I promise."

"Then also promise me you won't do any investigating without me at your side."

"You don't actually want to sit with me at the Duchess's studio while she sculpts Seedy, do you?"

"Do I want to? No. I wish we weren't even in this damn case. But you're not going alone. So do I get your promise?"

I thought he was overreacting to the danger level, but I made the promise. After all, marriage was all about compromise. Darn it.

We shut off the lights and returned upstairs, where Rafe was still cleaning. Everyone else had gone and the place looked tidy, so I had a feeling Rafe was hoping for a chance to make amends with his brother.

"What are you still doing here?" Marco snapped.

"I wanted to apologize for what happened," he said. "I did everything by the list. I swear I did, Marco."

"And yet someone got inside and was downstairs long enough to dig through the dirt."

"I don't know what else I can say," Rafe said.

Marco just looked at him, then turned and walked toward the back hallway. "Let's go home, Abby. Rafe can lock up. I hope."

"That was cruel," I said, as we got into the car. "How was Rafe supposed to know that the brawl was a diversion? Would you have known?"

"It's not about me."

"You're right. It's about your brother, who has very little experience with this type of thing. Yes, he keeps screwing up, but I wouldn't have thought to run to the back door when a fight broke out. Would you?"

"He wouldn't even answer me when I asked what he knew, Abby. Why wasn't he on top of things? What was he doing? Flirting again? That's what he seems to do best. How many times am I supposed to look the other way when he screws up? I wouldn't tolerate it from the rest of the staff. Why should I from him?"

Marco had a point, of course. "Then train someone else to be your manager."

He was silent as we made the trip home. But after parking at the curb in front of the apartment, he reached for my hand. "You're right, Abby. I wouldn't have thought to check the back door after a fight that broke out in the bar. Maybe I was too harsh with Rafe in this instance, but I think I will take your advice and advertise for a new manager. Thanks for being my voice of reason, Sunshine. I need you to keep me balanced."

That was one of the sweetest things he'd ever said to me. "Funny about that," I said. "I've always felt that you kept me balanced, too. It's one reason why we make a great team, Salvare."

Team Salvare. My wife doesn't understand how those words paralyze me with dread. She knows I love her, but she can't comprehend how strong that love is or what I'd do for it because I can't talk about those things with her. I'm afraid I'd scare her.

I've always had nerves of steel. Cool-headed, cold-blooded, my army buddies used to say. Killer instincts that came in handy as a Ranger, although I know Abby would disagree. *You don't fool me, Salvare,* she said once. *You're a lamb in wolf's clothing.*

At first I didn't know how to take her remark. I'd always liked the image of me as the Big Bad Wolf, although *badass* was more my style. It works to my advantage as a private eye. Abby saw the gentle lamb inside only because she brought it out in me. I preferred that news not get around, however. I value my tough reputation. A man of few words, Abby calls me.

I would say I'm a man of just enough words, but I don't mind her label because it isn't a put-down. Abby never puts me down. I don't know if she realizes how important respect is for a guy. Unlike other women I've dated, Abby has never tried to take me apart and put me together in a better way.

She likes me the way I am, flaws and all.

Well, except for a few minor things, but she needs to correct a few things, too. That's what's great about Abby. She believes in co-operation and compromise, and she gets it that people can have differences, arguments even, and still love one another deeply. In fact, she got it before I did.

But with that love comes the onerous responsibility of protecting her, and my gut instinct keeps telling me this investigation is putting her in jeopardy. Problem is, once Abby makes up her mind, there's no turning her back. So what can I do but take every step possible to keep her safe?

I turned to my wife, the woman I'd give my own life for. "Let's go see what our newest team member has been up to. It can't be any worse than what we just left."

Chapter Eighteen

Abby

It was amazing — make that shocking — what one little dog could do in a matter of three hours. For instance, she could drag every single shoe from the bedroom closet and the shelves by the fire exit door and pile them at the front door, making it nearly impossible to get inside. She could carry one end of the toilet paper from the bathroom to the front door, leaving a white path in her wake. She could pluck out a whole wastebasket of dirty tissues and make a small offering of them at the door. She could even pull down every towel from the bathroom and kitchen and pile them on top of the shoes.

In Seedy's case, she did all four, then stood proudly beside them, wagging her tail and giving a proud yip as we pushed our way inside, making it hard to scold her. But scold her I did, because we didn't want to encourage her. With her tail drooping, she crouched down and flattened her ears against her skull, watching us with the saddest expression I'd ever seen.

"She seems to like to bring things to us," I said.

"They're gifts," Marco said. "She thinks she's honoring us."

My cell phone rang, so I dropped the shoes to get it. "Let's hope this is good news."

"Aunt Abby?" Tara whispered. "You'll never guess who's at the sleepover. Haydn Cannon's sister, Hannah. Guess what she told me. That her dad's been acting weird, arguing with her mom, which he hardly ever does, and going into work early and staying late. Plus he keeps making private phone calls to her aunt in Maraville, and he doesn't even get along with her!"

"How did you get this information?" I asked.

After a hesitation, she said, "We were just, you know, talking about stuff."

"Stuff like the bones in the basement and how they might be connected to the Cannons?"

Silence.

"Tara, do you recall us telling you that this is a dangerous situation?"

"Don't you trust me, Aunt Abby? I'm not going to say anything stupid. Hannah doesn't suspect a thing. Oops. Gotta go. Our pizza is here."

"Tara, please be careful!" I said, but she had already hung up. "She's conducting her own investigation, Marco," I said, when he came back for more shoes. "What am I going to do to stop her? We've warned her. She knows the danger involved, but she's not taking it seriously."

"Wow. I wonder where she gets that trait. You know how I feel about this case, Abby. I think it warrants bringing in her parents, but she's your niece. It's your decision."

I scooped up the last pairs of shoes and followed him to the bedroom. "If I tell her parents, she won't ever trust me again, and I doubt they could stop her anyway."

"So much like you, it's scary," Marco said under his breath.

I sat cross-legged on the floor and began to sort shoes into a His pile and a Hers pile, although the His side didn't even qualify as a pile. "What if I told Tara that I'm pulling out of the investigation because it's too dangerous?"

"Here's an idea. What if you actually *did* pull out of the investigation because it's too dangerous?"

At my scowl, Marco said with a sigh, "I didn't think so. In that case, would it stop Tara?"

"It might. It's worth a call."

"Why did she phone you?"

"To tell me that Doug Cannon's daughter, Hannah, who's also at the sleepover, told her that Doug was argumentative all week, stayed at work from early in the morning until late at night, and has been making private calls to his sister in Maraville, with whom he doesn't get along."

"It sounds like we need to talk to Doug's sister. I'd like to hear her version of her father's disappearance anyway. I'll do some digging tomorrow to find out where she lives."

Seedy slunk up to me and dropped a used tissue in my lap as a peace offering, then raised her hopeful eyes to mine, as though to say, *Do you still love me?*

What could I do but gather her close and hug her?

Sunday

I hadn't yet convinced Marco to attend church with me, so I sat with my parents.

"I tried to call you last night," my mom whispered as we waited for the service to start.

Oops! Her voice mail. I'd completely forgotten to listen to it. "Sorry," I whispered back. "We went to see a movie and then had some . . . problems to take care of at the bar. And then it was too late to call you. What's up?"

"Didn't you listen to my message?"

I gave her a please-don't-hate me shrug. "Sorry. I forgot."

"I invited you to dinner today at five. Your brothers and their families are coming. I'm going to make a pork roast with all the trimmings."

"It sounds great, but can I take a rain check? We already have dinner plans."

Her lower lip came forward. It was her hurt expression. "It wouldn't be with Marco's family, would it?"

I gazed at her in surprise. "How did you know?"

"Francesca invited your father and me, too. I hope you'll save next Sunday for us — or will you be dining with them on every Sunday from now on?"

Great. Now we were going to have Sunday dinner wars. "I'll save next Sunday for you, Mom. We don't have standing dates with anyone."

Mom patted my hand. "Thank you, honey. I'm sorry I didn't make it to Bloomers with my new art yesterday, but it wasn't ready in time. So you'll get it tomorrow after school."

Amen?

After the service, I found Tara talking with a group of her friends and motioned her over to the side. "You have to stop investigating," I whispered.

"Why? I'm not in any danger."

"Tara, *I'm* pulling out. Marco says it's getting too risky even for me now."

"You are not," she said with a grin. "You love to snoop."

"Let's refer to it as investigating, please, and yes, I do love it, so you see how serious the situation is."

"I don't get it. Haydn and Hannah are really nice, and you don't get that way by having bad parents."

"Tara, it's too complicated to discuss here in church. Promise me you won't do any more snooping — yes, I said 'snooping' — until we talk again."

She studied my face. "You're really worried about me."

"Someone broke into Marco's bar again, Tara, and it's connected to the murder. That's all I'm going to say for now. Just promise, okay?"

She hesitated, then said, "Okay."

"What are you two whispering about?" my

brother Jordan asked, putting his arm around my shoulders.

Tara and I looked at each other; then she said, "Yogurt," just as I said, "Ice cream."

"We were having a debate about them," I added.

"Who won?" Jordan asked.

I glanced at Tara. "I did."

"For the time being," she said with an impish grin.

With Marco's experience at tracking people, it wasn't hard to discover the names and whereabouts of Kermit's daughters. Thanks to social media, Marco also discovered that Rona, the daughter who lived in nearby Maraville, was divorced, using her maiden name, and working at the Macy's store at the shopping mall. So on Sunday afternoon we made the thirty minute trip to the mall with Seedy and searched the ladies' department for a sales employee who matched the photo we had found online.

"Once we locate Rona," Marco said as we circled the store, "Seedy and I will make ourselves scarce." He stopped and turned me to the left. "There she is."

We stood near a rack of jeans so I could study her. Like Doug, Rona was tall and had brown hair, but she was much heavier and more jowly than either her brother or her Internet photo.

"I'm not certain how to start a conversation about her dad," I said.

"You could notice her name tag and claim to remember someone with her name."

"How would I know a woman her age?"

Marco pulled out the Web page he had copied. "She has a daughter named Karin who appears to be in high school. Maybe she knows Tara."

"If they live in Maraville, the girls go to different high schools. That won't work."

"She lists her hobbies as knitting and baking."

"Neither of which I do."

"Then just strike up a conversation and see where it leads you. You're inventive." He gave me a kiss on the cheek. "Seedy and I will be in the mall. Text me when you're done."

I sorted through the rack of jeans, trying to come up with an opening line before Rona got busy with another customer. I moved on to a display of sweaters, saw her coming toward me, and grabbed the closest garment. Fortunately, it was my size.

Rona walked up to me and said with a smile, "Finding what you want?"

"I think so." *Speaking of finding things, can*

I tell you what I found in my husband's bar's basement the other day?

Nope. Too insensitive. I held a turquoise sweater with a boatneck against my front, as though checking it for size. "I wear a medium, but this medium seems small."

Speaking of being small, when you were little, do you remember when your dad ran off with another woman?

I looked into her kind eyes and knew I couldn't do that to her.

"Why don't you try it on?" Rona asked. "The dressing room is right over there. My name is Rona if you need any help."

Speaking of help . . . "Um, Rona?"

"Yes, dear?"

I had to find a way to ease into the subject. "Would you stick around and give me your opinion? I don't see my husband anywhere."

With her okay, I scurried into the dressing room, shrugged out of my denim jacket, pulled the sweater on over my white long-sleeved T-shirt, and hurried out again.

"What do you think?" I asked, modeling it for her.

"It's perfect," Rona said. "The style suits you and that color is great with your hair."

I gazed at my reflection, pleasantly surprised. Not only did it accentuate my hair, but it also minimized my bust line. And how many times did that happen? "It is perfect, isn't it?"

Speaking of perfect . . .

Nope. I had nothing. I sighed in frustration. *For heaven's sake, Abby. Find an opening.*

"I love your boots," Rona said. "Where did you get them?"

And there was my opening.

"I got them at a store in New Chapel called Blazing Saddles."

She brightened at the mention of Rusty's shop. "My stepdad owns that place."

I pretended to be shocked. "Rusty Miller is your stepdad? My husband bought Down the Hatch from Rusty. In fact, we saw him yesterday. Rusty's an amazing guy for being, what, seventysomething, isn't he?"

Rona smiled. "He *is* an amazing guy, and a great stepdad, too. He was always so good to us kids."

"Did Rusty raise you?"

"I guess you could say that. More so for my sister and me. My brother was almost out of the house when Rusty married my mom."

"Oh, did your dad pass away?"

She gave me an odd look, as though she found my question intrusive but didn't want to say so. "No," she said lightly. "My mom divorced him." She moved to the next display table and began refolding T-shirts.

I had to find a way to get more information. "I think I'm going to have to buy this," I said.

"I'm sure your husband will love it."

"I think so, too. I'll be right back."

I changed out of the sweater and took it to the cash register to pay. As Rona rang up my purchase, I said, "So do you live in New Chapel?"

"No. I moved away quite a few years ago."

"I think I'd miss it if I moved away. I was born and raised there."

No comment.

I signed the credit card slip and handed it to her. "Do you see Rusty often?"

"Not as much as I'd like, but I may have to drive out there to get a pair of those boots."

"He has a big selection. Rusty actually picked these out for me."

Rona didn't appear to be interested in making conversation. She kept glancing around as though she were hoping to find other customers to wait on. But it was just Rona and me, and if I didn't act fast, it would be just me.

"So if you're Rusty's stepdaughter, then you have a brother named Doug, right?"

She looked at me curiously. “Yes. Do you know Doug?”

“I met him just recently. And of course Rusty talks about him. In fact, from what he told us, he took Doug under his wing at a time when he really needed a dad.”

Rona’s smile stiffened. “Rusty was always there for Doug.” She handed me the receipt and a shopping bag with the sweater inside. “Thanks for coming in.”

Unable to come up with anything else to say, I dug through my purse and found a business card. “I own a flower shop on the square called Bloomers. Come in to see me, and I’ll give you a discount.”

“Thank you. That’s very kind.”

I walked away, then stopped in front of a display of shirts so I could glance back. Rona was watching me, a puzzled look on her face.

I left the store, glancing around for Marco, and saw him and Seedy standing to one side of the pretzel shop. “Want a bite?” he asked me, holding out a partially eaten crusty pretzel.

I tore off a piece. “I didn’t have much luck getting information. When I first mentioned Rusty’s saddle shop, Rona seemed delighted, but then after I asked a few questions it became apparent that she wasn’t interested in talking about Rusty or Doug. All she would say was that Rusty had been there for Doug." I popped the bite in my mouth.

"Do you think she suspected anything?"

"I don't think so."

Marco crouched down in front of Seedy to adjust her leash. "Don't look now," he said, "but Rona is standing behind a big potted plant watching us." He raised his head. "And she just took your picture with her cell phone. Yep, she suspected something."

We started walking toward the exit. "What do you think she'll do with the picture?"

"Probably send it to her brother. If Tara's information is correct, then Doug has been in contact with her, and I would bet any money that their conversation was about Kermit. So if Rona is aware that there's an investigation, as soon as you started asking about Doug and Rusty, she was probably on alert. I wouldn't be surprised if we heard from Doug tomorrow."

It didn't take until Monday for that to happen, but it wasn't Doug who called.

"Salvare," Marco said, answering his phone later that afternoon as we took Seedy for a walk in his neighborhood. "Hey, Rusty.

What's up?" He hit the SPEAKER button so I could listen.

"I hate to bother you, son, but I need a favor from you and your lovely bride."

"What can we do for you?" Marco asked.

"Well," he said hesitantly, "I don't mean to interfere with your work, but I'd appreciate it if you didn't involve Lila's girls in your investigation. They was just little kids back then and didn't really understand what was going on when their papa ran off. Lila and Doug tried to shield them from the publicity, so all they knew was that their papa got so unhappy, he went away."

"They're adults now, Rusty," Marco said. "They must have heard the rumors."

"Course they did, son. I'm not saying they don't know what their papa did. What I'm trying to tell you is that they don't have the particulars. You bring all your questions to me, and I'll do my best to answer them for you. I'll be completely open with you, just like I've been doing. But please don't bother the girls. They don't need to know the sordid details. It's bad enough they know their papa was a drunk. You hear what I'm saying?"

"I hear you, Rusty. We didn't mean any harm. Actually, your stepdaughter noticed Abby's new boots, and that's how the conversation started. So let me put your mind at ease. We won't bother Lila's girls with questions. We'll come to you or Doug or Henry."

"I'd appreciate it if you'd leave Doug out, too, Marco. Kermit's running off was hard on him. Between me and Henry, we should be able to answer your questions."

"I can't guarantee that I won't need to talk to Doug again," Marco said, "but I'll do my best. How about you answer a question for me, okay? Who phoned you to tell you that Abby talked to your stepdaughter?"

"Is that important?" Rusty asked.

"I'd like to see how open you really are, Rusty."

There was a long pause, and then he said, "It was Doug."

"Did he ask you to get in touch with me about it?" Marco asked.

"He said he thought I should know what was going on."

"Thanks for your honesty, Rusty. I'll be in touch." Marco ended the conversation. "Interesting, isn't it? After all these years, Rusty is still very protective of Lila's kids."

"They're hardly kids now."

"Exactly. Doug's a fifty-two-year-old man. Why didn't he call me if he had a complaint? Why is he turning to Rusty?"

"Because maybe that's what Doug always does when he needs help."

"Good point. So why is Rusty still rushing to his and the girls' defense?"

"Once a parent, always a parent?"

"That's it, Abby. Rusty is still taking care of their problems as though he's the dad. It makes me wonder whether he did that in nineteen seventy-six, too."

"Meaning that he took care of Kermit for them?"

"For himself, too. Look at all the motives. He was frustrated that his bar's basement wasn't getting fixed. He had to have been resentful that Kermit was abusive to his sweetheart. And he saw how much Kermit was hurting Doug and the girls, whom he seemed to have bonded with.

"So what better opportunity than to have Kermit working in his bar basement, with a dirt floor that was about to be cemented? As Rusty pointed out, the shovel was sitting right there."

"And so was the trowel, apparently. What I don't understand is why Rusty would have had garden tools in his bar basement in the first place."

"He may have had a rooftop garden. I've run across this before. It was part of a new green movement downtown during the seventies. I'll bet Lottie would remember."

"Then are you eliminating the other suspects to focus on Rusty?" I asked.

"No, of course not. But from where I'm standing now, Rusty is at the top of the list."

For Marco maybe, but I was still struggling with it. I had such fond childhood memories of Rusty.

With that to chew on, we headed over to Marco's sister's house to have a big, happy Italian feast. I hoped.

CHAPTER NINETEEN

How did one say *help* in Italian?

"Let's remember not to take Seedy with us next week," my grouchy groom said as we drove home from his sister's house that evening.

"How about let's remember to say we're busy next Sunday?" I replied, also grouchy, holding the dog in question in my lap. The dinner hadn't gone well, but it wasn't all Seedy's fault. Part of it was that I had been out of sorts with Marco. "Seedy likes to bring us things. As you pointed out, she's honoring us."

"Well, she has to stop honoring us, because bringing us feminine products from my sister's bathroom drawer, and dirty underwear from my nephew's hamper, and Mama's expensive Italian leather shoes isn't cutting it with anyone."

"They're just *things* to Seedy, Marco."

"Things or not, we have to train her not

to do that."

"She's not the only one who needs training," I muttered, gazing out the window.

From the corner of my eye, I saw him give me a surprised glance. "Meaning?"

"Meaning that I'm tired and shouldn't be discussing touchy subjects like having Sunday dinner at a parent's house every week."

"We don't have to go every week."

"You've got that right. We don't. And they shouldn't expect us to, either. My mom was hurt when she found out that we were going to your sister's for dinner, and your mom has already scheduled us for next week."

"We can go on another day."

"I don't care if we see your family on a Sunday, Marco. Sundays *are* family days. My point is that we need to make it clear that we are going to *alternate* Sundays. I don't want to start a war over something that should be a pleasant get-together."

Marco mulled it over as he parked the car. He turned off the engine and sat there for a moment. "You're right, babe. I shouldn't have agreed to next Sunday without discussing it with you first. I'll talk to Mama and you talk to your parents." He turned my chin so he could see me. "Don't look so solemn, Abby. We'll work it out."

His gaze was so full of love that I felt my anxiety melting. "Thanks for understanding."

"Did you think I wouldn't?"

"You seemed to be enjoying your family so much that I felt guilty saying anything."

"Abby, if you're not happy, I'm not happy. I could tell you were tense, but I thought it was because of Seedy's behavior, because she was making me tense. If you want to hire that fancy dog trainer for Seedy, we should be able to swing a few lessons. Why don't you call Jillian and get the guy's phone number? Let's nip this in the bud before it becomes a habit. And that goes for you, too. When something's bothering you, speak up, sweetheart. Don't keep things bottled up. That just causes tension, and that's not good for either one of us."

"So when I see a problem developing, you want me to tell you about it."

"That's what I'm saying."

"What if it offends you?"

"Abby, come on. Give me some credit here. You're not going to offend me."

"Okay, then how about cutting your toenails over a newspaper instead of on the carpet?"

Marco was silent for a moment; then he

said slowly, "All right. If that bothers you, I'll cut them over a newspaper."

"Thank you."

He gave me a skeptical glance. "Anything else?"

"I'm thinking. How about if I get back to you on that?"

Marco opened his door. "Let's get out of here, Seedy, before she hires a trainer for me."

Monday

The day started out as every other Monday did, with Lottie's scrambled egg and toast breakfast and cups of Grace's special blend of coffee. We sat in the parlor eating and discussing the weekend's events before moving on to business. Seedy sat beneath my chair munching contentedly on a dog biscuit.

"Look how well adjusted she is," Grace said, smiling at Seedy.

"She has a few habits that we need to break," I said, and explained what a nuisance she'd been at the Salvares'. It hadn't helped that Marco's nephew was an active little boy who spent most of the time chasing Seedy around the house until he was plunked into his booster seat for dinner.

"Don't be surprised if Jillian stops by," I

told Lottie. "I called her last night to get the name of her dog trainer but my call went to her voice mail."

"There's something to look forward to," Lottie said.

"It's art day, too," I reminded them. "Mom will be in after school with her latest project."

"Good morning, everyone," Francesca sang out, stepping into the parlor.

And it was a Francesca day. I took a deep breath and turned to smile at her.

"What a *fantastico* day, no?" she asked. "The sun is out, there are orders on the spindle, and, oh, look, there is our little imp Seedy under the chair. I should guard my shoes, eh, *bella*?"

Lottie and Grace laughed nervously.

"I apologize for Seedy's behavior," I said. "I'm going to hire a trainer for her."

"A trainer?" Francesca raised her eyebrows, her gaze on Lottie and Grace, as though to say, *What kind of crazy idea is that?* "Don't waste your money, *bella.* I know how to train dogs. Give her to me for a day and I will shape her up in no time."

The last thing sensitive little Seedy needed was a drill instructor. "I'll think about it."

There was a rapid knocking on the door and then I heard Jillian call through the glass, "Abby? Are you in there?"

Francesca let her in, and in a moment Jillian came into the parlor pushing her baby stroller. A pink bundle was strapped to the seat. "Sorry I didn't get your call until this morning, Abs. Princess got out yesterday and we couldn't find her for hours."

Seedy immediately got up and went to investigate the stroller, but this time no little terrier face appeared at her sniffing. Seedy backed away as though she'd smelled something bad.

"We finally found her in a neighbor's backyard eating food left out for a feral cat," Jillian said. "Dr. Hammertoes was very upset."

"Dr. *Hammertoes*?" I asked.

She wrinkled her nose. "Maybe it's Hammerstein. He's Princess's psychiatrist."

Grace gave a tiny gasp, while Lottie clamped her lips to keep from laughing, and Francesca folded her arms under her breasts, looking dubious. "There is such a thing?"

"Of course," Jillian said. "If people can have psychiatrists, why can't animals? Anyway, after Johann quit on us — which I totally blame on you, Abby Knight — we had to call someone."

"Wait a minute," I said. "Time-out. Why

are you blaming me?"

"Because Johann was fine when we left him in your care Friday night, and the next morning he called and quit. Two plus two equals four, Abs. Do the math."

"You just *did* the math, Jill, and Johann was not fine when you left him. He had a migraine caused by —"

"Let's not play the blame game," Jillian said. "Getting back to my story, we called the psychiatrist's hotline yesterday morning and got in on an emergency basis. He did an assessment and put Princess on doggy tranquilizers immediately, but we knew by evening that they weren't strong enough, so when I called this morning, he said to double the dose." She pulled back a corner of the blanket, revealing Princess's face. Seedy backed out of the room.

"Jillian, this dog looks strung out," Lottie said, crouching in front of the stroller. "Poor little thing. She can hardly focus her eyes."

"The doctor said it was the only way to calm her down," Jillian said, looking hurt.

"What rot," Grace said. "Dogs have been trained for centuries without resorting to brain-altering chemicals. You must not subject this poor creature to drugs any longer, Jillian."

"Then how do I control her?"

"Give Princess to me for a day, Jillian," Francesca said. "I will teach her how to behave."

"Do you have dog-training experience?" Jillian asked.

"I raised six *bambini* alone," Francesca said with a lift of her chin. "Dog, child, it doesn't matter. You simply must let them know who's in command. You'll see."

"Okay," Jillian said, pressing her hands together excitedly. "When can I bring her over?"

"I will come to *your* apartment. I finish here at noon and will stop at the store to buy ingredients for my pasta sauce. You'll get a well-trained dog and the best spaghetti in town."

"I can't wait," Jillian said, and threw her arms around my mother-in-law. "Francesca, you're a dream."

Seedy chose that moment to drop a packaged tampon at my feet.

"That little devil," Lottie said, scooping it up. "She got that out of my purse."

Francesca turned to me and lifted one eyebrow.

"Guess who showed up at the bar at nine o'clock," Marco said, as we headed to the Duchess's studio on Tenth Street. "Reilly and a forensic team. They've been working in the basement all morning. Reilly said he'd keep me informed of their progress."

"That's great, Marco. Finally, some movement! And I have news, too. Your mom is going to train Princess for Jillian."

"What?"

"I'm not kidding. Jillian stopped by this morning with Princess, who now has her own psychiatrist. The poor dog was in such a drug-induced fog, she couldn't even get out of the stroller. It was pathetic."

"That's bordering on abuse, Abby."

"I am in complete agreement. Anyway, your mom told Jillian she could train Princess, and Jillian accepted. Francesca is on her way to Jillian's apartment as we speak." I took a breath, then added, "Your mom wants to train Seedy, too."

"Let's see what kind of results she gets with Princess first."

Which meant he would consider it. Damn. But in the spirit of cooperation, I said, "So if she gets good results, then I guess we'll let her work with Seedy."

"No guesswork, Sunshine. You have to be happy with the decision or we don't do it."

I smiled at him. This marriage thing wasn't as hard as I'd feared.

As Marco pulled into a parking spot down

the street from Parthenia's art studio, I said, "Do you want me to do the questioning again?"

"Let's play it by ear and see what kind of mood she's in. You have the photo, right?"

"The photo and our little marvel. If you have the notepad, then we're set."

We walked toward the studio just as a man burst out the front door and hurried across the street. Parthenia came out behind him wearing another colorful, belted caftan and brandishing a glossy black-and-white clock. "Do not ever cross my doorstep again!" she shouted. "Do you hear me? Ever again! Peasant! Geniuses do not bargain!"

She turned and caught sight of us, then made a show of checking her watch, as though to say we were late. At that moment Seedy lifted her leg and let loose a stream of urine on the rear tire of the black-and-white bicycle standing in the bike rack.

Muttering something in Greek, the Duchess spun about and marched into her shop.

"Yeah," Marco said, "I think I'll let you do the questioning."

I was surprised by the amount of work Parthenia had already done on Seedy's sculpture. The clay form was about fifteen inches tall and showed Seedy sitting on her haunches, one leg missing, and her tall ears perked forward, her head tilted. All that was needed were the finer details.

"It looks wonderful so far," I said as I placed Seedy on the table.

"A work in progress," she said casually. She glanced around at Marco, who was leaning against the wall, arms crossed over his chest. "You may approach if you like."

"Thanks. I'm fine here," he said.

"Suit yourself." She studied Seedy for a moment, then began to sculpt the face with a tool that had a small blade on the end. "This will not take long. Just try to keep the dog still, please."

"Okay," I said, petting Seedy. "But I do have a few more questions for you."

She paused to glower at me. "More questions about Kermit?"

"Some new information has come to light that I thought you might want to comment on."

"Your mother is annoying me," the Duchess said to Seedy. "Tell her to make it fast."

"I will, I promise," I said, then pulled the list we'd made out that morning from my pocket. "Have you ever heard the name Pete Morgan?"

"No."

I glanced over at Marco. He had taken

out his notepad and pen and was writing. "When you settled in the artists' colony," I said, "were you aware of anyone following you?"

"No."

"Were you pregnant when you left New Chapel?"

"Same answer as previously. No."

"Is Columbus the name of the town where you lived?"

"Yes." She narrowed her eyes at me. "How did you know that?"

"We've learned that a private detective named Pete Morgan was hired to find Kermit, and he found you instead."

"How do you know he found me?" she snapped. Then in a completely different tone, she said to Seedy, "Hold still, little one."

I pulled out the photo and showed it to her. "This is you, isn't it?"

By the sudden reddening of her face, I thought she was going to throw a fit, but then she tilted her head and studied the photo as though examining a painting. "I looked good, didn't I?"

"Beautiful," I said, grabbing Seedy before she could leap off the table, "and pregnant."

Frowning in concentration, Parthenia went back to sculpting. I waited a moment, then glanced at Marco, unsure of whether to say anything further. He put his fingers to his lips, so I stayed quiet and scratched Seedy behind the ears.

It seemed like an eternity before Parthenia spoke; then she said softly, "I lost the baby."

"I'm so sorry." I waited for her to say more, and when she didn't, I said, "It must have been a terrible time for you. Was it Kermit's child?"

"Yes."

Doug had been right.

Again Parthenia worked without talking, until finally she said, "Was it Kermit's wife who hired the private detective?"

"That's our best guess. The only other person it could be is Henry."

"Why would he hunt for the man he wanted out of his life?" she asked.

"How do you know what Henry wanted?" Marco asked, stepping forward.

"Pah! It was obvious to me. Remember, I heard Henry and Rusty discussing Kermit. I saw Henry's face when Rusty told him about Kermit's behavior. If it hadn't been for Rusty, I believe Henry might have done something to Kermit that day. That's how angry he was."

"What did Rusty do?" Marco asked.

"Put his arm around Henry and said, 'Don't get yourself so worked up, son. I only told you this so you'd know why I have to fire him. Don't you worry. I'll take care of Kermit.' " Parthenia shook her head, her expression bitter. "As though anyone could control Kermit."

"You said before that Kermit called Henry a girl," Marco said. "Then you went on to say that Henry wasn't secure in his manhood. Are you implying that Henry is gay?"

"I liked you better standing against the wall." She waved him away.

Marco moved back, giving me a nod to go ahead with the questioning.

"Could you explain what you meant about Henry?" I asked.

"I don't know Henry," she said sharply. "I told you what I observed back then and what Kermit told me about him. Now, silence, please! I must concentrate so I can finish."

Marco's cell phone rang, so he quickly muted it and left the room.

Parthenia sculpted in silence for several minutes, then, still working, said, "Your husband, is he good to you?"

"Very good to me."

"Consider yourself fortunate."

"I do."

"I wish to stop answering questions about Kermit. I've told you all I know, and in truth, it's painful for me. I pray that you never know what's like to be abandoned or lose a child."

"I understand, but we'd really like to solve this case."

"This little dog," she said, standing back to examine her sculpture, "knows what it's like to be abandoned. Don't you, *aschimos*?"

"Is that a Greek name?"

"It's a Greek word."

"It's pretty."

"It means ugly. I am finished. You may leave."

With that, she walked away.

"Wait," I said. "Can I ask you one more question?"

She heaved a big sigh and turned to face me, her full lips pressed together in annoyance. "One more. That is all."

"Do you think Rusty could have killed Kermit?"

She gazed at me for a moment, as though considering how to answer. "Let me ask you this, and it is my last word on the subject. You have given this dog a home, food, and love. Do you think your little *aschimos* would ever turn on you?"

I turned to study Seedy, who was wiggling her whole body as though she couldn't wait to get off the table. I picked her up and put her on the floor, snapping her leash onto her collar. "I don't know. I suppose if I treated her badly or she felt threatened, she might."

"Then how can one say for certain that one man would never turn on another?"

"One can't. But I have a hard time believing Rusty could have killed anyone."

"Then why did you ask?"

"I wanted your opinion."

"No, you wanted *your* opinion confirmed. *My* opinion is that the murderer is either Doug or Henry." She walked to the doorway and waited for me to leave. *"Yia sou."*

"Oops. I'm so sorry. One more." Before she could object, I blurted, "Do you know what happened to the ten thousand dollars Kermit took from the business checking account?"

Parthenia had opened her mouth to put an end to my question, but upon hearing it, she tilted her head to one side like Seedy did when she was puzzled. "What ten thousand dollars? This is the first I've heard about any money of Kermit's. Who said this to you?"

"It doesn't matter."

"Pah! You don't need to tell me. I know it was Henry. He blames me for Kermit's death, doesn't he? Of course he does, so why wouldn't he blame me for taking the money? He was always jealous of the attention Kermit paid me. Now go away."

"Efharistó," I said. Thank you.

I met Marco outside just as he was ending his phone conversation. "It was Reilly," he said, as we walked to the car. "The forensic team just came across something interesting — a key." He opened the door for me. "Maybe that will help us identify who was buried down there."

Chapter Twenty

"So what did we learn from Parthenia?" Marco asked on the ride back to the bar.

"That she lied about carrying Kermit's child, which makes me doubt the rest of her story."

"I thought her comment about Rusty assuring Henry that he would take care of Kermit was noteworthy," Marco said.

"I know what you believe, Marco, but I'm still having a hard time accepting that it could have been Rusty. And couldn't Parthenia be making that up, as well? She didn't mention Rusty as a suspect before we showed her the photo. Now suddenly she remembers Rusty's incriminating words? That's suspicious to me.

"But when I asked her about the missing ten thousand dollars, she seemed genuinely shocked. She wanted to know who had told me, and when I wouldn't say, she said it had to be Henry because he had been jealous of the attention Kermit paid her."

"If that's true, Abby, we have a stronger motive for Henry."

"If we can trust Parthenia."

"Anything else come out of the interview?"

"Nothing about the investigation." I rubbed Seedy's head. "Parthenia called Seedy *aschimos.*"

"Which means what?"

"Ugly."

"Aschimos," Marco said. "It has a nice ring to it."

"Don't listen to him," I said to Seedy, stroking her fur. "You're not ugly."

She rubbed her bristly muzzle against my hand, then turned to gaze out the window, her lower teeth protruding in profile.

"Not very ugly, at least," I said.

I had only a few minutes before I needed to be back at Bloomers, but I wanted to see the key that the police had found, so I followed Marco down to the basement, where the team was still sifting through dirt in marked quadrants.

One of the officers Marco knew from his stint on the force obliged him by showing him the key that was now bagged and tagged for evidence.

"What is that?" I asked, because it certainly wouldn't open any door that I'd ever seen. It was half the size of a house key and had a narrow barrel-shaped shaft.

"It looks like a briefcase key," Marco said, taking a photo.

I pulled out my phone and got a photo, too, for backup. "I doubt that Kermit carried a briefcase to work. Could it be for a suitcase? Parthenia would have had a suitcase with her."

"Why would her suitcase key be on Kermit's key chain?"

We puzzled over it as the men worked; then Marco said, "Maybe Kermit *did* have a briefcase with him that morning, Abby, and maybe it was full of the money he took from the business."

"Then whoever killed him took away a lot of cash but had no way to open the briefcase."

"They're not that hard to open. What I'd like to know is where the ten thousand dollars went." Marco turned back to the cops and said, "Any sign of clothing, a wallet, ID, money?"

"This is all we found," the other cop said, and showed us a bag with five buttons in it.

They were creamy white and less than half an inch across. "Common shirt buttons,"

Marco said, "the kind you see on just about every men's shirt made. Someone must have been in such a hurry to get the clothes off the body, he popped the buttons."

"We're done here," the first cop said. "Once we leave, you can seal up your hole."

"Great. Thanks," Marco said. As we headed upstairs, he said, "Finally, I'll be able to get the floor fixed. I'm thinking of asking Doug Cannon to give me an estimate."

"Are you serious?"

"I think I'll ask Henry to come, too, so he can give me a quote on putting in a bathroom."

"Why would you put a bathroom down here?"

"I wouldn't. My intention is to see how they react to the scene of the crime. Nothing like bringing a suspect to the murder scene to see what comes out."

"Are you going to bring Rusty here, too?"

"I haven't decided that yet. What I'd like to do is get back out to Blazing Saddles so I can question Rusty in more detail about how much money he put into the basement. Remember that he had Henry build the storage room and remodel the bathrooms and kitchen upstairs. That would take a good chunk of change. Figuring that the dollar was worth a hell of a lot more back then, I'd guess it would have cost him ten thousand dollars."

"Let's talk about it at dinner," I said, giving him a kiss. "I have to get back to work."

Lottie and I worked hard all afternoon filling over thirty orders, while brave little Seedy sat in the shop's bay window to do some people-watching. By the time my mom got there at three thirty, I was ready to take a break. What I wasn't ready for was her newest art project.

"What do you think?" she asked, gazing proudly at her sculpture.

I studied it from one side, then walked around the table to study it from the other, and the whole time my brain was saying, *Think of something nice to tell her!*

She had made a doglike creature using a neon green skateboard for the body, stubby blue metal cylinders for the legs, red ping pong balls, halved, for the feet, the white insole of a shoe for the face, a glossy green child-sized party hat for the snout, and a small red rubber ball for the tip of the nose. Around the floppy pink suede ears, about a dozen foot-long, half-inch-wide turquoise blue metal strips, twisted like peppermint sticks, stuck up all over the head. A shorter pink strip represented the tail.

But that wasn't the end of it. Riding on the skateboard was a miniature version that used a flip-flop sole painted purple for the body.

"Dogs?" I asked.

"Dachshunds," she announced. "A mother and her precious little daughter. I was thinking of calling it *Madachshund and Child* to keep my theme going, but I'm open to suggestions."

I had a feeling she wouldn't like the name running through my mind.

"Is Francesca gone?" she asked, looking around.

"She left at noon. She went to Jillian's house to train her terrier."

"Oh," she said in a clipped tone that told me right away I shouldn't have opened my mouth. "I didn't realize Francesca was also a dog trainer."

"She's not, but she volunteered to help because Jillian's trainer quit. It was nice of Francesca to offer, Mom."

Mom huffed to show she was disgruntled. "I suppose you're right."

I put my arm around her. "Why did hearing about Francesca upset you?"

"Not upset so much as . . . I don't know, Abigail. Worried me maybe."

"Worried you about what?"

She shrugged, looking suddenly young and vulnerable. "I don't want to be usurped."

The jealousy thing again. "Mom, no one could ever usurp you."

"I just feel so inadequate around Francesca. I can't cook like her. I can't help out here because I'm teaching. I don't speak a second language or have a voluptuous figure or . . ."

"I don't care about those things, Mom. You've got a lot going for you. So what if you're not Francesca? Would I want a mother just like my mother-in-law? Someone shoot me now!"

That made her laugh. "Really?"

"You just be my mom, the greatest mom anyone could ask for, the best kindergarten teacher in town — and a pretty darn creative artist, too. Okay?" Thank goodness I'd remembered to use *darn.* She hated when one of her kids used a curse word.

She gave me a hug. "Thank you, honey. I never knew you saw me that way."

"Well, I do. So will you promise not to feel jealous when Francesca is here helping?"

"I promise." We hugged, and then she

said, "Where will you display my new piece?"

When cornered, punt. "I'll let Lottie decide. She decorates the shop."

"Maybe I'll have a chat with her on the way out." She kissed my cheek. "I have to run. I promised your dad we'd go to the park. We won't have many of these lovely fall days left."

"Give Dad a kiss from me," I said.

Soon after Mom left, the curtains parted and Lottie peered in. "What did she make?"

I picked it up by the skateboard body and got stuck in the chin by a piece of twisted metal. "Ouch! This," I said, holding it up. Seedy came through the curtain, saw the large, dangerous-looking object in my hands, and gave me wide berth to get to her doggy bed.

"Oh, Lordy," Lottie said. "What the heck is it and what are we gonna do with it?"

"With what?" my niece asked, scooting under Lottie's arm. She had Seedy's puppy, Seedling, on a leash, and the puppy immediately ran to her mother, where the two had a happy reunion.

Tara took one look at the dachshund duo and clapped her hand over her mouth so her laughter wouldn't be heard by the customers in the shop. "It's a wiener dog on drugs!"

She put it on the floor as though to skateboard on it. "Grandma made it, didn't she?"

"Yes," I said, picking it up before she could attempt to ride it. "And it doesn't roll. What am I going to do with it?"

"Your mom suggested I put it in the bay window," Lottie said.

"Then we'd need to sell it fast," I said, "and I don't even know how to price it."

"Want me to sell it for you?" Tara asked. "I can list it on eBay. Take a photo of it and I'll put it up right now. My mom has an account."

"What if your mom tells Grandma what we're doing?" I asked. "She'd never speak to me again."

"Mom won't even know. She hasn't bought or sold anything in months, and I have her password. But first let me see what to charge." She sat at my computer, slipped off her bungee cord bracelet that held her keys and began to type. "Wiener dog made from skateboard. There. Now let's see what the search engine can find."

The bell over the door jingled, so Lottie said, "Good luck," and slipped through the curtain to wait on the customer.

I took photos of Mom's art from two

angles, e-mailed them to Tara, then took Seedy and Seedling outside for a quick walk while she worked.

"Okay," Tara said when I returned. "Photos are up. What do you want to say in the ad?"

We worked on the ad copy for ten minutes, trying to make the dachshund duo sound wildly artistic and desirable. Then we figured out a price, and just like that we had a live ad.

"I can watch the bids for you," my niece said, "but it'll cost you."

"You're becoming quite the little extortionist," I said. "What's the cost this time?"

"Fifteen percent of the profit or twenty bucks, whichever is higher."

"Deal," I said.

"Awesome," Tara said, swiveling the desk chair in a circle. "So what's the latest on the murder case?"

"Nothing new to report," I lied, then, remembering that I was supposed to be off the case, I added, "or at least that's what Marco tells me."

"Like I believe that. Maybe I'll wander down to Down the Hatch to see what I can learn."

"Do you really think Marco will tell you anything?"

"You're not the only one who loves a challenge," she said with a grin, slipping on her bracelet. That was when I noticed one of the keys dangling from it.

"Tara, what is that?"

"My bicycle lock key," she said, showing me.

I slipped the bungee cord off her wrist so I could examine it. Then I pulled up the photo of the mystery key and placed them side by side. "What do you think?"

Tara hung over my arm. "It's not exactly like mine, but it could be for an old-fashioned bike lock. Why don't you bring it over? Dad still has his ten-speed with his bike lock on it."

"How did he get to keep his bike? Grandma sold mine." I studied her key and the photo, then handed her bracelet back. "I'll be over as soon as I close the shop."

At five thirty, I locked up the shop and headed to my brother's house. I phoned Marco to let him know what I was doing, and we agreed to meet for dinner at Down the Hatch afterward. My brother and sister-in-law were out, but Tara was waiting for me in their big three-car garage.

"Get any new info from Uncle Marco this afternoon?" I teased.

She made a face. "He wouldn't talk about it."

"I told you so."

She turned away, but not before I saw her grin. "Tara, what are you keeping from me?"

"Nothing. I'm off the case, remember?"

The sly gleam in her eye said otherwise. "Please don't do anything dangerous."

"I won't do anything you wouldn't do," she said. It did nothing to quiet my stomach.

The garage was amazingly well organized, with white cabinets along the back wall that had labels on them, each cabinet holding items from garden supplies to tire polish.

"Did my brother do this?" I asked, running my fingers across one of the labels.

"Yeah, Dad's slightly OCD," Tara said. "He says it makes him a good doctor."

She showed me the bump-out storage room on the back where my brother kept his old Schwinn. The storage room had cabinets, too, but they were labeled for the various sports equipment they held.

Tara opened one. "Can you believe this? He still has all his high school soccer stuff." She opened another one to show me all his trophies. "Mom won't let him keep these in the house."

I examined his bike, which looked to be in mint condition. "I don't see a lock."

"You have to look in the cabinet marked *Locks.*" Tara opened another door and pulled out a bicycle chain with a green rubber coating and a padlock hooked onto the end. In the lock was the key. I put it below the photo of the unknown key and had a virtual match.

"Fantastic! This is it!" I gave my niece a hug. "Tara, you may have helped" — I caught myself before I said *us solve the case* — "Uncle Marco."

She scowled at me then walked to the open door and stood in the doorway, her arms crossed. "If you want out, you have to tell me how this helps the investigation."

"Like you could stop me." We had a stare down contest for about a minute; then I said, "Fine. I'll tell you, but you can't say a word to anyone."

She made a zip-the-lips motion; then we walked out of the garage together. "The police sifted through the dirt and found the key you saw in the photo, so it's a piece of evidence."

"A piece of evidence that means," she said, tapping her chin, "that someone involved in the murder had a bike and a bike lock."

"If the key they found is actually a bike lock key."

"What else would it be? So you're looking for a person who would have been the right age to ride a bike. Let's see. How old would Haydn's father have been back in — what year did the murder happen again?"

"Never mind what year it happened."

"All I have to do is get on the *New Chapel News* Web site and do a search for the article. That'll tell me what year." She smiled. "See? I can be a detective, too."

"You're too smart for your own good, and I mean that as a warning."

She gave me a hug. "I'm just smart like my favorite aunt."

"Yeah, well, your favorite aunt has nearly gotten herself killed a few times. Just remember, Tara," I said, getting into the car, "you promised to keep out of this."

"And you remember," she said, leaning in my window, "that you promised to keep me in the loop."

Tara stepped back from the car and waved as I pulled away. I had already broken my promise. Would she keep hers?

When I got to Down the Hatch, Marco was in his office with his brother, and from what I could hear, Rafe was getting a lecture. When he stamped out five minutes later, I stood back to let him pass, then went into the office.

Marco was seated behind his desk, an irritated look on his face, but when he saw me, he brightened and stood up. "Sunshine, come see what I found."

"Everything okay with Rafe?" I asked, following him up the hallway to the bar.

"Is everything *ever* okay with Rafe?"

I knew better than to pursue that lead.

Marco led me behind the bar, where Rafe and another bartender were mixing drinks. Rafe gave me a half smile and went back to his business.

Marco took one of the old framed photos off the wall. "This is the picture Rusty told us about," he said quietly. "I had Gert help me with this earlier today. See any familiar faces?"

I studied the 8 × 10 faded glossy. It showed a group of smiling men standing in front of Down the Hatch. They were dressed in colorful striped shirts, bell-bottom pants and jeans, and most sported mustaches and long sideburns. One man had on an orange leisure suit.

"By the Western clothes, this is Rusty," I said, "but I don't recognize anyone else."

"Kermit," Marco said, pointing to a tall, good-looking man with jaw-length sideburns. "And see this younger man he has his arm around? This is Henry."

Henry was the best dressed of the lot, wearing a yellow shirt with royal blue stripes and matching blue bell-bottom pants. He, too, was clean-shaven, with sideburns that were shorter and thinner than the rest. Unlike the others, however, he looked miserable.

"Now check out the left side of the group," Marco said. "Can you see the tall guy standing behind the others, almost like he's hiding? You can just see part of his face peering over the top of this man's head. This is a young Doug Cannon."

"What would Doug be doing at a bar party?"

"Doesn't matter, Abby. What matters is what's standing beside Doug." He pointed to a black circular object visible behind a pair of legs. "This is the rear tire of a bicycle."

Chapter Twenty-One

I studied the photo as the full implication of what I was seeing sank in. "Marco, if that's Doug's bike, then that little key the cops found could be for his bicycle lock!"

"It would appear so, but we have to consider that could have belonged to any of the men in the photo, including Henry."

"Impeccably dressed Henry? I hardly think so, Marco."

"Do you remember what was hanging on the wall in Henry's office? A bicycle helmet. Think of the hybrid vehicles in his parking lot. Doesn't Henry seem the kind of socially conscious guy who would have used a bicycle for transportation back then? Granted, it's more logical that it's Doug's bike because of his age, but we need proof."

"Okay, then just listen to what I found out," I said excitedly.

"Let's go back to my office so we have some privacy."

I followed Marco to the back of the building, where we sat facing each other in the leather sling-back chairs in front of his desk.

"I just came from my brother's house," I said, barely able to contain my excitement, "where I did a comparison between the key from the basement and my brother's old bicycle lock key. It's a virtual match, Marco. If the key is Doug's, then the key chain is most likely his, too. Doesn't that tell you who the murderer is? And don't you think we should call in the detectives now?"

"And tell them what? That based on a key chain and an old bike lock key, we think Kermit was murdered by his son? We don't even have proof that the bones were Kermit's, Abby, and without the bones, there's no way to do a DNA analysis or use dental records to find out. For the detectives to believe that Kermit was murdered — not by his son, but just murdered period — we'd need irrefutable proof, like a confession."

"Okay, then where do we begin?"

He took my hands in his. "I think we should be saying, here's where it ends, Abby."

"No, Marco! I feel like we're so close to solving this."

"Sweetheart, we're not close at all. I know

you think that the evidence is pointing straight at Doug, but there are signs pointing toward Rusty now, too, and we're learning more about Henry that makes him a stronger suspect. And there's another possibility that we haven't discussed in a while."

"Which is?"

"Collusion. Think about it, Sunshine. Doug was fifteen years old when Kermit disappeared. Would he really have been able to kill his father, bury the body, strip the clothing, and smooth over the floor without Rusty knowing? And then cold-bloodedly help pour cement over the top?"

I sighed and sat back. "When you put it that way, it does sound far-fetched."

"Who does Doug always turn to for help?"

"Rusty. But would he have back then? He didn't know him well then."

"Considering what we know about Rusty's history with Kermit, how much would it have taken to convince Rusty to help Doug cover up the crime? Remember that at first, Rusty claimed that the floor had never been disturbed while he owned the bar. We know now that his memory isn't as bad as he claims. It's possible we're looking at two men who are desperate to keep this case from being solved, and that makes the situation doubly dangerous."

"Then what's our next move?"

"*My* next move is to have a talk with Rusty. I'm going to pay him a call tomorrow when the saddle shop opens."

"Then see him at noon so I can go with you."

"Did you not hear what I just said about this being doubly dangerous?"

"Hey, what can happen to me in the middle of the day at his shop?"

"Hey." He put his arm around me and ushered me out from behind the bar. "Let's get something to eat."

"That's not the end of this discussion."

"It is for now. Come on, our booth just opened up."

Tuesday

At twelve fifteen, Marco and I approached the counter at Blazing Saddles and asked the same young salesperson if we could talk to Rusty. Marco wasn't at all happy about me coming along, and we almost got into an argument about it. But I reminded him how a team works, and he finally gave in, with the stipulation that he do most of the questioning. I could tell by the set of his jaw, however, that he was still on edge. It was very unlike him.

"You handsome folks lookin' for me?"

Rusty asked.

I turned and saw him coming across the floor, limping more than the last time I'd seen him. "I hope you've got some good news this time," he said with his big smile.

"I hope we do, too," Marco said.

"Come on into the break room," Rusty said, motioning for us to follow. He offered us sarsaparilla, but we declined.

"Whatcha got for me this time?" Rusty asked, easing into a chair.

Marco showed him the key photo on his phone. "This was found in the dirt in the basement. What do you make of it?"

He brought it close to his eyes. "Looks like the key to a briefcase."

"Did you ever see Kermit carry a briefcase?" Marco asked, slipping the phone into his pocket.

Rusty sighed in exasperation. "We're back to Kermit again. I keep telling you that Kermit took off with that Duchess woman. Why don't you want to believe me?"

"Why are you avoiding the question?" Marco snapped.

Rusty shook his head as though he couldn't believe what he was hearing, and frankly, Marco's sharp retort surprised me, too. "Why would a carpenter need a briefcase, Marco? Kermit carried a toolbox."

"Would Kermit have locked his toolbox?"

"What for? He worked alone and always had it with him. That key you're wanting to connect with him could be a hundred years old. Who knows how long it's been in the dirt and, frankly, who cares? The bones you found belonged to some itinerant. End of story."

Marco seemed to relax after that, and I could tell he was changing tactics. He leaned back and hooked one arm over the seatback, talking to Rusty like he was an old friend. "Let's test your theory about one homeless guy killing another. How old would you say those itinerants would have been back in the seventies?"

Rusty shrugged. "I don't know. Maybe somewhere in their thirties or forties."

"Which would make them at least seventy now, senior citizens anyway," Marco said. "Is it realistic to think that one of those vagrants would still be around town today?"

"Maybe," Rusty said.

"Is it realistic to think that this homeless man would read about the bones, then break into the bar to steal the bones — and return a *second* time to sift through the dirt?"

Rusty scratched the back of his head but said nothing.

"Look, I know you don't want to believe that your old buddy was murdered, but Abby and I have done a lot of investigating, and the most likely scenario is that the bones did belong to Kermit. And whoever killed him came back twice to make sure there was no evidence that tied him to the murder. Hardly the actions of a senior citizen, are they? Do you see what I'm getting at?"

At Rusty's reluctant nod, Marco said, "Good. Now let's move on. Did you ever see the Duchess at your bar?"

"Never," Rusty said. "That Gypsy wouldn't have stepped foot in my bar. She was uppity even then."

At least we knew that the bike in the photo couldn't have belonged to Parthenia, not that I'd ever seriously thought it could.

"Did you have a rooftop garden back in the seventies?" Marco asked.

"I don't remember," Rusty said, his gaze shifting away.

"Are you sure?" Marco asked. "I really need you to think back now, because we found a set of garden tools in the bar's basement, and I can't think of a reason to have them unless there was a rooftop garden. But don't sweat it. If you can't remember, I'm sure Gert can."

Marco was certainly showing his interrogation skills. I could tell by the way Rusty kept rubbing his chin that he was thinking hard, probably hoping to find a way to refute Marco's claims. Throwing Gert into the picture was pure genius. Gert remembered everything.

"I seem to recall a garden up top," Rusty said. He ran his fingers along the tabletop, as though trying to appear nonchalant. "What's so important about the tools anyway?"

"The murder weapon may have been a garden trowel," I chimed in. "We uncovered a trowel in the dirt near the bones that matched the other tools in the basement."

He turned to me with a look so haughty and so irate that I scooted back. "Young lady, are you trying to tie me to the murder weapon?"

"Whoa," Marco said. "There's no reason to get upset with Abby. She's being straight with you, that's all."

"Well, I don't like what she's implying," Rusty retorted.

"Look," Marco said, "we came here for help because you owned the bar when those bones were covered up. Who else would we ask, right? The reason for Abby's question is that it seems likely the trowel was lying with the rest of the garden tools and the killer picked it up. We were simply hoping you had some memory of the tools. Okay?"

Rusty looked down at the ground and grumbled, "Okay."

"On a different subject," Marco said, "Abby, would you show him the picture of your brother's key?"

I took out my cell phone and pulled up the photo, enlarging it so he could see the detail. When he wouldn't look immediately, Marco said, "Rusty, please cooperate with us. You're making this harder than it needs to be. You may have information that you don't even realize you know that may help us crack this case. Now please, take a look at the photo on Abby's phone."

With a huff, he looked at my screen.

"This is my brother's bike lock key," I told him. I put my phone on the table beside the photo. "It looks identical to the key that was found in the dirt."

Rusty studied the photo, then sat back and folded his arms across his chest, a stubborn look on his face. "I see it."

"Did you ever see one of the itinerants with a bike?" Marco asked.

"Of course not," Rusty grumbled.

"Did Kermit own a bike?" Marco asked.

"Kermit wouldn't have been caught dead

on a bike," Rusty said.

"Then it would be highly unlikely for Kermit to have had a bicycle lock key in his possession, wouldn't it?" Marco asked.

Rusty shifted in his chair, looking uncomfortable.

"Did Doug have a bike?" Marco asked.

"Are you kidding? That ol' stingy Kermit wouldn't buy him one," Rusty said sullenly.

"Did you buy him one?" Marco asked.

"Why would I buy someone else's kid a bike, Marco?"

"Because you felt sorry for Doug."

"If I had bought that boy a bike, Kermit would have been angry as all get out."

"Somehow I don't think that would have bothered you," Marco said. "Didn't Doug ride over to the bar after school to see his dad?"

"Who told you that?" Rusty demanded. His chest was thrust forward, his arms back, giving me a glimpse of the tough guy he must have been at one time. "Was it that Duchess woman? Sure it was. She'd say anything to take the heat off herself."

I made a note of his second defensive reaction.

"Rusty, come on now," Marco said. "You know we can't reveal a source."

"Now you're going to get all secretive on

me?" Rusty shook his head sorrowfully. "I never expected this kind of treatment from you, Marco."

Marco gave him an exasperated look. "Don't play the guilt card on me. I don't expect that kind of treatment from you. Now I'm going to ask you once more. Did Doug have a bike?"

"And I'm going to give you the same answer," Rusty said. "No, he did not."

I took the framed 8 × 10 photo out of a tote bag I'd brought with me and laid it in front of him. "Is this the photograph of Henry's party you told us about?"

"Yes, ma'am, it is. There's Kermit right in the middle."

"Do you see this man's head above the man in the back row? Do you recognize him?"

With a frown he said, "That's Doug."

"Do you see this?" I pointed out the bicycle tire.

Rusty blinked at the photo, rubbed his eyes, took another look, then shoved it away. "I don't care what this old picture shows. That wasn't his bike. If you're saying that boy killed his papa, you've got it all wrong."

"You keep referring to Doug as a boy," Marco said. "He's a middle-aged man, Rusty."

Thrusting his chin defiantly in the air, Rusty said, "He's a boy to me."

"If you're protecting him, Rusty," Marco said, "you have to stop right now."

Rusty scraped back his chair, his face turning an angry red. "Get out of my store." He stabbed a gnarled finger at the doorway. "Get out and don't you ever come back."

"Rusty, take it easy," Marco said, rising.

"You can't go accusing my friends of murder willy-nilly and expect to be welcome!" Rusty shouted.

Fearing he would have a heart attack, I picked up my purse and started toward the door. "Marco, let's go," I said quietly.

"You know how to reach me," Marco said, and walked out behind me.

"That was rough," I said as we got into the car. "I was afraid he was going to keel over."

"I didn't want that to happen, but I did want to scare him." Marco started the car and pulled out of the lot. "If I'm right, in a few minutes he's going to head over to Cannon Construction to warn Doug about the key."

Marco parked on the side street, where we sat and waited. Within ten minutes, Rusty drove past in his pickup truck. Marco followed some distance behind until he saw

Rusty turn into the construction company's parking lot.

"Bingo," Marco said, and took a photo with his cellphone of Rusty walking into the building. "I wouldn't be surprised if Doug showed up at the bar this evening to convince me I'm wrong about his involvement. Or maybe he'll be frightened enough to pull a disappearing act. But please make sure you talk to Tara after school and emphasize the importance of staying away from the Cannon residence. If Doug is the killer, he'll be running scared. We don't want Tara anywhere near him."

"What are you going to do about Rusty?"

"I'm not sure yet. It was obvious that our bicycle information took him by surprise. But why? Because he didn't want to believe that Doug could have killed Kermit or because he didn't think there'd be any proof?

"So here are our possibilities. I think we can safely rule out the Duchess. She might have had a strong motive, but it's not likely that she would have met Kermit at the bar no matter what time of day it was, or snuck into the bar to steal the bones, or have hired college students to create a diversion while she sifted dirt. I'm also moving Henry to third on the list. He might have had the means and opportunity, but his motive was the weakest of the three men.

"So the first and most likely possibility is that Doug killed his dad, and Rusty found out about it when Doug came to him for help. The second is that Rusty didn't know until just now, when he figured it out after he saw the key and the photo. The third is that Rusty and Doug worked together to kill Kermit."

Marco stopped and pointed straight ahead. "That was a quick visit."

I glanced up and saw Rusty pulling out of the Cannon lot. But instead of turning left to head back to the saddle shop, he turned right toward town.

"Let's see where he's going," Marco said, and started the engine.

As he eased into traffic, I checked the time. "I need to be back at Bloomers soon. Not that I'm complaining, but we've been inundated with orders."

"I'd hate to lose track of him now, Abby, but if you need to get back —"

"Forget I said that. I'm sure everything is fine. I haven't had any emergency phone calls, so that's good news."

I didn't want to tell Marco that I'd been hoping for a phone call telling me that Francesca's experiment with Princess had gone badly. That hadn't happened, which meant that she'd want to work with Seedy next, and I really didn't want to turn my little rescue dog over to her. But if I said no, I'd offend Francesca.

"Penny for your thoughts," Marco said.

"Just thinking about Seedy."

Marco glanced over at me. "By the worry line between your eyebrows, I'd say it was Seedy and my mom."

How well he knew me.

"Do you want my opinion?" he asked. "Seedy's not ready for my mom. It's too soon."

I breathed a sigh of relief. "But how do we tell your mom that?"

Marco gave my hand a reassuring squeeze. "Why don't you let me handle that, babe?"

"I would love that, Marco. Thanks." I sat back with a pleased smile. Sometimes there was an *I* in team.

We followed Rusty around the town square, where he turned south and headed across the railroad tracks. Both of us were surprised when he pulled into Greer Plumbing's lot.

"From Doug's office to Henry's?" I asked. "What does that mean?"

Marco took a photo of Rusty entering the

building. “I’m not sure what it means, but it certainly puts a twist in my theories.”

Chapter Twenty-Two

Ten minutes went by without a sign of Rusty. Because we were so close to the square, I left Marco doing surveillance and walked back to Bloomers. Seedy was in the window again, and scratched at the glass when she saw me coming. As soon as I stepped inside, she was in front of me, her hind end wiggling so hard I thought she would fall over.

I scooped her up and held her. "Hello, little girl. Did you miss me?"

She gave a yip then licked my cheek until I put her down.

Two women were just leaving, and both stopped to tell me how much they admired me for taking Seedy in. "Grace told us all about her," one of the women said. "You did a wonderful thing. I've had my rescue dog for five years, and he's the best dog I've ever owned." She smiled at her friend.

"Now I'm trying to talk Kim into adopting one."

I chatted with them for a few minutes, then, with Seedy following right behind, headed into the back where Lottie was hard at work. Seedy went to her pile of toys beneath the table, chose one, and took it to her doggy bed.

"Any calls from Jillian?" I asked.

"None," Lottie said. "It's been blessedly quiet."

Just what I'd feared.

Grace came through the curtain carrying a tea tray loaded with cups, saucers, a teapot, and scones. "I thought you might need refreshment," she said, setting the tray on the worktable.

"Thanks," I said. "Marco didn't bring any food, and I'm starving."

"Did you make any progress on the case?" Grace asked.

I put a dollop of clotted cream on the blueberry scone and took a bite. "Oh, this is so delicious, Grace. Yes, we did make progress."

I filled them in as I ate, answered their questions, then rolled up my sleeves and got back to business. I read over a new order, then looked at Lottie in surprise. "The customer wants a wedding bouquet and boutonniere, and that's all? No floral arrangements, no bridesmaids' bouquets, nothing?"

"Apparently they're going to be married in front of a judge," Lottie said. "They're a nice older couple who want to keep their wedding simple. You can see on the slip that she wants a bouquet of purple-and-green flowers with something a little surprising in it."

How fun! I went to one of our walk-in coolers and studied my stock. I pulled green hydrangea and green tea orchids, then purple dendrobium orchids and purple statice. I looked around for something a little exotic and spotted peacock-toned *Craspedia,* and that gave me an idea for the surprise. Peacock feathers.

"That's a knockout," Lottie said when I was done. "Maybe you can use a peacock feather with a green tea orchid for the boutonniere. That'd be a surprise, too."

I finished the order and started on the next, and by four fifty-five that afternoon, Lottie and I had cleared the spindle. I'd never worked harder or felt more content. I had a new husband, a new mattress, two fantastic assistants, a sweet new dog, and a thriving business. It didn't get any better than that.

And then my cell phone rang. I saw my sister-in-law's name on the screen and got an instant knot in my stomach that I couldn't explain.

"Abby, is Tara with you?" Kathy asked, the worry evident in her voice.

Now I knew the reason for the knot. "No, I haven't seen her today. What's up?"

"She was supposed to go home with a friend to do their math assignment and then be home by four thirty. I called and texted her twice, but she didn't answer, so I called her friend's house, and she said Tara was never there. I don't know what's going on, Abby. She's been really secretive lately, and that makes me worry even more."

I had a strong hunch about what was going on, but I sure didn't want to tell Kathy that her daughter was playing detective in a murder investigation. "I'll be leaving Bloomers in about ten minutes, so I'll check around. I know some of the places she likes to hang out. In the meantime, if she shows up, let me know."

"Trouble?" Lottie asked, sweeping the floor.

"Tara isn't home, and Kathy is starting to worry."

"And you're worrying, too. That little crease between your eyebrows is back. You better go look for her. Gracie and I will close up shop."

"Thank you," I said, giving her a hug. I grabbed my jacket and purse and headed for the curtain, then came to a stop. "Oh, wait. I forgot about Seedy."

"I'll take her down to the bar," Lottie said. "You're going to call Marco anyway and let him know about Tara, so just tell him that I'll bring Seedy down."

"Perfect." I made sure I had my cell phone with me. Then I took off.

Once in my car, I phoned Marco, but it went to voice mail, so I called the bar directly and Rafe answered. "Hey, hot stuff, if you're looking for Marco, you'll have to wait. He's on a phone conference."

"Okay, when he's done, have him call me. I'll be driving around looking for my niece. You haven't seen Tara, have you?"

"Not recently."

"What do you mean *not recently*? Was she down there today?"

"Yeah, after school. She said she wanted an update on the investigation, but Marco was busy, so I filled her in."

That little redheaded sneak. "What did you tell her?"

Rafe suddenly sounded nervous. "Just what, you know, Gert pointed out to Marco in that photo on the wall."

"How do you know what Gert told Marco?"

"I was standing right here."

My stomach knot grew bigger. "Tell me exactly what you said to Tara."

"I showed her the photo, and then she wanted to know who the people were in it, so I pointed out the guys that Gert had pointed out to Marco."

Then Tara knew that Doug Cannon was in the picture. "Did you show her the bicycle tire?" *Please say no please say no please say no.*

He paused. "Um, yeah, I think I did."

Crap! Unless I was way off base, I had a pretty good hunch where Tara was — at the Cannons' on a hunt for Doug's bike. Because her dad still had his old bike, to her it would be perfectly logical for Doug to still have his. I wished I'd never shown her the photo of that key.

I did a fast Internet search, and found an address for the Cannon residence. It was in a township outside of New Chapel's borders, in a wooded area where the homes were scattered. Guided by my GPS, I followed a country road east for six miles before turning north onto a road that led to a smaller road that circled a retention pond.

I finally found the house on the backside of the pond, a two-story gray Colonial with white trim, and a long asphalt driveway that led to a big four-bay garage at the rear of the property. No cars were parked in front of the house or in the driveway and all garage bays were closed. I didn't see Tara's bicycle.

There was no place to park near the house where a vintage banana yellow Corvette wouldn't be seen, so I had to leave it on the other side of the pond and hike, staying in the shelter of the trees. I hadn't planned on having to sneak around someone's house, and I feared my orange checked shirt hadn't been the smartest thing to wear. Luckily, it was an hour before sunset and the cloud cover was thick with impending rain. I hadn't brought an umbrella, so I crossed my fingers and hoped the rain held off.

I came out of the trees as close to the garage as possible and saw Tara's bike in the grass behind it. It made sense that she'd start there since that was where her dad kept his bike. I tried to look through a side window to see what was going on, but the glass was so grimy, I couldn't make out the shapes I was seeing.

I dug a tissue out of my purse to clear off a small circle in the dirt. I felt something on my hand and glanced down to see a tiny spider crawling along my thumb. With a shriek, I brushed it off with the tissue, dropped both on the ground, and stamped on them, then checked my hand carefully to make sure there were no more.

With a shudder, I examined the pane carefully before cupping my hands and gazing through the glass. Now I could make out two shiny modern bikes, one silver, one blue, and Haydn's red Mustang on the far side. The other bays were empty.

I was about to turn away when I saw a small form with a familiar red bob coming down a set of pull-down stairs. I waited a moment to make sure no one followed her, then rapped on the glass. At once, she dropped out of sight behind the car only to reappear toward the front, peeking over the hood. She saw me and her eyes widened in surprise.

I motioned for her to come out but she shook her head and reversed the motion. I shook my head, but she kept waving me in, bouncing with excitement. She pointed toward the side of the garage by her, where I saw a service door, then again waved for me to come in.

I hurried around the back of the garage, and when I entered the door I was immediately hugged. "Wait till I show you what I found, Aunt Abby. Come with me."

"Tara, forget it. I've got to get you out of here before Haydn's parents come home."

"They won't be home until after six o'clock," she said, tugging me toward the steps.

"That's only half an hour from now. It's too risky."

"I'm about to solve the murder case for you, and you're saying to forget it? Wow. I never thought I'd hear you say that, Aunt Abby."

"Tara, if anything were to happen to you —"

"All we need is five minutes," she whined. "What could happen?"

Why did that remind me of myself? "What if Mr. Cannon comes home early?"

With a huff of exasperation, Tara dropped my arm and hurried to the stairs. "Fine. You stay there, and I'll bring it down."

Before I could stop her, she had scuttled up the steps and disappeared through an opening overhead.

"Don't tell me you found Mr. Cannon's bike."

"No," she called back. "This is even better."

Now she had me excited. But then

Marco's warning sounded in my head. "You shouldn't tamper with evidence, Tara. We need to bag it."

"Who has a bag? Just come up and see it."

I gazed up apprehensively. *Crap.* An attic. What did attics have? Spiders.

My heart was thumping as I climbed after her. I stepped onto a wooden plank floor and glanced around. Spiderwebs hung all around me — from the attic vents, under the eaves, along the support beams . . . My skin was crawling already.

"Over here," Tara called. She was at the front of the garage under the slant of the roof in what appeared to be a cozy hideaway. I could see an old patio lounge chair, a chrome floor lamp, a small black trunk, a dormitory-sized refrigerator, a blue throw rug, and stacks of magazines. It was probably the only space in the entire attic that was clean.

"You need to phone your parents," I said, making my way across the plywood floor, one eye on the webs overhead. "Your mom is worried."

"I phoned about ten minutes ago and said I was here with Hannah but hadn't been able to get a signal, which is almost true. It happened last time I was here."

I'd had no idea how much my niece and I thought alike until this very moment.

"Oh, and by the way, no bids on Grandma's art yet."

Hard to care about Mom's art when the spider alert was at the orange level. I circumvented half a dozen large storage boxes. One of them was open, and I could see sports equipment inside. "Where's Hannah?"

"In the house with Haydn doing homework. I saw them through a window. Hurry up. Don't think about spiders."

"Easy for you to say." I rubbed the goose bumps covering my arms. "How did you get Hannah to let you come up here alone?"

"Simple. I didn't ask. I knew the side door was open during the day because Hannah showed me."

"Dear God, Tara. That means we broke in. Do you know the risk we're taking?"

"You do it all the time. It's fun!" She thrust an open book at me. "Read this. It's Haydn's journal."

"*This* is your evidence? A teenage boy's private journal?"

"Would you just read this page?"

I began to read silently:

Holy shit. It's my dad. He was in the garage right below me talking to Mr. Greer and Rusty and I think they did something really bad. Really, really bad, like killed Grandpa Kermit. Thank God they didn't hear me. I couldn't even move, I was so scared. They were saying shit like, We've got the bones. They can't prove anyone was even buried there. If you'd put in new plumbing when you had the chance —

I can't remember everything but it was something about Grandpa's bones.

They're saying my dad was the guy who did it. I remember Dad telling me what a mean bastard Grandpa was, and Dad never liked talking about him. I mean, we had no pics of the guy in the house or anything. I know why now.

My dad is a murderer but he's my dad. I can't tell Hannah, I can't tell Mom. No one can ever know. So I guess it's a secret that me and my dad will always share, even though he'll never know.

I stared at the neatly written page in shocked silence. All three men had been in on the killing.

"See?" Tara asked proudly, tapping the journal. "Didn't I tell you I had evidence?"

Not only evidence, but Tara, without even

knowing it, might have solved the case. I flipped to the next page to see if there was more, but Haydn had written about school, so I used my cell phone to take a picture of the single entry.

"Aren't you going to take the journal with us?" Tara asked.

"Not on your life. I don't want the Cannons to know we found it. How did you know about the journal anyway?"

"Hannah wanted me to see the poem Haydn wrote about me, which is pretty sweet, by the way."

I handed her the slender book. "Put it back where you found it, and then we need to get out of here fast. My car is on the other side of the pond."

"I can't leave my bike," she said, following me down the stairs.

"I'll have Marco come back for it. How did you pull the steps down?"

"They were already down."

At the door, I leaned out to be sure the way was clear. "Okay, Tara, we're going to run behind the garage and then head into the woods —"

A black Lexus SUV turned into the driveway.

I jerked back inside. "What kind of car does Mr. Cannon drive?"

"A black SUV."

Crap.

A car door slammed. I peered out and saw Doug walking up the long drive heading toward the garage. He had his cell phone against his ear and was talking to someone. Behind him, Rusty's red pickup pulled into the driveway followed by Henry's hybrid.

I leaned against the door, heart racing, mind going in ten different directions. Should we run for the woods? Hide in the attic? What if they saw us? What would they do? Come after us?

"What is it?" Tara asked in a frightened voice.

I could hear the men's voices in the distance. "Mr. Cannon and his friends are here. We'll have to hide in the attic."

"I'm scared, Aunt Abby," she said at the top of the steps.

I was, too, but I didn't want to frighten Tara more than she already was. "I'll text Marco. We'll be fine."

I had her climb into one of the boxes of sports gear and covered her with an old blue-and-gold Bears stadium blanket. "Whatever happens, Tara, do not make a sound and don't come out unless Uncle Marco tells you it's safe, okay? Promise?"

"Promise," she said in a muffled, little

girl's voice. "Where will you hide?"

I looked around, but the other boxes were sealed with tape. "I'll find a place where I can listen. Don't worry."

I moved away from Tara's box and closer to the opening. Checking for spiders, I hunkered down behind the largest container I could find. Then with shaking hands I texted Marco: *In Doug's garage attic w/Tara. D, R, H, all here.*

Damn. Where was *here*? What was the address? My mind was a blank.

I heard men's voices directly below and ended with: *Hurry!* Then I put my phone on mute and set it in front of me so I could see his reply.

"Okay, we've got two options. Either we get rid of the Salvares or convince them to drop the investigation."

I was voting for option two. I knew the speaker was Doug. Their voices were distinctive enough that I had no problem identifying them.

Henry: "Convince them to forget a murder? He was a cop. It'll never happen."

Rusty: "Not so fast now. Marco's a reasonable guy. And Miss Abigail has a heart of gold. If we present our case well enough, they'll understand."

Henry: "Understand that Doug killed his

father, and we helped him cover it up? In whose lifetime?"

Something tickled my hand. I glanced down and saw a brown spider with long legs crawling across the back of it. I shook my hand hard, biting my lower lip to keep from letting loose with a bloodcurdling shriek. I took deep breaths to steady myself as it scuttled away. I *had* to keep quiet. No spider in the world would make me put Tara in danger.

Marco, why haven't you texted me back? Shuddering, I pulled my knees tightly against myself and wrapped my arms around them, trying to make myself into an invulnerable ball. I tuned back in to the men below, trying not to think about the webs all around me.

Rusty: "They know what a bastard Kermit was. If they're not convinced, we'll give 'em more. Right, Doug?"

Doug: "They haven't heard half of what that asshole did to us. But I have to agree with Henry, Rusty. Marco was a cop, and Abby worked for a lawyer. Would they be able to turn a blind eye to murder? I don't think so."

Rusty: "Hey, now. Remember, she worked for a public defender who represents all types of people, including criminals and those wrongly accused. She'd be the most likely to be impartial, and a woman knows how to convince her man. Come on, boys. Listen to the voice of experience here. No one likes abusers. Abby and Marco will listen to me. They respect me."

Silence. Then Henry: "I don't know . . . I suppose we could try."

Doug: "And if they won't go along with us, what then?"

Henry: "Then they'll disappear. You're the builder, Doug. I'm sure you can find an excavation site waiting for a load of concrete."

My stomach turned over. They were plotting our deaths. Even Rusty. I didn't think I'd ever say this, but thank God Tara was a snoop; otherwise, we wouldn't have known what the three were planning until it was too late.

I began to listen again.

Rusty: "Let me contact Marco and have both of 'em meet me out at the saddle shop after hours. It's far enough out that no one drives past after six."

Right. Like we were going to fall for that now. My cell phone vibrated against the wood, making a humming sound. I snatched it up and read the message: *Stay hidden. I'm on my way.*

Marco was coming. *Thank you, God.*

I felt something fall into my hair and quickly brushed it off. Three small spiders fell onto the floor in front of me. Pinching my lips with my fingers to keep from screaming, I shot to my feet, my body racked with shudders. *Keep it together, Abby. Think of Tara!*

I glanced up and saw a white bag of tiny spiders dangling above me. My scalp prickled. There were more.

I stopped myself from screaming out loud but I couldn't keep in my terrified whimpers as I jumped away from the nest, slapping the top of my head. Still whimpering, I bent over to brush my hair furiously. When I looked up, Doug Cannon was halfway through the opening, staring at me in shock.

CHAPTER TWENTY-THREE

Marco

"A train? Now?" I pounded the steering wheel with a curse, then remembered the little dog sitting on the passenger seat next to me. She was watching me fearfully, ready to leap off the seat and dive for cover. My fault.

I used a soothing voice to calm her. "It's okay, girl. I didn't mean to frighten you. Everything's okay."

Except that my wife was in danger at this very moment, while I sat at the railroad crossing waiting for this mother —

I was working myself up — very unlike me. I needed a cool head.

The train seemed to be crawling past.

I hit my fist against the steering wheel before I remembered not to. "Sorry, Seedy."

She was shivering again, her eyebrows drawn together in fear, so I reached across and ran my hand down her bony back.

"Don't worry. We'll find Abby and Tara. By God, we will. Once the train passes we're maybe fifteen minutes away."

It had taken me a few minutes to decipher Abby's text, to understand that Doug, Henry, and Rusty were meeting in Doug's garage. Obviously they had all participated in the murder. Was it a strategy session?

Son of a bitch, my wife is in danger and I get caught by a damn train.

I wanted to phone Abby, but knew better than to draw attention to her. I decided to try a text. She was smart enough to have muted her phone: *R U OK?*

It wasn't much but it said what needed to be said. I set my phone in my lap and waited for her reply. I drummed my fingers on the steering wheel and checked the rearview mirror. Two cars waited behind me. Very little traffic on country roads at that time of day. I glanced up and saw the gates rising. Finally.

"Now we're moving, Seedy. Get on the floor, girl. Down. There you go. We're going to travel fast."

Another benefit from my Army Ranger days: I learned how to drive defensively, maneuver out of dangerous situations, save lives. With both hands on the wheel, I gunned it through the countryside, taking turns faster than most people could handle. Just let a cop try to stop me now.

You don't get it, man. I'm trying to save my wife's life. Two people's lives. They're depending on me. So step back and arrest me later.

I checked the time and clenched my teeth. Still about ten minutes away. Why hadn't she texted back? I willed my thoughts to my wife: *I'm almost there, sweetheart. Hang on. You'll be safe soon.*

Abby *had* to be safe. What the hell would I do without her?

"Thank God. Here's the pond," I said to the dog, who raised her ears and tilted her head, as though to say, *What's a pond?*

I jammed on the brakes when I saw the hood of Abby's yellow Corvette through a stand of trees. No time to analyze why it was there. I pulled off the road, hopped out, and jogged to her car. She'd locked it. Good. It would have to stay there until I found her. *Until,* not if.

I drove around the pond, watching the addresses on the curbside mailboxes until I was close to the Cannon residence. Baseball cap and sunglasses on, I drove past, but no cars were in the driveway. Was it the right house?

Using my cell phone, I did a quick Internet search and the same address came up. I parked on the street between two homes separated by a huge expanse of plush green lawn and tall evergreens. Both houses seemed quiet — sun was setting but no lights on, no cars or bikes around — so I grabbed Seedy and walked her on her leash straight up between the yards to the back, where the grass abutted a wooded area. From there we wound through the trees to Cannon's property until we were near the garage; then I crouched down to observe the environs. I gave it five minutes. I didn't dare wait longer than that.

I crept up to the window on one side and looked in. Red Mustang, two bikes, no men. The steps to the attic were down. That alarmed me.

Seedy whined and pawed at my leg. I looked down at her and saw a filthy, balled-up tissue in her mouth. "Seedy, let it go."

She dropped it at my feet, then put her nose in it and sniffed, whining like it bothered her. I picked it up to make sure nothing was rolled up inside. "Just a dirty tissue, Seedy. Nothing here except a dead spider."

I tossed the tissue, then led her along the backside of the garage and entered through the service door. I checked the Mustang quickly then left Seedy at the bottom of the steps and climbed cautiously into the attic. I walked between the boxes, keeping my head down so I wouldn't bump my head.

They weren't there.

Shit.

I started down the steps and met Seedy coming up, dragging her leash behind her. Somehow she'd made it halfway. I snapped my fingers, trying to get her to follow me down, but she wouldn't buy it. She was determined to get to the top.

I climbed after her just as she made the last stair. She put her nose to the floor and sniffed along a path straight to an oven-sized cardboard container marked Sports. Glancing back at me, she gave her little yip, then scratched at the side of the box.

"What did you find, Seedy?"

A muffled voice said, "Uncle Marco?"

What the hell? "Tara?"

A blanket was flung aside; then Tara's red head appeared. She saw me and began to cry, holding out her arms like a child. I picked her up, lifted her over the side, set her down, and hugged her to me. "You're safe, Tara. We'll get you out of here. Where's Abby?"

"They took her," she sobbed.

My gut twisted so hard I wanted to puke. "Where?"

"I d-don't know." Tara's teeth rattled violently. She rubbed her arms, shivering, her face white. She was in shock.

I picked up the blanket and wrapped it around her. "Tell me what happened."

"I f-found Haydn's journal where he talked about the m-murder, so I showed Aunt Abby. We were j-just ready to leave when we saw the m-men coming toward the garage. Aunt Abby had me get into the box; then she hid out here s-somewhere so she could listen. All I could hear were muffled voices, so I d-didn't know what was happening until I heard her moving around and slapping herself and trying not to cry."

Tara paused to glance around, then pointed out a dozen smashed spiders under the slant of the roof. "There."

No wonder Abby freaked out. The tissue outside must have been hers, too. Seedy would have recognized her scent.

"Then I heard Mr. C-Cannon's voice. He was angry, s-so angry at her. I heard scuffling sounds, like she was fighting with him, and then I heard other men and they were all talking at once, and then their voices got softer and softer, and then nothing." She began to cry again. "What are they going to do to her, Uncle Marco?"

I couldn't let my mind go there. All I knew

was that if they harmed my wife, they'd wish they'd never been born. "Nothing's going to happen to her, Tara. I'll see to that. Go get the journal, and let's get out of here."

I picked up Seedy, tucked the journal inside my shirt, then proceeded down the steps far enough that I could lend Tara a hand. I didn't think she was steady enough to walk it on her own.

"M-my bike is here. Can we g-get it?"

I didn't want to take the time, but I couldn't tell her no.

A misty rain was falling now. Tara carried Seedy and I rolled her bike back the way we'd come. On the drive to her house, I questioned her again about what she'd heard, but she had no new information.

My phone dinged with an incoming text. I checked the screen and immediately pulled off the road.

"What is it?" Tara asked, holding Seedy on her lap.

"Hold on." It was Abby. Thank God.

But it wasn't Abby. The message read: *Abby is safe. No police and she stays that way.*

Sons of bitches. They were using Abby's phone. I texted back: *What do U want?*

No reply.

"Tara, I need you to keep a secret. Will

you do that for your aunt Abby? It's important."

She nodded, her big green eyes wide with apprehension.

"Those men you heard in the garage want to meet with me. Your aunt is with them. Everything will be fine as long as I don't bring police with me. But here's the problem. If you go home now, your parents will want to know what happened, and there's no way in hell that they won't call the cops if they hear that Abby is being held. Do you understand?"

She nodded again, clutching Seedy to her.

"You okay with coming to the bar? You can sit in my office and play on the computer. Rafe can keep you company. You can tell your mom and dad you're on a sleepover at our apartment. I'll explain everything to them once Abby's safe, all right?"

She shook her head. "My mom won't let me spend a school night away from home."

"Then you're going to have to get dropped off at home and tell a lie. It's the only way to make sure Abby doesn't get hurt. Are you good with that? Can you be convincing?"

Tara nodded. "Will you text me when she's safe?"

"You bet."

I dropped Tara off, waiting outside until her mom came to the door. Then I gave a shrug, as if to say, *Kids!* Tara wiggled her fingers to say good-bye, then stood there watching as I drove off. *Do a good job, Tara.*

Now to find my wife.

The windshield wipers had a hard time keeping up with the sheets of rain that were falling now, slowing traffic. There wasn't any sign of Rusty's pickup or the other two cars at Cannon Construction. No cars at the saddle shop or at Greer Plumbing either. I made the circuit twice. Where the hell were they?

I checked the rearview mirror. Seedy had climbed into the backseat and was curled up for a nap. My phone dinged, so I pulled into a convenience store parking lot. This time the message read: *We want to meet with you.*

I replied: *Where. When.* I watched the screen until the phone shut off. *Come on come on come on. Answer, damn it.*

The ding came minutes later: *After the bar closes wait for further instructions. No police or Abby's dead.*

When I saw those last two words, my insides froze. But it didn't make sense to keep searching. I wouldn't find them until they wanted to be found. I returned to the bar, tucked Seedy in my office with a hunk of steak and a bowl of water, stashed the journal in my safe, then tried to distract my mind by mixing drinks, talking to customers, anything to pretend my world hadn't stopped.

At two in the morning, I sent my staff home. "We'll clean tomorrow."

"Thought you should know, boss," Gert said. "Someone propped that back door open again, but I caught it. I think one of the cooks did it going out for a smoke."

"You caught it, not Rafe?"

"He's off tonight."

Damn, I hadn't even noticed. My mind was too focused on my wife. But for once I couldn't blame my brother. A dubious silver lining.

"There weren't any muddy prints in the hallway," Gert said. "Looks like we lucked out."

"Thanks." There wasn't anything left for the killers to take but dirt anyway.

I locked up and paced from front door to back, checking the time every few minutes. At two thirty, I got a new text: *Open the back door and wait in the basement. No police.*

That was the third time they'd warned me, as if I were a novice. But it was better that way. If they wanted a rookie, they'd get a rookie.

I replied: *No Abby, no deal.*

I took my pistol out of the safe in my office, tucked it in the back of my waistband, put my knife inside my sock, wedged a piece of cardboard between the back door and the jamb just enough to keep it from locking, grabbed a flashlight and went downstairs so I could turn the light on over the hole. I had no intention of waiting down there. If anyone was going to be a sitting duck, it wouldn't be me.

CHAPTER TWENTY-FOUR

Marco

"Glad you could join us, son."

Rusty's voice came out of the darkness. Before I could react, two men grabbed me from behind, preventing me from reaching my gun. It was yanked from my waistband. A hand felt down my pant legs and found my knife. I'd been ambushed. Like a rookie.

A light went on over the hole, illuminating my wife tied to a rusty chair, her mouth gagged, her eyes wide, alert, relieved, frightened. I saw that and my insides twisted. If my hands had been free, I would have killed the nearest man. I locked gazes with her as my wrists were tied behind me. *I'm sorry, Sunshine.*

It clicked in my head then. Gert had found the back door open. The men had brought Abby in while I was out searching for them. They'd been down here the whole damn evening.

I was pushed forward to the other side of the hole, where four dilapidated barstools had been resurrected from the pile of junk and put in a circle. "Have a seat," Doug said.

"You assholes really think gagging my wife is going to make me cooperative?" I asked. "You want to talk to me, untie her."

"In due time," Henry said. "She hasn't been hurt, have you, Abby?"

She glared at him. That was my Fireball.

I sat on the stool and studied each man in turn, not giving them the satisfaction of asking what they wanted. Rusty flicked his fingers against his boots, clearly uncomfortable. I gave him a look that said, *What the hell are you doing?*

"We need to explain a few things," Rusty said, his expression pleading. "We want you to understand how it happened."

"Why it happened," Henry said.

I sat and waited. Silence unnerved people.

"You don't know everything about Kermit," Doug said. "It would take hours to tell you everything he put my family through — the abuse, the lies, the shame, the neglect — for years before the drinking got bad."

"Not just his family," Henry said. "Kermit knew I was a hard worker and wanted to make money, so he promised me whatever it took to reel me in. He treated me like a son, and I actually fell for it. My father left my mother when I was two, so I'd never had a dad. Kermit became my dad."

Henry looked down. "The abuse started slowly — a criticism here, a complaint there — making me try harder to please him. I worked from early morning until late in the evening, all week and every weekend, doing all the jobs Kermit was too lazy to do. Then the criticisms escalated, especially after he started drinking heavily. I blamed it on the alcohol at first, but then I started to see him for the selfish, mean-spirited bastard that he was."

"My mother knew Kermit had cheated on her over the years," Doug said, "and she suffered in silence because she believed divorce would be harder on us kids than living with him. I was the one who saw him with Parthenia. I heard Kermit plan to take the money from the business account and make a new life with her. 'Away from those stupid, whiny brats of mine' were his exact words."

"You told me he was undecided," I said.

"We were hoping you'd think Parthenia did it," Henry said.

"So you dropped off a photo of her, pregnant, from nineteen seventy-six."

At Henry's nod, I asked, "What happened to the money?"

"We put it back into the account," Henry said. "We would have gone into bankruptcy otherwise."

"That ol' bastard was ready to leave them all with a foundering company without so much as a pang of regret," Rusty said.

"I hated him," Doug said through gritted teeth. "I would lie in bed at night and wish I could make him disappear. I would drag him home from the bar and think about driving him to the lake and pushing him in. The same day I heard him make his plans with Parthenia, I found him here late in the evening, drunk out of his mind, and I knew I had to stop him before he destroyed all of our lives."

"So you killed him with a garden trowel that Rusty kept down here," I said to Doug matter-of-factly, with a quick look at Abby. Her body was as tense as a coiled spring.

"I didn't plan to kill him," Doug said. "I threatened to spread it around town about Parthenia being pregnant, unless he dumped her. But all he said was, 'I'm leaving, and you can't do nothin' about it.' He was so drunk, he couldn't even stand. He asked me to help him get up, and I told him he could just die there." Doug began to sob quietly. "He laughed at me."

"It's okay, son," Rusty said. "You don't need to say anything else."

"They need to know," Doug said through gritted teeth, wiping his face with his sleeve. "They need to know that he laughed so hard, he vomited all over himself. That was when I picked up the trowel. I wanted to hurt him for all the times he hurt us. I swear to God I never meant to kill him."

But he did kill his father, and then he covered it up. I looked at Rusty. "Damn those brawling itinerants."

Rusty had the decency to look ashamed. "So you were in on it, too," I said to him.

"Yeah, I was in on it. Doug called me down here and showed me what he'd done. Poor boy was hysterical, sobbing, shaking all over, even had the dry heaves. I called Henry, and we met here and did what we had to do to protect the kid."

"And you're still trying to protect *the kid,*" I said.

"We didn't want it to come to this, Marco," Rusty said. "But here we are."

They all looked at me, waiting.

"So we sing 'Kumbaya' and everyone goes home happy?" I asked.

"We're hoping you'll work with us, son," Rusty said. "Drop your investigation. Tell the cops you reached a dead end or whatever. You'll know what to say."

"Otherwise?" I asked.

The men glanced at one another. Rusty looked down. The other two gazed at me with cold eyes. "Otherwise you both end up in cement," Doug said.

I didn't want to look at Abby. She was waiting for me to get us out of this, and I wasn't seeing a way yet. All I could do was stall for time so I could think.

I fixed my gaze on Doug first. "You know why I became a cop? Because I believe in justice. So what you're telling me is that you meted out your own justice that day."

"That's it, Marco," Rusty said. "The way it worked out, Kermit got what he deserved. The world became a better place with him gone."

"Kind of a vigilante thing," I said to Henry.

"I guess you could say that," he said.

"Yeah, I get it," I said. "The abuse ended, Henry got rid of a negligent partner, Doug got rid of his cheating father, and you got your high school sweetheart back, Rusty."

They looked at one another with congratulatory smiles. Assholes.

I glanced around, checking for anything that I could use against them, but they'd cleared all the junk to the far end of the basement.

"See how well it all worked out, son?" Rusty asked.

"Rusty, do me a favor. Don't call me *son* anymore."

They looked at me skeptically.

"What's it going to be, Salvare?" Doug asked. "Are you going to work with us?"

I had an idea. "Take the gag off my wife's mouth."

"No, I think you need to answer first," Henry said.

"No, I think you need to take her gag off first," I said, letting my temper show.

At Doug's nod, Rusty got up and went to her, untying the bandanna in back. She spit it out and made a face, as though the taste in her mouth was bad.

"You okay?" I asked her.

"Just thirsty." She was signaling me with her eyes: *Don't you dare give in to them.*

"Now her hands," I said.

"You're not serious," Henry said.

"Now. Her. Hands." I used a tone that meant business, and they listened. I've known men like these. They weren't really brave. They were just desperate.

"Go ahead, Rusty," Doug said. "Henry, guard the doorway."

Shit. There went my plan.

Abby rubbed her wrists and glared at Rusty. "I used to admire you." She pulled off her new boots and tossed them in the dirt. Her symbolic gesture of *Up yours.*

"Your answer?" Doug reminded me.

"Are you crazy?" Abby asked defiantly. "You're asking a former United States Army Ranger to cover up a murder? Are you *all* crazy?"

"Abby," I said.

"How do you propose to kill us?" she demanded of Doug. "Shoot us, drag our bodies up the stairs, through the alley, and into your SUV? I don't think so. Imagine all the trace evidence you'd have to scrub off, not to mention having to carry two dead-weights all the way to the end of the alley without anyone seeing you. Or maybe you think you can just bury us like you did —"

"Shut up!" Doug said, running his fingers through his hair. "Rusty, tie her up again." He was tense, unraveling. "We'll bury them here."

Abby looked at me as Rusty bound her wrists, willing me to hurry with our rescue. And I had nothing. What the hell could I do? I didn't care about me, but I had to get her out of this.

The men went into a huddle by the doorway, but I could hear their whispers.

"The basement has been cleared by the detectives," Doug said. "They'll never look here, especially once we get the new cement floor in."

"How do we, you know, *do* it?" Rusty asked, giving me a guilty glance.

"Marco's gun," Henry said. "It's loaded."

"But *who's* gonna do it?" Rusty asked. He was the least sure of them.

They said nothing for a few seconds; then Doug let out a breath. "I'll do it."

Abby sprang from her chair and ran to me, curling up against my chest. I wanted to hold her and tell her she'd be fine, but I couldn't. I'd never felt so helpless in my life.

"They're bluffing," she whispered.

"They're not bluffing," I said against the top of her head.

She looked up at me. "What are we going to do?"

"Just go along with whatever I say. Don't antagonize them."

"Get away from him," Doug snapped, his voice edgy. He came toward us, pointing the pistol at me.

"Get as close as you can to the doorway,"

I whispered, then said aloud, "Do what he says, Abby." I watched her back to the side of the hole, but before she could step up onto the cement floor, Henry dragged her back into the middle. *Shit.*

Doug moved behind me, so I twisted around so I could see him. It was always better to face the man with the gun. "We agree," I said. "We'll drop the investigation."

"Good to hear that, Marco," Rusty said, his shoulders sagging in relief.

"It's too late for that, Rusty," Doug said. "Abby's right about him. He's too honest." My gun was shoved against my spine. "I knew it was a waste of time to talk to you, but the other two thought you might give us a break, that you'd understand Kermit was better off dead."

"You can't play God," Abby burst out. "You can't decide that another person has no right to live."

"Shut up," Doug snapped. He jabbed me with my pistol. "Kneel down in the dirt."

"No," I said. "You'll have to shoot me here. More of a mess to clean up."

Doug swore under his breath. "Henry, help me drag him into the hole."

Before Henry could move, I snapped my head back, hitting Doug in the diaphragm. As he gasped for a breath, I jumped to my feet, pivoted, and kicked the chair at him, then used one booted foot to send him crashing to the ground. Doug landed hard on the floor, but didn't let go of the pistol. With my hands tied, I was helpless to go for it.

Rusty grabbed my arms to hold me as Doug got to his feet, dusting off his pants. "You son of a bitch."

"Just shoot him and be done with it," Henry said.

I heard Abby struggling and turned to see Henry leading her back toward the dirt. She must have tried to make a break for the stairs.

I was shoved toward the hole so hard I lost my balance and fell face-first. Abby broke free from Henry's grip and knelt beside me. "Marco, whatever happens —"

"Get up," I ordered through gritted teeth, struggling to my knees. "Get out of the dirt. Now. Don't make this easy for these bastards."

Abby rose and turned toward the men. "You won't get away with this. You're crazy if you think you can."

"Hold her," Doug said. He put the pistol to my temple. Rusty glanced away.

"No, please!" Abby cried, her voice strangled, tears flowing down her face.

"We'll do whatever you want. Just don't kill my husband!"

Suddenly, lights came on in the storage room and a barrage of footsteps sounded on the stairs. Shocked, I turned to see Reilly round the corner, gun drawn, followed by half a dozen of New Chapel's finest. I'd never been so happy to see cops in all my life.

"Throw the gun down!" Reilly shouted, as the other cops took aim at Doug. "Throw it down now!"

Doug backed away, startled, and tossed the pistol into the dirt.

"Hands up, all of you. Now!" Reilly ordered.

As the cops handcuffed the three men, Reilly cut through Abby's restraints and then mine. She wrapped her arms around my chest and squeezed tightly, but I did her one better. I picked her up in my arms and carried her upstairs, kissing her all the way.

At the top, I saw my brother pressed against the wall, biting his fingernails. He smiled in relief. "Thank God! If the cops hadn't gotten here when they did, I was going to go down myself."

"You called them?" I asked, setting Abby down.

He nodded.

"How did you know we were here?"

"I found the back door propped open with a piece of cardboard, so I snuck downstairs to see if anyone had gotten in. When I heard what those guys were saying, I called the cops."

"Why were you here?" I asked.

He shrugged ashamedly. "I've been coming here after the bar closes to guard it."

"You've been sleeping here?" Abby asked, glancing at me to see if I got it.

"I wanted to make it up to Marco for screwing up so many times," Rafe said. He wouldn't look at me.

Abby began to laugh and cry at the same time. "You're a hero, Rafe. You saved our lives." She threw her arms around him and gave him a big hug. When she finished, she gave me a look that said, *Say something!*

What was I supposed to say? You've come through at last?

I could tell by Abby's expression what she was thinking. *Rafe's trying, Marco. He looks up to you. He needs your encouragement. Don't be an ass.*

That was another thing I loved about my wife. She kept me in line.

I held out my hand and Rafe shook it hesitantly. "Good job, man."

"Thanks, bro."

Abby beamed at me. *Perfect,* her eyes said.

Not quite. Instead of letting go of Rafe's hand, I pulled him to me and hugged him, then ruffled his hair. My little brother, the hero.

Chapter Twenty-Five

Abby

Two evenings later, Marco closed the bar for a private party to celebrate what we were calling *The Grand Reopening of the Basement Floor.* We weren't actually in the basement — that would have been some party — but everyone who was invited knew the significance: A new cement floor had been poured, and the hole where we'd almost been buried was gone.

It hadn't been easy to get it covered quickly. A new plumbing company had been called in and extra money had been paid to fix the bad pipes. Then Marco, Rafe, and I had stood on the side while a buddy of Reilly's mixed the cement and troweled it on.

Speaking of trowels, Doug wouldn't admit to the cops what he'd done with Rusty's garden trowel, but Marco and I were betting it had gone the way he'd wanted us to go — in the foundation of a building. At that moment, Doug, Henry, and Rusty were sitting in jail. They'd been charged with murder, accessory to murder, and attempted murder. They would sit in the county jail for months awaiting their court dates. Let them see how it felt to have someone decide whether they should live or die. But how tragic for Doug's wife and children.

Tara had recovered well and was taking credit for discovering the first piece of solid evidence that connected Doug to the murder. The prosecutor had been thrilled with her discovery. Tara sat beside me now in a booth, her skinny arm around me, her head on my shoulder. Seedy sat on my lap under the table, nervous because of the men present. Across from me were my mom and dad and Marco's mom, who was telling one of her long but humorous stories, making them laugh.

At the next booth, Jillian sat holding a wiggling, barking HRH Princess Moon Petal something-or-other, with Claymore beside her. By the way they kept snapping, "Princess, no! Princess, down! Princess, stop eating that napkin," it was obvious that Francesca had not succeeded in training the terrier. Good news for Seedy.

Opposite them were my brother Jordan

and sister-in-law Kathy, Tara's parents, who had just about had strokes when they'd learned what had happened in that garage attic. Tara was now grounded for a month from extracurricular activities. They would have grounded me, too, if they could have. Instead, I was banned from seeing Tara alone for two weeks.

Grace and Lottie sat on barstools across from the booths, turned to face us. They, too, were listening to Francesca's story, occasionally sharing a whisper and a laugh. Every so often they would smile at me and nod, as if to say, *You pulled off another one. We're so proud.*

Parthenia had been invited but had declined to come. Marco and I had made a special trip to her studio to give her the news so she didn't have to read about it in the paper. Her reaction had been: "Pah! I knew there was a good reason why Kermit didn't show up that day. Did I not tell you it was Doug and Henry? But Rusty? This shocks me. You see why I don't trust men? You, I make an exception for, Marco. Now go. Leave me alone. *Yia sas.*"

My other brother, Jonathan, and sister-in-law Portia were here, too, as were Gert, Mary, and other staffers, who were seated at the bar enjoying their night off.

And where was my handsome husband right now? He and Rafe were circulating, making sure everyone had enough champagne, and keeping their eyes on the platters of hors d'oeuvres at the bar to ensure they remained well stocked.

My gaze followed Marco as he made his rounds. We'd come so close to death that for the first twenty-four hours after our release, I hadn't wanted to be separated from him. Our experience had made me realize that I should trust Marco's instincts the way I expected him to trust mine.

Was I sorry that we'd brought murderers to justice? No. But it would take me a while to sleep through the night without having bad dreams about being buried downstairs.

Marco slid in next to me. "How're you doing, Sunshine?"

"Good. Better now that you're here."

"You know what we're going to do come Monday?" he asked, putting his arm around me. "Go house hunting. I don't care what kind of case pops up. I don't care how important, intriguing, or challenging it may be. We — that's you and me, lady — are going to concentrate on finding the perfect little house for the three of us."

So sayeth the king. The queen did not respond, although the idea of hunting for a castle was appealing.

Seedy got up and stepped over to Marco's lap, facing him so he'd scratch her behind the ears. He obliged her, then leaned forward to see Tara. "Doing okay, kid?"

She nodded happily. "We make an awesome team, don't we?"

"Don't get any ideas," Marco said with a scowl.

Tara's eyes twinkled impishly. "Ideas about what?"

"Marco," I whispered, "remember who she takes after. But don't worry. I'm on top of it."

"Why don't I feel better?" he asked.

"Aw, look at the newlyweds," Lottie said. "Can't keep their hands off each other."

Everyone laughed, and then Grace cleared her throat loudly, waiting until the voices quieted to say, "I believe a toast from Sir Walter Scott is in order. 'To every lovely lady bright, what can I wish but faithful knight? To every faithful lover, too, what can I wish but lady true?' Abby, I believe you've found your gallant faithful knight. Marco, you've definitely found your lady true."

"You're right on both counts, Grace," I called. There was more applause as Marco and I kissed each other. It was like our wedding dinner all over again.

Marco put Seedy in my lap, then rose and held up his glass. "I'd like to propose a toast, too." He turned toward Rafe, who was standing at the end of the bar. "To my brother."

Rafe looked stunned.

"Thanks for being there for us, man."

My husband, a man of few words. But it was enough for Rafe, who beamed as everyone applauded.

As if she knew what was happening, Seedy jumped down from the bench and hobbled over to Rafe, putting a paw on his pant leg and giving him a yip. He picked her up and cuddled her, and I was stunned to see her lick his chin. That made a whopping two males she wasn't afraid of. It figured, though. Both had that Salvare magic.

My dad spoke up next. "My toast is to Abby and Marco, of course. We are so relieved that you're both safe. A thank-you to Rafe, too, for your great work. But I'd also like to add one to Abby's mom, my beloved Mo, who received some very exciting news today."

To clamors of "Tell us, Maureen," and "Share!" Mom slid out of the booth and stood like a teacher in front of her class.

"Parthenia Pappas, whom you may know

as the Duchess of Tenth Street, a highly acclaimed artist, saw photos of my latest work of art, *Madachshund and Child,* and has commissioned me to do a whole set of dogs for her. And the best part is that she wants to have a show for me at her studio."

As everyone cheered, I glanced at Marco with raised eyebrows, as if to say, *Who knew?* At least I was off the hook.

"But," Mom said, quieting everyone down, "I told her I wouldn't do it."

Amid cries of "What?" and "Why not?" and Princess barking like the crazy dog she was, Mom clapped her hands teacher style to get our attention.

"Because," she said, then turned to gaze tenderly at me, "I said I would have it at Bloomers instead. If anyone is going to benefit from my creative ability, it's going to be my precious daughter and my new son-in-law."

Everyone clapped except Marco and me, who looked at each other in shock.

"Speech, Abs!" Jillian cried, and everyone joined in, while I sat there frozen.

"Abs," Jillian hissed, "get up and say something."

Marco squeezed my hand for support then got up to let me out of the booth. I slid out slowly, my mind searching desperately for the right words. *Thanks, I think?* just wasn't going to cut it. I glanced at my dad, my ally, and he gave me an encouraging nod. *You can do this, Abracadabra.*

What could I say? That I was overjoyed? Could I pull off the lie?

Then I saw Rafe in my peripheral vision and remembered the look on his face after Marco had hugged him. His eyes had glistened with grateful tears, his chest had puffed up, he had smiled radiantly from ear to ear. He had finally felt accepted by his big brother. Yes, Rafe had screwed up many times, but he'd come through when we really needed him.

Hadn't my mom always been there when I needed her? Well, most of the time anyway. Now I wanted her face to light up like Rafe's had. I knew this would be a moment that would be etched in her mind forever.

"Mom, I'm so excited for you — and proud, too — and honored that you chose Bloomers for your show. And I promise that we'll make it the best damn show this town has ever seen."

Applause filled the room. Everyone was smiling. Marco gave me a nod that said, *Way to go, Sunshine.* Dad gave me a thumbs-up.

I'd done it! A memory forever etched not just in Mom's mind, but in the minds of everyone here.

My mom cleared her throat, no doubt husky with tears, and turned toward me. But instead of smiling radiantly and holding out her arms for a hug, she pursed her lips.

"*Darn,* Abigail."

"What?" I asked.

"The best *darn* show." She leaned toward Francesca and said in a loud whisper, "I don't allow my children to curse in my presence."

The employees of Thorndike Press hope you have enjoyed this Large Print book. All our Thorndike, Wheeler, and Kennebec Large Print titles are designed for easy reading, and all our books are made to last. Other Thorndike Press Large Print books are available at your library, through selected bookstores, or directly from us.

For information about titles, please call:
(800) 223-1244

or visit our Web site at:
http://gale.cengage.com/thorndike

To share your comments, please write:
Publisher
Thorndike Press
10 Water St., Suite 310
Waterville, ME 04901

CPSIA information can be obtained
at www.ICGtesting.com
Printed in the USA
FFOW03n1009220814
7030FF